SMOKE AND MIRRORS

SMOKE AND MIRRORS

BY

TINSLEY COLLINS

Also by the author

Design For Death
Séance
Send in the Clowns

Before....

OLD MIN HAD BECOME SOMETHING of a National Treasure in South London, not something that anyone had got round to telling her, but she was noticing that she was regularly being given smiles and waves in the street, and that people she'd never seen before suddenly seemed to be on first name terms with her. Originally from Catford, she had gone up-market in late middle age and had moved to the Clapham, Wandsworth and Battersea triptych, switching between them as and when she felt like it. For the last couple of years she had favoured Belleville, a close but poor relation of the other three, but this was the nineteen nineties and it was clearly moving up the property ladder at a pace. Min had a nose for that sort of thing. She had noticed an increase in hard-hatted men busy working on those houses that were on their way up, and an abundance of what she called lollypop trees in galvanised planters gracing the doorways of those already there. She knew it was a good idea to grab a prime site in the early stages of an area being gentrified and before property values went sky high so she had staked her claim when it was all in its infancy.

Her current residence was a quiet little spot between the launderette and the halal butchers at the less busy end of the High Street. It was just a foot or so back from the main pavement so she could see everything that was going on, but there was no danger that anyone would tread on her when she was having her afternoon nap. It was nicely furnished with an orange box for a dining table and two wooden chairs that someone had kindly left out on the pavement next to the common. She even had a comfy arm chair she had had to push the length of the High Street to get home, but keeping it dry was sometimes a problem and she didn't want her rheumatism to get any worse. Pride of place went to an elaborate standard lamp. She wasn't able to plug it in to see if it worked, but even without a bulb it gave her home the touch of class it needed. But what she could badly do with was a new carpet as the current one had become very damp and smelly, so doing her early morning rounds with her supermarket trolley, she was thrilled to find what looked just the thing rolled up in a low skip. There was a ton of joists and rubble piled on top of it but she had never been afraid of a challenge. With the quiet patience of someone who has all the time in the world, item by item, brick by brick, she cleared and manoeuvred all this stuff out of the way till most of the carpet was free, then holding it firmly, she jiggled and pulled until it was more or less out.

Underneath the carpet was a body, nicely dressed by the look of it, but coated with a thick layer of builder's rubble. This had done quite a good job of soaking up the blood that had leaked from the head, but could not disguise the extent of the injury.

She had seen a lot in her time on the streets, but nothing quite like this. She was already off balance with the weight of the carpet and suddenly felt herself go dizzy with shock. She reached out for something to hold on to, but the only possible support was her trolley which was of little help because of its wheels. Still clutching the carpet like a new lover she collapsed in a messy heap on to the pavement sending the trolley speeding off into the distance.

After....

ONE

PLEASE, PLEASE, *PLEASE!* NO! NOT a sodding demonstration! John's instincts had been right – there *was* a conspiracy against his getting to work! In the distant past having nearly been destroyed by the rail service from Belleville into town he had eventually been driven in to the arms of the Northern Line which was Club Class in comparison, but still a refined torture in its own right; and then after months of string pulling he had finally managed to secure the use of one of the coveted parking spots in Lincoln's Inn so he could travel to work by car. Provided he left home at the crack of dawn he could get a reasonably clear run into the office, and for the last few weeks had bellowed his TVR down the Trinity Road serenaded by Pavarotti or The Pogues depending on his mood, and his will to live had cautiously crept back, non-committal, but prepared to give things a short trial period. But today there was *a sodding great demonstration blocking the entire road!* He banged his head against his steering wheel in disbelief. This was Belleville, not Trafalgar Square! Barely ten minutes from his own front door, he was in complete grid-lock, hemmed in fore and aft, and wholly unable to move. He couldn't even jettison the car and take the tube. He wasn't yet late as such, but that was not the point. Solicitors don't have office hours; you had to stay ahead of the pack or you got eaten by them, and there were enough bites out of his bottom already. Only a reluctance to draw attention to himself so near to home stopped him from leaning on his horn and wailing.

Desperate to rescue something from it all he attempted to dictate some memos into his portable Grundig, but the ever louder chorus of *'What Do We Want'* was making it impossible. For God's sake didn't they know he had a job to do? Whatever their problem might be, all he cared about was getting out of this jam and on his way, but it looked hopeless. Normally easy going in his relations with the world at large, frustration drove out any question of being rational, particularly knowing that it wasn't possible to win against people like these. A banner meant a cause, and a cause meant the moral high ground and the right to hob-nail it over anyone in its path. It wasn't as if they were the only ones with principles; he had his own deeply felt belief system too: *Work Hard/ Play Hard*, a simple creed beyond the possibility of criticism and jewel like in its neatness, but he didn't shove it down people's throats and hold people up on their way to work.

Looking round him he noticed that the majority of the demonstrators were female. He strained to hear what they were maundering on about, and caught the reply to their interrogative chant as *'More Schools!'* Oh give me a break! The last thing Belleville needed was *More Schools* as that would bring the inevitable *More Kids*. Belleville certainly wasn't short of things it needed to drag it further up market, but not schools. A Connolly shop wouldn't do any harm, and a local branch of Harvey Nichols, plus a few more decent cafes and wine bars; thinking about it, a Hempel Hotel would top it off nicely. While he was on the subject of upgrading life as a whole, what England needed was a bit more global warming, cheaper petrol, and fewer tourists cluttering the place up. What John personally wanted, his Fantasy Wish List regularly amended and added to as it was always conveniently available in the deep recesses of his mind, was an Aston Martin, a villa in the South of France, and while he was about it, Young Tracy From Accounts kindly standing on his desk to change a light bulb in that miniskirt she was wearing week ago last Thursday while he held her by the waist to make sure she didn't fall off. His spirits briefly lifted as he wondered how all this would look written on a placard, and he spent a few happy minutes trying to devise a short punchy chant to go with it, eventually having to stop himself humming it out loud. At least, as a man with an education he never need be bored by his own company.

Oh God, when was this going to clear? Another ten minutes had passed, and even devising rhyming couplets with a real edge to them could not keep his temper below a vigorous simmer. He drummed his fingers on the steering wheel noticing that the temperature gauge was creeping into the red sector and the exhaust note getting lumpy. His TVR was comfortably past its first youth and even at its best had problems with *sotto voce*, but he was having to blip the throttle to keep it from stalling, and it was beginning to sound distinctly unhappy. Panic added to his misery as he realised he was locked into a particularly nasty Catch 22. He couldn't risk turning off the ignition as the car could be such a bastard to start once it had overheated, but if he kept it idling in this jam there was a risk that it would boil over. At thirty four he should be way beyond all this and not stuck in a traffic jam potentially late for the office in a car that was beginning to attract the wrong sort of attention. He wouldn't be having this problem if he had the latest Porsche Boxster like Ian, or a state of the art Alfa like Simon, but the fact was, for all his appearance of affluence, cars like that were comfortably outside his financial limits. Splintered glass under the fingernails would not have made him say it publicly, and even thinking it made him look around nervously in case he had inadvertently said it out loud and someone had heard.

His frustration at being held up flowed into a general all over resentment, and dragged his mood even lower. In a world that now seemed to be dominated by the rich and the beautiful not to be seriously affluent or successful was as humiliating as being jealous, such afflictions being un-acknowledgeable as they marked you as a loser and therefore an untouchable. In day to day terms he was perfectly well off, but there was a chasm between that and being where he felt he should be at this stage of his life, and it was this lack of real financial clout that had caused him to buy an admittedly sleek and elegant flat in Belleville rather than in South Kensington or Notting Hill where he really wanted to be. Belleville was tipped to be the next South London borough to take off into the stratosphere of Cool Britannia, but although it had moved up market a notch or two since he had moved in, there had not exactly been a flood-tide of media millionaires or super-models trying to elbow their way into the local property market. He couldn't wait much longer for it to happen; he wanted it now, or preferably a bit sooner. At thirty four he already saw life slipping past him. The current crop of Dot-Com millionaires and legal whiz kids with Met Bar memberships and weekend Ferraris still had their thirtieth birthday on the horizon, so he was already into borrowed time.

"What Do We Want......?"

Oh, who cares what you want, you ugly bunch of toad breathed, spotty bottomed, badly dressed turn-offs. He mentally compared these dreadful women with their stupid banners and British Home Stores anoraks to the sleekly tailored City wine bar girls or South of France topless goddesses they could have been, and shook his head in disbelief that they had had decided to opt for being down at heel housewives instead. And whoever they were, why had they chosen to have their stupid protest so close to where he lived making it impossible for him to get to work? If he gave into his instincts and bashed their heads in with their own banners, it would be the end of any quality of life for as long as he lived here. His Fantasy Wish List may have included a Clerkenwell loft or a Holland Park penthouse, but for the time being, home was a flat above Boomtown Videos in Belleville and one of the few lessons in life that he tried hard to live by had clear references to poo and one's own doorstep, and how it was considered tactically advantageous to keep a good distance between them.

Oh sod these bloody people! His car's temperature gauge was rising even further and the tick-over beginning to sound terminal. Please God if you have any sense of natural justice at all, *please* don't let me boil over! He leaned as far out as he could to try and see what was going on. The protest was not that large considering the impact it was having, and to be fair seemed to be free of the usual rent-a-mob crowd. Most of them were ordinary looking young mums plus a handful of New Agers, but there were still enough of them to keep the traffic from moving. A handful of bored looking policeman were in attendance, but doing little more than keeping a watchful eye. Clearly he was not the only impatient one and horns were sounding and drivers looking round trying to find ways to escape. A few of the protesters were taking advantage of the stationary traffic to hand their leaflets through car windows, and the driver in front of him was now being ear-ached by a kaftan clad female who was so heavily wrapped in scarves as to be nearly invisible.

Oh bugger this! He was next in the queue, and in his open car John was conscious of being a captive audience. How was he going to deal with it? Even frothing with anger, faced with someone who was female and therefore potentially fanciable his instinctive need to be fancied in turn kicked in. The little he could see of her behind the drapes and the John Lennon glasses looked perfectly OK with milky skin and good bones, so his mating urge went straight in to automatic pilot. Instinctively he checked his appearance in his rear view mirror to ensure the effects of his morning grooming had not deteriorated too much since he had left his flat barely half an hour ago; the trouble was that it was simply not possible to launch into a tirade of complaint about any subject on earth without adding ten years to your age, and instantly transforming yourself from *Affluent Young Hedonist* into *Disgusted of Tunbridge Wells*. Even if he blew her away with a battery of well-chosen words, he would still be ugly with self-righteousness. There was clearly a void in the market when none of the style magazines explained just how you could go ballistic with anger and still remain the man to whom most women in a random survey wanted to consume with their morning cuppa. She and her cohorts had single handedly turned him into someone he didn't want to be, and the angrier he became about this, the closer the resemblance grew, a self fulfilling prophesy that stoked its own fires. It was touch and go whether he or the car would boil over first.

"Would you like to sign this?" She had finished with the car in front and his turn had come. "It's a petition against the new development." She took a thick sheaf of paper from her beaded bag and thrust it into his hand.

It was the wrong moment for him to be asked about anything. He saw his temperature gauge suddenly jerk up a notch and whatever he might otherwise have said was lost in a red mist of frustration. "There's no point in pushing that stupid leaflet in my face as I'm not interested so will you all just bugger off so we can all get away from here!" Image and political correctness were lost in the horror that he might boil over in his own high street.

She flushed briefly, but otherwise let his hostility ride over her. "I'm taking that as *No,* but you haven't read our leaflet yet. Don't you want to see why we have to do this? "

"I'm sorry, but I don't give a toss for your petition or your leaflet, and I'm certainly not going to sign *anything* with a gun to my head." Fizzing with self-righteousness he turned in his seat and pointed to the queue of cars behind him, "Don't you see that none of us can get to work because of you!" She'd done it of course. In ten seconds flat he had become a pompous middle aged tosser making *Disgusted of Tunbridge Wells* sound quite moderate, but he was now painted into a corner and might just as well run with it. "Every one of us is losing money because of you."

"You think that profit is more important than children's rights to an education? That's the issue here."

"There can't *be* education without profit. There can't be *anything* without profit."

Sounding like a parent with a difficult child she carried on, her voice quiet and earnest. "If this new development goes ahead, the whole character of the area will change. There has to be a balance between profit and the community. I think you're stuck here for a bit longer, so why don't you read what we've got to say. That's the very least a reasonable man could do."

"Community!" He was in danger of losing it completely and had to fight the urge to grab the ends of her scarf and strangle her with it. "For God's sake, this isn't the 1960s you know. Did you and all your fellow harpies sleep through the last couple of decades?"

They stared at each other with growing hostility, her eyes now glittering behind her glasses. He even hated himself for sounding like this, but he had started on a slippery slope and seemed to have lost all control of his momentum. He gave her full marks for persistence though as she kept her cool and continued to chip away at him. "It's only a question of considering the bigger picture. If we don't look after the immediate neighbourhood….."

He didn't really hear the rest of what she said as he was suddenly mesmerised by a tell-tale wisp of steam coming through one of the ventilators in the dashboard. His car was on the very edge of boiling over and nothing else mattered. Somehow he had to get out of this before it was finally too late. In desperation he blipped the throttle and clunked into reverse, hoping against hope he might just be able to turn the car through a right angle and then off into the next side street and get away. Unaware of his intentions she renewed her appeal, pushing the petition into his hands and sending him completely over the top. Blind with panic he ripped it to shreds and threw the pieces back into her face, ignoring her yell of protest as he desperately looked for that necessary inch that might give him turning room. Unconscious of anything else he completely failed to see her own eruption into anger or to do anything to protect himself when she lunged forward and pulled her beaded bag over his head, enveloping him in darkness and a slight smell of incense. Totally blinded by the thick material, he struggled to free himself, and it was the sound of the steam jetting out of the radiator and up through the bonnet seams rather than the sight of it that told John that his car had finally given up and was vigorously boiling over.

T W O

"YOU'RE LATE."

"How perceptive you are!" After what he had been though John was in no mood for his secretary's sarcasm, or in fact for anything other than curling into the foetal position on his office floor. On the plus side he would be back home again in about ten hours and have all the time in the world for dying quietly in the night, or, if he was really unlucky, surviving to live through another day. On the good side, at least she had got the percolator on the go and experience told him that after a good strong coffee he would be ready to do battle again.

"Andrew was in at quarter past eight."

She was not going to give up easily. Three years in the south had done nothing to soften Marjorie's Hartlepool accent nor her conviction that all southerners were limp wristed wimps and that John was the worst of them. She had come down because of her husband's job, but hated it from day one and was determined that everyone should know it. She was known round the office as Rancid Marge because of her permanent sour expression. "Stella was about half an hour before that – I heard her say so in the ladies."

He poured himself a coffee and could feel new life flow into him even after just one mouthful. "Have I missed anything?"

"He wants to see you."

"Who does?"

"*He* does – The Prince of Darkness. Who else?"

His poor deluded parents were under the impression that his secretary called him "Sir" and knocked before coming into his room. Never mind that, Luke Chaplin who was both the head of his department and Managing Partner needed him and he had got in late. Bugger it! It was mere trivia in any real sense, but he knew that Luke would store it in his mental data base for retrieval when it could do most damage.

"What does he want?"

"Search me. It was a good hour ago so it's probably too late now anyway." She looked at him with something approaching pleasure. "If you're really lucky, it'll only be the sack."

* * *

"Hi Luke. You wanted me?"

His light tone was a thinly disguised attempt to cover his apprehension as Luke's office was universally acknowledged to be a hard hat area. Luke's air of studied calm initially lead you to feel safe but you never knew what might suddenly fall on you. He continued to study the document on the desk in front of him, John's arrival not important enough to interrupt what he was doing. On the edge of forty, he was not that much older than John in the scheme of things, which made this demonstration of seniority all that much more galling. On a mahogany side table he had used his toddler as an excuse to display a number of photographs of his lovely house and garden, and even his boat, the worst of them showing him looking tanned and relaxed and clutching the child in question as the two of them laughed. This of course was blatant discrimination. The parents in the firm could put out as many photographs as they liked of them enjoying bath time frolics with their children and it was considered a good thing, but if any of the single guys showed photographs of them enjoying bath time frolics with their latest girlfriend, it would likely lead to a written warning.

"So you're here." Luke finally looked up, his face neutral and controlled, so only John heard the unspoken words to the effect that John was late, and it was a further example of his not really being a Grade A Big Hitter. John knew there was no point in making excuses as there was nothing so pathetic sounding in these situations as tales of traffic jams or train cancellations. They surveyed each other for a moment, as always their shared secret hovering silently over their heads. The two of them operated on terms of armed neutrality, tied to each other by an invisible thread known only to themselves. Every day, John walked a tightrope, the mastery of which kept him from falling from the comparative comfort of the frying pan into the terminal implications of the fire.

"George Stavros phoned just before nine. Shame you weren't here. He tried your mobile but it seems it was switched off." Having left in a hurry to avoid the traffic that morning, John had left it in his living room. "I shouldn't have to say this, John, but client communication is vital in this business, they like to know that we are always there for them. They feel insecure if they can't and that's when they call another firm, and we lose their business. Didn't Russell and Brooks care about that sort of thing?"

Luke had been the managing partner of a firm called Hart-Stanley and a year ago had spearheaded that firm's takeover of Russell Brooks and Keeling. The combined firm was now called Hart- Russell and was very much under Marcus' control. He was a good solicitor and a ruthless administrator, determined to mould the firm into his vision of a cutting edge modern practice. His obsessive attention to detail however was not to everyone's taste and there had been a number of resignations.

"Had a few problems this morning."

"Solicitors don't have problems, John. Clients have problems and we sort them out."

He could have added that we also charge them a fortune to do so, but that was wholly understood. There was no issue between John and Luke on that one. That was why they were both there. No hours are too long and no effort is too much for a client, and it is vital at all times to get it right, but for that you charge premium rates for every phone call, letter, memo and microsecond of consideration time, otherwise there would be no point. John knew that there were solicitors out there who dealt with social problems for clients at legal aid rates and handled messy landlord and tenant and immigration problems on a shoestring budget, but they were hardly the real thing. John had once seen a beggar on the tube with a notice which read "*I wouldn't be doing this if I could do something else.*" He thought that had to be the case with Legal Aid lawyers. Try as he might he couldn't think of any other reason.

"Anyway, George wants you to ring him. He wants you to attend a meeting with him to do with one of his developments."

"What sort of a meeting?"

"With one of these resident's associations. They're all up in arms about something he's up to. Usual NIMBY stuff."

It didn't take John more that a second to realise that the noise echoing through his head was alarm bells. "That sounds like a job for Planning."

"Not exactly. This is just a meeting to appease the locals. He wants to get them on his side and convince them it's all in their best interests."

As an experienced and able litigator, John's instinctive reaction was to run and hide. The result of a court case depended on your convincing the Judge that your client was legally in the right. End of story! Morally in the right did not come in to it, and you certainly did not have to convince your opponent that you were in the right. The chances were that at the end of the trial your opponent wanted to cut your dangly bits off with a rusty saw, but that was all part of the fun. The meeting described by Luke sounded everything John hated. There was no neutral Judge to convince or to keep things in order, it would be unstructured and unprofessional and everything turned on getting a bunch of hysterical locals with a vested interest to approve what George was up to. As that almost certainly involved his making a massive profit regardless of the consequences to anybody else, John had his reservations about his ability to achieve it.

"Luke, this is nothing to do with litigation. I don't think I'm the right person for it. Why don't you try Andrew, he's red hot on his planning stuff."

"But George wants you to do it."

"What about Stella?"

"Stella's a family specialist."

"Exactly! All that mediation stuff – she's good at calming people down."

The expression on Marcus' face hardly changed but a hint of wish fulfilment tinged his voice. "Perhaps you'd just like to go and work for someone else who won't make so many demands on you. Plenty of firms out there looking for experienced litigators."

Yes, and I'd vastly increase my salary, but I can't because you've got me locked in you bastard! "OK! OK! Of course I'll do it"

Luke started fiddling with a paper knife. "I believe in horses for courses too, but George insisted it was you. Whatever we all think of George, he gives us a lot of business and we've got to keep him happy."

"I just don't want him to find I'm the wrong person."

"He won't."

"But seriously Luke, supposing I mess it up?"

Luke looked at him coldly. "Hart-Russell don't ever mess things up. I thought you knew that."

"OK. OK. I'll phone him."

"Keep me posted." Marcus' eyes started to glaze over and he picked up a file. The meeting was over, and all going well they might be able to avoid each other for another few weeks.

THREE

GEORGE STAVROS ALWAYS INSISTED ON John. A few years before, John had won a piece of sink or swim litigation for him and had not only saved him from losing a big chunk of his business, but had also recovered in costs the sort of money that most people would be pleased to earn over a couple of years. Now the adrenaline rush of all that was behind him, John would rather that it had not happened; George was not the sort of client he wanted. George had learned the rudiments of business as a petty criminal on the streets but during the process of moving himself up to the fringes of organised crime he suddenly declared himself to be legit and moved into the building industry. From there he upgraded to property development where he was a natural. His company, Dragoon properties, had gone from strength to strength, but John could never be sure how much was due to an astute understanding of the market, and how much from utilisation of back alley diplomacy when things got tough.

Even telephoning George made John nervous. Standing on a rocky pedestal was not a comfortable place to be, and one of these days he would do something to upset the balance and would crash to the floor, and George would be looking down at him with a smile of regret that John should have disappointed him so badly.

"*Johnny boy how are you?*"

John had to suppress a nervous shudder at the sound of George's voice at the other end of the phone. "Fine, George. And you?"

"Never better. Got a bit of a problem and I know you'll sort out for me. You know there's nothing I like more than a problem that's been sorted. Like getting a pip out from your teeth. Such a relief when it's gone."

Yes, but what if the probe hits a nerve and you land up with tooth-ache? John felt a sudden need to go off to the loo for a quiet hour or so. "Is it my sort of thing, George? Horses for courses and all that."

"Course it is. You'll walk it."

"I hope so. Luke gave me some idea. Can you expand?"

"Just a lot of silly old tarts objecting to one of my developments."

"Tarts?"

"You know, Do-Gooders with tits. The Jam and Jerusalem set."

"That's not going to worry you is it?"

"Not really, but I want to earn myself a bit of goodwill with this one. I've got the planning more or less tied up so it's all systems go. It's just there might be a follow on job, so I don't just want to beat them, I want them on my side if you get me. You know, think I'm a great guy and that it's a good thing for the area, so I can just get the next one through on the nod. Lot of money riding on this one, John. Not going to let me down are you?"

John could visualise him ordering the cement boots even as he spoke. "Which one is this?"

"The Belleville development."

John felt the siren call of suicide. He knew he sounded like a character from a cheap soap opera, but he had to verify what he had just heard and that it wasn't a cruel joke being played on him by a weak telephone connection and too much wax in the ears. "Belleville?"

"That's right. Do you know it?"

Not for anything would he tell George where he lived. "I think I know someone who lives there."

"We've all got a few sad friends. It's a dump for the losers who couldn't afford Clapham."

"But isn't it, you know, up and coming?"

"Fuck off, John! There's not a piss-stained alley anywhere in London that

some estate agent won't say is up and coming. If I were you I'd tell your friend to sell up now while he's ahead."

John felt himself punch drunk with information overload. "Look, I think I need to know a bit more. Tell me about the development and what you want me to do."

"No probs. I need some lunch anyway. I'll send the car round for you."

Please no! Not that dreadful car – a Mercedes stretch limo with a TV in the back permanently showing porn videos. John had only been in it twice, but each time wanted to shroud his head with a raincoat as he got in and out like a serial killer avoiding flash bulbs. At least the windows were black so once inside no one could see you.

"Hang on, George…."

"About 12.30. Try and be ready."

* * *

When Marge rang and told him the car had arrived she asked him in her flat voice if he needed some Kleenex for the journey. Who had told her about the porn videos? People knew things in this office before they happened.

'"Can you talk – what does the chauffeur look like?"

"Started off ugly, but then someone hit him in the face with a hot shovel and spoiled his looks."

It had to be Sid, a human rottweiller who frightened John to death. His head was so square you could cut your fingers on the corners, and his neck had the same dimensions as an oil drum. His hands could double as a builder's shovel and looked as if they could unscrew wheel nuts without a spanner. He was always impeccably uniformed, but the Nazi dagger tattooed on his neck disappearing into his shirt collar somehow spoiled the effect. The only thing going for him was that he never wasted time on small talk and could normally convey all he needed to by grunting. The car was his baby and he kept it gleamingly perfect, but as a result resented anyone but George sitting in its doe-skin interior. Under other circumstances John might have enjoyed being ferried around in this behemoth while he played with the cut crystal glasses and helped himself to the cigars, but terror of what Sid would do if he scuffed the carpets or spilled a drink meant that he had spent his few journeys in the car rigidly upright and horribly uncomfortable.

Marge was at the front door as he left and had her sniffy '*It's all right for some*' look on her face. If only she knew! He would have happily swapped places and tucked into one of her mushy pea sandwiches instead, but it was a done deal. As he left his office he looked longingly behind him as if this might be the last time he would ever see it.

* * *

John tried to use the journey to George's Mayfair office to persuade himself that it wasn't all bad. Lunch with George might not be John's idea of a good time, but it would almost certainly be lush and expensive. George had no truck with new kids on the block like Chinawhite or Momo, but stuck to the long established biggies like The Ritz or The Dorchester where you knew where you were and whose place in the pecking order was beyond challenge. Everything that touched, went near, or was trodden in by George had to be not merely the best but recognisably so by a blind man on a dark night. For John, having started the day having a bag pulled over his head by a New Age protester while his radiator boiled over, this had to be some sort of an improvement.

When he arrived at Bruton Street Sid pulled to a halt then went in to fetch his employer giving John no more than a few minutes of precious solitude before George's unmistakable silhouette waddled into view down the stone steps. No matter how many times he saw him, John was always surprised to see what a massive blubber mountain George was. He always practised in advance, mentally visualising the vast bio-mass, the sheer enormity of the man, but still was hit by an overwhelming sense of awe that without complicated scaffolding and ferro reinforcement this weight could be transported from place to place on anything a low tech as legs. As with every other time, he managed to underestimate the effect that being in the presence of such bulk had on him.

"Johnny boy, nice to see you." George settled into the seat next to him and the whole balance of the car changed, and John had to cling to the leather covered handle next to him to avoid sliding down into George's side of the seat. When George was in the car it stopped being huge and pretentious and became little more than a runabout with just about enough room for two.

"And you, George. You're looking well."

"Mustn't grumble. You've not seen this one already have you?" He indicated the generous blonde doing her stuff in bright Technicolor on the screen in front of them in a bravura effort to prove just how good women could be at multi tasking. In fact, during his entire time in the car John had been doing his best to avoid eye contact with any of the sexual gymnastics being performed for his benefit. After an early drive in the car when disgust had lost the battle with curiosity and he had given in to watching the endless permutations being demonstrated, he had learned things about the human anatomy that he really didn't want to know, and he had found himself virtually impotent for days afterwards. For nearly a week, the only way a girl could make herself of any interest to him at all was by being fully and modestly dressed

."No problem, George. You can turn it off if you like."

George aimed the remote at the screen, and as if by magic, there was Julie Andrews singing about her favourite things to a bunch of children in an Alpine hillside.

"You won't tell anyone about this will you, John. We all have our little weaknesses."

"Well, it's a bit more sophisticated than the previous one." He desperately tried to find something to say that would cover his embarrassment. "Anyway, I think it was about to descend into a custard pie comedy."

George gave a token laugh that was completely devoid of humour. "Glad you can see the funny side of things, John. We might need that if things don't work out." He fished in to his side pocket and passed a photocopied sheet to

John. It was a flyer from the Belleville Resident's Association and listed the various horrors that Dragoon's new development would bring if was allowed to proceed, not the least because the development was planned for the only possible site where a new primary school could be built. Should it go ahead, the area's chances of having a forward thinking progressive school would be gone forever.

"Look at this John- '*Kids before Kapitol*.' It's just a bunch of tarts talking through their panty liners, but they can still make things difficult. They've wangled a meeting tomorrow at the Town Hall to debate it all. I want you to talk to them and convince them it's all a good idea. "

"And what do you have in mind?"

"Tell you in a minute."

The car stopped outside the Ritz and the two of them went in to the golden splendour of the dining room, John doing his best to look as if this was the sort of place where he popped in for a light bite on a daily basis. He noticed that the second chair at the table reserved for them was larger and heavier than all the others in the room and looked as if it were made out of gilded railway sleepers and he guessed that George's previous visits had convinced them that if damage to property was to be avoided, this man needed serious underpinning. Without consulting John, George ordered champagne then prodded his fat fingers at just about everything on the menu and asked for it to be brought quickly. John would have liked to take his time over ordering but he could see that what George wanted was bulk and that he wanted it now, so made a hurried choice.

When the first course arrived, George went at it as if the plate was about to be whisked away. He consumed his food like a chain smoker lighting one from another, each fork-full following the previous one with the regularity of a metronome and mastication being a middle man he seemed to be able to do without. John was sure that he really couldn't be appreciating anything he was putting away, and once George had got enough inside him to risk pausing for breath, he confirmed John's impression.

"I don't need all this fancy stuff you know." He indicated the pomp and plush surrounding them. "I'm really a simple bloke at heart. Give me a plate of ham and mustard sandwiches and a video and I'm as happy as Larry."

John was doing his best to savour his Dover sole but watching George's chomping jaws was putting him off. He steered the conversation back to the development hoping that if he concentrated on that, he might be able to get through the rest of the meal.

"Listen," George threw a few more chunks of untreated carbohydrate down his throat followed by a pint of champagne. "What you've got to do to start with is show them that it's generally good for the area. That's easy. It's part offices which will bring employment, and it's part leisure complex where all the yuppie girls in their leotards can drink liquidised bird seed. The rest of it is restaurants and bars so the locals don't have to schlep it to Clapham or Chelsea when they want some char-grilled swordfish. All right so far?"

Definitely all right! John heard his heart singing arias. This sounded exactly what was needed to kick up the value if his flat. If this worked out he might make a killing on it and move up a post code, or it might even make sense to stay put.

"The next bit is a bit more subtle." In fact it was so subtle that three or four buckets of meat and potatoes had to be tipped down George's gullet before he could go on. It would have taken the average person most of an afternoon to masticate and swallow what had just consumed, but as George seemed to be able to digest industrial sized chunks of food without chewing, there was only a short pause.

"The big thing all these douche bags are going on about is they want one of these funny schools to open in the area." He reached in his pocket and fished out the leaflet he had shown John earlier. "Here it is. A Saul Liebling school. It's one of those places where the teachers spend all day telling the kids about getting in touch with the haunting magic of their sub-conscious instead of smacking their heads and kicking their arses. Currently there's not much building space in Belleville and there's only two possible places where they could build it. One is the Old Brewery site where we've got in first and our current development is going to happen, and the other is the Gambols site where there's a big empty department store." He cleared his throat with an unusual modesty. "We own that as well."

John could tell from the look on his face that there was some history here and gestured to George to tell him. George finished a plateful and mopped his now sweating face with his napkin.

"Gambols was a big department store, one of the old fashioned family ones. Usual problems, undercapitalised and couldn't quite keep up with the times. Few years ago it was close to collapse so we thought we'd try and help them out. Like to do people a favour when we can. We brought the freehold to give them a bit of working capital, then leased the land back to them. We didn't ask for much, but they still couldn't cut it and so the poor bastards went under." John tried to meet George's eye, but it was focussed elsewhere. "Luckily we had insisted on guarantees from the directors, so after Gambols had liquidated and we took possession of the shop, we recovered the leasing costs under the guarantees. Directors had to sell their houses and everything, but in the end we got back just a bit more than we had paid for it. Of course it we hadn't actually laid out any money ourselves – we'd borrowed the purchase money from a finance company." He threw down a goblet of champagne and then felt strong enough to meet John's eye again. "Not a bad bit of business one way and another."

The words *"Help them out"* had not gone unnoticed, and John was not surprised George had not been able to meet his eye. Well, it was business and it was long over now. His own problem was still that he was going to have to front the meeting tomorrow. How was all this going to placate a hall full of angry women who wanted their school?

"So how does this help?"

"Because we can let them have the Gambols site so they can build their fucking school." He looked at John, his eyes guileless. "I'm prepared to enter into a legally binding agreement that Dragoon Properties will sell the Gambols site to this Saul Liebling lot for seventy percent of its value for them to build their school on, provided of course that the Old Brewery development goes ahead and we get the first stage payment from the lessees."

"Who's that?"

"Clarendon"

John was impressed. "This is a bit out of the way for them isn't it? I thought Clarendon only dealt with prestige property in prime central London sites."

"There's money enough in this one to make it prestige, John. The down payment from them is about five mill. That's not peanuts. That's why we're not agreeing to sell Gambols to the school unless we've got that as otherwise we'll need to develop the Gambols site instead."

It suddenly felt as if the Dover sole in John's stomach was trying to swim up-stream. With five million at stake, and the words *Legally Binding* hovering in the air, the look of open honesty on George's face made him fear the worst.

"Legally binding?"

"Hundred per cent. That's your job to draft that."

Why me? Did I do something dreadful in a past life? "You really want to be committed to that?"

John searched George's face, but it was like looking down an endless tunnel where whatever was at the other end was beyond the limits of human sight. George's pale eyes were like coloured glass, and he simply nodded his agreement.

"And you want me to tell the meeting, that as your solicitors we are authorised to tell them that, and that we are in the process of drafting an agreement now."

"That's right, John."

John's brain went into overdrive. If he screwed this up for George, he'd probably be found nailed to a garage door in Brixton. If it turned out to be illegal in some way, he'd probably lose his job and never get another one. Suddenly being in a traffic jam with a bag over his head seemed quite a nice place to be.

FOUR

THE BIG DISADVANTAGE OF JOHN'S flat was its position above the video shop so that sometimes coming home at night he had to negotiate a crowd of the Schwarzenegger and six-pack set, but tonight the coast looked clear. Unlocking the front door he was interrupted by his mobile ringing and stuck it under his ear as he undid the second Chubb.

"John Foxton."

"*John, it's Alfie.*"

"Can you speak up? I can barely hear you."

"*It's Alfie, John. I need to talk you.*"

Oh for God's sake! "If you ring me at the office in the morning I can make an appointment to see you. What are you whispering for?"

"*Now, John! It's urgent!*"

Oh please! Well past his first youth, Alfie, a retired burglar, was one of John's few criminal clients. He was a nice enough bloke and he always paid his bills on the nail, but it had been an arduous day and John was in serious need of some food and a good half bottle of red.

"It can't be that urgent. Where are you?"

"*About a yard or two away, but I think I'm being watched. Just go on in, and I'll slip in behind you.*"

For Christ's sake! John froze on the spot with his brain working overtime. If he didn't go along with it he would probably lose more of his evening than he would otherwise. If he dealt with him quickly, he might be able to salvage a bit of time to himself. Gritting his teeth he went through the door in slow motion, and a moment afterwards Alfie's overcoat clad body cannoned into the back of him. They went up the stairs in single file, and John let Alfie into his flat. Once indoors, Alfie looked around him and started to loosen up.

"Blimey! Is this Snoopy's kennel?" He took in the large white space that opened out once through the door. "Where's the furniture?"

"It's minimalist."

"Is that a posh word for practically empty? Very nice though." He dropped down onto the large creamy couch that dominated one end of the room. "Bet you've had some fun on this haven't you? Lucky sod!"

OK. Enough of this! "Alfie, what is this? How did you find out where I live for starters?"

"Come on, John, I'm a burglar! It's my job to find out where people live."

"Is that supposed to make me feel more comfortable? What's the being watched bit, and why's it so urgent to see me at nine thirty in the evening when you could easily have made an appointment to see me at the office?"

"Look I'm really sorry about this, but you know how things can be in my game, John."

"What game is that then? Aren't you supposed to be an honest man these days?"

Alfie got off the couch looking sheepish. "Don't give me a hard time, John. This is just a friendly visit, not a professional one. Just wanted to run something across you."

Oh for God's sake! At least there was no harm in Alfie, unlike some of his clients and a lot of the people he worked with. "I'm going to cook myself something. Do you want to join me?"

"Blimey, John. That's nice of you. Don't go to any trouble on my account."

"I'm cooking anyway. Let me get some jeans on and I'll knock something up. You can lay the table, the stuffs all in there." He pointed to the door to the kitchen. "Don't steal anything while I'm gone."

"No chance! Looks like someone beat me too it."

* * *

"I have to say, this is really good, John." Alfie was making short work of the stir-fry John had thrown together. "You'd make someone a lovely wife."

"Glad you're enjoying it."

"Good as anything my missus does." He looked round appreciatively. "It was a shock at first but this place is beginning to grow on me. How do you make a place that's practically empty look so expensive?"

"That's the trick of it."

"Things have changed round here haven't they, all the yuppies moving in and prices going through the roof. I can remember when you could get a house with a garden for about eight grand."

"That must have been a while back."

"Thing's haven't changed that much though. Did you read about that local counsellor who was all bashed up and left in a skip? Poor sod! Must have annoyed someone." He speared the last vegetables from his plate. "I've never gone in for this violent stuff, gives criminals a bad name." He looked hungrily at the bowl in the middle of the table. "There wouldn't be a bit more of that would there?"

John topped him up then took the last of it for himself. "Can we get on with it, Alfie? It's getting on, and I get up at six."

"I suppose we'd better" Alfie fidgeted in his chair and scratched his face. "Can I just talk round it for a bit?"

"Whatever you want."

"I just don't know what to do about something, John. Look, I've more or less retired now, but I don't know." He got up from the table and paced the floor. "I'm bloody brilliant at what I do, that's really no exaggeration. I can do anything in the breaking in business, cars, houses, safes, security gates. I've done the lot, but it's all been a bit domestic, you know, cash when I can, cameras, bits of jewellery, stuff I can fence or stuff done to order. Nothing significant. And then I started asking myself, what have I got to show for it?

Nice little house, nice little wife, but what else? No recognition, nothing like that. I'm more or less retired but with nothing to say that I'm a top guy who can really cut it. Can you imagine how that feels?"

Suddenly he had a captive audience. John had to be up early, but so what? He opened another bottle and topped up Alfie's glass.

"Go on."

"So I thought I'd do something memorable, something that I could look back on and feel proud of myself." He looked round. "I don't suppose you've got a paper from last week have you. What I want to show you was on the front pages most days."

John disappeared and came back with a handful of Guardians and passed them to Alfie who after a second's scanning waved a headline under John's nose. *"Jimmy Parker's Vermeer Stolen."*

John had already read about it. Lord Parker was an all purpose Aunt Sally for journalists and a lot of truculent politicians who considered him to be a tacky arriviste. From a pinch and scrape childhood he had set out to make money and success at any cost, starting at his school which enforced a clean plate regime in the lunch hall, thus giving him his first business opportunity which was eating his class mates' sprouts or other school lunch nasties for a few pence a plate. He made enough from this over his last three years at school that when he left at fifteen he had the funding to start selling shirts from a market stall. He went from that to a corner shop, and in due course built up a massive retail empire. Having made himself wealthy he then bought his way into politics with contributions to the government who may have despised him but not enough to turn down his gifts. He had no real political ability but had a knack for fund raising, so both he and the government were kept reasonably happy. Now as a peer of the realm and a millionaire several times over he wanted to get himself some cultural cred and he was trying to earn this by building up an art collection. Because of his sheer spending power he had managed to buy a large number of works that any national collection would have been thrilled to own; one of these was a small Vermeer which had been stolen from his London house last week.

"That wasn't you!"

"It bloody was!" Alfie lost his hang-dog look, a glow of triumph on his face. "How's that then, John!"

"Well you've certainly got my attention. You've stolen a *Vermeer!* Christ!"

"Thought you'd be impressed!" Alfie took the paper from John's hand, beaming at the story. "Nice headline, but shame it didn't say *"Police Baffled"*. That would have been a really nice touch."

"But for God's sake, I mean what are you going to do with it?"

In front to his eyes, Alfie shrank like a burst balloon, all his recent cockiness gone. "Exactly, John! That's the whole sodding problem."

He explained that he had got so involved in the idea of this one big heist that he hadn't thought any further. He could get all the usual stuff fenced, but this was too specialist and he didn't know what to do with it. Worse still, although he had not left any traceable evidence, apparently the entry had all the hallmarks that the police associated with him, and had had him in for questioning twice already. To cap it all, they were watching him day and night. They were doing it discreetly, but he knew they were there, and it was beginning to give him the creeps. It was cramping his style, and even Beryl was being checked on. "I can't get on with anything. There's all sorts of people I need to contact, and visits I need to make to do with some of the old jobs, but I'm completely buggered. Even my phone calls are being monitored."

Alarm bells rang. "But you just phoned me. Won't they trace that?"

"That call was all right. I nicked that mobile from the pub on the corner just before I phoned you."

Well that was all right then! "But you thought they were watching you here."

"I think I'd shaken them off. I was just being paranoid outside. Anyway, I'm allowed to visit my solicitor aren't I?"

Yeah, sure! With a stolen phone in your pocket! "Look, I think you should get rid of it."

"I've thought of that, but I can't. I liked the idea of making some big gesture, you know, sending it to the Queen Mum as a birthday present, something like that, but I can't get at it any more. I've got it stored in a warehouse but the fuzz are watching me the whole time and waiting for me to lead them to it." He looked round the large white space that was John's flat. "If you didn't mind picking it up yourself, it would look pretty good in here. What about just to the left of that stone bowl, sort of balancing it."

"I think you'd better go, Alfie."

He got up ruefully. "No suggestions then?"

"If they put you inside, I'll send you a copy of it. You can put it on the wall of your cell."

"You're all heart, John!"

"Ring me if they pick you up again. I'll come to the station with you." Refusing his offer of a free mobile, John let him out.

F I V E

"I CALL THIS MEETING TO order!"

The Chairman, clearly a junior council employee who would rather be anywhere else but in this hall cleared his throat nervously and did his best to avoid the eye of everyone in the room. The body of the hall was heavily populated with a large number of the more vociferous members of the local community and conversation amongst them was vigorous and loud, in marked contrast to the cautious silence of the few people on the stage. In his element in court, John sat there facing a clearly hostile and potentially unruly mob, his stomach in a mess and his brain working overtime as he tried to plan answers to questions yet to be put to him. It would be hell. Badly formulated and emotionally charged questions would be fired at him by people who would not listen to, or believe his answers. Even before things had started he could here mutterings of *"It's disgusting!"* from different corners of the room. Sitting on his left was George who had insisted on being there, even though he wanted John to front things and answer all the questions. He sat there in his overcoat, which must have cleared an entire desert of camels, vastly physical and monolithic and looking like an oversized inflatable model of the entire Kray family.

The chairman continued. "Before getting on the main business, I should briefly mention the absence of Counsellor Martin Fletcher, who would otherwise have chaired tonight's meeting. Most of you know that he is currently in intensive care in St George's hospital having been attacked and thrown in a skip recently. All I am able to tell you is that Martin is in a serious but stable condition, and that as soon as there is any progress, information will be released. Visiting is currently out of the question, but I can give a telephone number at the end if any of you want to get any information direct from the hospital." His voice took on a new note of confidence now that his part in the proceedings was nearly over. "I will now pass you over to Mr John Foxton of Hart-Russell who will give an opening address on behalf of Dragoon Properties, and then you can all ask him questions."

John had arrived separately from George and had thrown down a double scotch in the pub twenty minutes before entering the hall, and in case there was any danger of this impairing his thought processes, had followed it up with a couple of powerful espressos at the new coffee lounge next door. The barista there certainly understood what triple shot robusta was all about, and although an overdose of stimulants had had put some courage in him, John's heart seemed to be attempting the land speed record and he felt hyper and edgy. Looking round at the people in the hall he wished he had skipped the coffee and just carried on with the hard stuff and was now happily lying on the floor of somewhere friendly and congenial while people carefully stepped round him.

Screwing up his courage he got to his feet and made a start. "The purpose of this meeting tonight is to give you some information about Dragoon's proposed development which I know you are all concerned about. I'll explain why it will be of benefit to the local community, and I'll then move on to tell you what Dragoon have in mind to ensure that Belleville gets its new progressive school."

Not bad so far! He looked at the thick wedge of A4 he had prepared and prepared to settle in. "The concept of the … …"

"But what about our shop?"

"Look, I've barely started and…."

The young Asian who had interrupted had a glazed look in his eye and appeared not to have heard. "It's the local shops that suffer, init. We don't want no long speeches or nuffin. We just want our shops. My dad's shop…"

He was interrupted by an earnest looking woman in half glasses and a baggy cardigan. "But it's the school that really matters, the Saul Liebling school. We mustn't let individual vested interests confuse the main issue."

Several women from different parts of the hall *Hear Heared*, and nodded vigorously in agreement and John tried to nip this in the bud. "I suspect that you will all find that your questions will be dealt with as I proceed. It might be best if I explain…."

"Yes, but can we speed things up. A lot of us have baby sitters waiting at home."

For God's sake, if only you'd all shut up! "As I said, the concept of the development is multi-use, multi- occupation on the site of what was once…"

"Yes, but what about the school? That's what we want to know about. You can't go on fudging the issue."

Someone else cut in protesting that the problems that some of the shops faced trumped the question of the school and instantly others raised their voices in disagreement. John could see civil war breaking out before things even got started and looked to the chairman for support, but clearly was not going to get any. All he could do was to soldier on as best he could and he raised his voice an octave. "I'm sorry, but if you don't listen to me we are not going to get anywhere." He could feel his gorge rising, his lawyers hatred of anyone who could not listen and consider before speaking, at heavy simmer. "If we don't deal with this in a methodical fashion, we are all going to waste a lot of time." He took a deep breath, desperately searching his mind for the quickest and most concise way of getting the most important facts across. "The three principal elements of the development are retail outlets, mixed domestic accommodation and a health club with associated amenities. What my client…"

"But what about the school though! It's the school…."

"Will you SHUT THE FUCK UP!"

The stunned silence that greeted this was so intense he could hear his own heart thumping against his ribs, but horrified as he was at what he'd just said, now he'd let his feelings show he couldn't seem to stop himself. "I'm sorry I had to say that, but if you're all too stupid to listen, there's no point in any of us being here is there?" He glared round the room daring any one to speak, the alcohol and caffeine banging drums inside his head. "I'm coming to the school *and* the shops. OK! *Did you all hear that?* I'll be covering everything, but it will all take a moment, so just be patient, and when I've got to the end, if there's any point of detail you want to know more about you can ask questions."

He picked up his notes, the hiss of each sheet of paper against the other clearly audible in the sea of silence, then, self-conscious, but confident that he could now take them all on if it came to it, he delivered his address to the end, a note of smugness in his voice when he explained that Dragoon properties were prepared to enter into a binding contract to sell the Gambols site to the Saul Liebling School at comfortably less than its market value.

He sat down to indicate that he had finished, risking a glance in the direction of George who continued to stare straight ahead, his rubbery features giving nothing away. The hall was in total silence, and for a moment it looked as if this would continue indefinitely, until from the third row, a slim female hand was raised in question, the owner of the hand totally hidden from John's view by a large elderly Sikh sitting directly in front of her, his turban blotting her out almost completely. This modest show of life and movement, the first since John's outburst, was enough to break the tension, and in a sea of relieved throat clearing, a number of people got up and scurried out, including the Sikh. Now that he could see the woman properly, all Johns' new confidence evaporated. She was blonde with magazine cover bone structure, and had her face not been so beautiful John would have been blinded by the sight of her silky legs, elegantly displayed in a short-skirted city suit. She presented herself with the big glasses/tortoiseshell hair-clip combination that invited simultaneous removal so that some smooth operator could say *"Why Miss Jones, but you're beautiful"*, even though that was blindingly obvious anyway. She was a clear ten out of ten, and John couldn't believe that he had not appreciated that the previous day when, scarved and kaftaned and looking nothing like this sleek city siren, she had pulled her bag over his head.

She stood up to ask her question, her eyes fixed on his but amazingly showing no flicker of recognition. "Mr Foxton – it is Mr Foxton isn't it?"

He tried to answer but his throat was too dry and he just nodded lamely.

"This contract you mentioned. As it seems we were all too stupid to listen to what you were saying, isn't there a danger that a clever lawyer could draft it in terms that we wouldn't understand, and as such, not necessarily give the school and the community what it really wants?"

Let me die now! Let me have a heart attack and not recover. "We had assumed that lawyers for the school and the Resident's Association would satisfy themselves that it really is watertight."

"Well, assuming that people who are too stupid to listen know how to instruct lawyers, isn't that an additional expense for them, and how is it to be paid for? Do we assume that Dragoon will be footing the bill for any legal costs?"

George hadn't mentioned that. "Well…."

"Course we'll pay, Babe." John was startled to hear George's unmistakable voice growling from his left side. He turned in his direction to see him igniting a massive Havana. "We'll see you all right, darling. Leave it all to us." He blew a stream of blue smoke skywards and winked at her, then as if to make things incapable of rescue, he turned to John and winked at him as well, locking the two of them together in a conspiracy of arrested development. How much worse could it get? George's stretch Mercedes was outside taking up a street's worth of parking space with Sid circling it like a Rottweiler with a grudge, there was an entire forest fire lightly disguised as a cigar smouldering away in George's fat mouth in a strictly No Smoking meeting, and John had been Effing and Blinding the very people he had come to get on their side.

As John pondered if there was any conceivable way he could rescue himself, a conspicuously tall man in a shiny suit at the end of the front row stood up, a disposable ballpoint in one bony hand, and notebook dangling ominously from the other. "Belleville Chronicle. Who will be drafting this watertight contract Mr Foxton – will it be your firm?"

Punch drunk and with the anaesthetising effect of the caffeine and alcohol wearing off at a rate, John nodded as if somehow this was less committing than speech.

"And your firm is...?"

There was no avoiding it. "Hart-Russell."

Desperate to regain control, he was about to ask if there were any final questions when a woman he was horrified to recognise as the high street lollipop lady stood up. "Haven't I seen you in Tesco's? You live local don't you?"

"Oh yes! I recognise him now." Mr Patel from the corner newsagents stood up to get a better look. "You come in regular for The Guardian and Time Out. Sometimes GQ."

Now open season on John Foxton had been declared, the back row now joined in the artillery. "He's that chap with that noisy open .car – the blue one"

"Oh *that's* who it is!" The woman's face was straight out of a Christmas pantomime crossed with Viz. "He really frightened my cat the other day revving up. Telling *us* to shut up! Bloody cheek!"

"Look, *please!*" His instinct for survival kicked in and pumped a little of the adrenaline back into his system. "You now know what the development is all about, that it's going to benefit the area, and increase the value of your businesses and property. In addition there is now a much greater chance that you'll be getting the school you want. This is all thanks to Mr George Stavros here, so unless there are any more questions that are directly relevant to these issues, I suggest that you give Mr Stavros a round of applause for his generosity and then we can all go home to our families."

Out of habit they did just that, not with much enthusiasm, but it was a gesture, and behind his curtain of smoke, George had a smirk of self satisfaction on his face, but then the girl in the city suit stood up again, and raised a questioning hand. "I'd like to see that contract as soon as there's a first draft. I suspect that consent from the Resident's Association will depend on just how water tight it is"

John's answer was instinctive. "You appreciate that the contract will of course be confidential between my clients and the School and its lawyers"

"Of course. Let me give you my card." She negotiated her way to the platform and handed a card to John. '*Wendy Vyne*' it said in embossed letters. '*Ormorod and Co, Solicitors.*' "As well as being on the Resident's Association I'm representing the school." She took of her glasses and looked him in the face, then did a double take, recognising him for the first time. For a moment they just looked at each other, wondering how to react, then she extended a hand and took his, a beaming smile lighting up her face. "I'm sure we'll be able to do business with each other."

SIX

FRIDAY EVENING AT LAST AND cocooned in the smoky depths of Drum's Wine Bar in Chancery Lane, the air perfumed with Claret and Bulldog Special even Luke seemed borderline human. John was approaching the top of his curve, nicely mellow and full of love and well being, but not yet an embarrassment to himself and others and still some way before either weeping over how badly he had treated his mother or trying to pick a fight with the cigarette machine.

It wasn't a bad turn out for an ordinary Friday night, the usual suspects were here, Michael, Chris, Julia, and Ron plus Luke, Linda, and Simon. Even a couple of the secretaries had pitched up, plus the unutterably edible Young Tracy From Accounts. Life had nothing better to offer, especially as Tracy was wearing a particularly short skirt tonight, this one with a tantalising slit up one side to add a touch of *Now You See It, Now You Don't* to today's leg exhibition. A skirt this short meant of course that she had to be wearing tights rather than stockings, but try as you might you couldn't have everything in this world, a fact bemoaned by Ron as he poured the last dregs of the bottle he was sharing with John into his glass. Comfortably over any conventional retirement age, Ron looked like a house that had somehow managed to resist all attempts by the demolition ball to bring it down. Cobwebbed with structural cracks, the big question was whether individual chunks would start fall off one by one, or if instead, without warning, the entire edifice would suddenly come crashing down.

"If she had any sense of fair play, she would wear that skirt with stockings." Ron's voice had a wistful edge to it. "Only reasonable to give us the odd flash of suspender as she walks round the office. Wouldn't cost her anything."

John was hit with a cocktail of conflicting reactions. It was one thing to have guilty thoughts like this, but quite another to share them with other people. Having said that, Tracy was such eye candy it was hard at times not to keep thoughts to yourself and as Ron had started this particular ball rolling he might as well run with it. Yes it was adolescent but it was Friday night and he was only human.

"Do you think," John said, leaning across the bar to call for another bottle. "Do you think that when she was a little girl she gave sweets to dirty old men?"

"If she did, I bet they landed up paying for them in the end!"

Trying not to make it too obvious John took a few moments to assess Tracy's petite silhouette. "Tell me, on the basis that no one can ever score a perfect ten, what do you think she is? Nine and three quarters?"

Treating the question with the seriousness it deserved, Ron carried out a lengthy visual examination before replying.

"Eleven and a half."

"No, come on, Ron! I know she's way ahead in the bimbo league, but for a score like that you've got to have a pedigree as well and all the usual add-ons."

"But bims don't need class. If they have class, then they're not a bim. The first hint of brains or an education and they start asking to be treated like one of us, and the next thing you know you might just as well have a wife."

Ron was one of the original partners with Russell Brooks and Keeling from the days before it hooked up with Hart – Stanley. A perfectly capable corporate lawyer but long resigned to not being a big hitter, in late middle age he had quietly settled into lazy cynicism. Before the amalgamation life had been cosy and undemanding, and he had no intention of allowing it to be any other way and the constant stream of memos and instructions about billing targets and time records that landed on his desk since the new regime were scarcely given a glance before he dropped them in the bin and got back to his racing paper. He had always regarded his career in the law as a means to an end, and now his house was paid for and his children long grown up, it had served its purpose. He would have retired, but as that meant the prospect of spending his days at home with Clarissa he quietly hung on, fully aware that one day, warnings about failure to meet targets and objectives would in due course mean the chop and permanent incarceration with his wife. Until then, the office served him as a cross between a club and a library.

He took out another Benson and lit it. "Tracy's one shortcoming is that she's brilliant with the computer which could mean she might have a brain."

"Is that right?"

"She's fixed mine for me two or three times; just taps away at the keys and it does party tricks for her. It's 'cos she's so young I expect. The closer to a school kid you are, the easier it is."

John was still thinking about what he had said earlier. "Must be nice being a bimbo. That's all that's asked of you, just be sweet and sexy and that's the end of it. Must be tough on girls like Julia and Linda who have to score on all the career stuff and still have to compete with bims when they go out on Saturday nights."

The constant calculation and re-calculation of people's status was an integral part of any conversation between the two of them, even if it meant carefully side stepping any question of where they fitted in. With his nicotine stained eyebrows and sagging suits Ron tacitly accepted that he was now well out of the game but he was prepared to put in considerable effort to fine tune the precise score of anybody who qualified for consideration. As the subject headings included such diverse matters as postal district lived in, make and model of car, quality of degree, calibre of firm, status within it, status of current squeeze et al, the final score involved complex considerations. If, for example, someone had a double first from Oxford plus a Porsche and a flat in Islington, the final score could still be dragged down if the person in question happened to be a spotty nerd who hadn't pulled since three Christmas parties ago. It was unspoken that anyone over forty was best left out of the game as pondering on the quality of their sex life could be off putting, although an exception was always made for Augustus Melville QC, who not only scored ten plus in just about every category, but also had looks that were on the cusp between a Greek god and an Easter Island sculpture. They had long ago agreed that his intellectual credibility was not damaged in the slightest by his frequently being seen in the best watering holes with A-List actresses and models so his position at number one seemed pretty safe for the foreseeable future. .

Pondering on the whole complex subject John swept his eyes round the group who had pitched up here tonight. In a far corner, Luke was in animated conversation with Linda and Simon, none of them dedicated alcoholics but well into their second bottle of champagne and visibly loosening up. Simon was a long way from being a genius but with his long hours and impressive attention to detail he was likely to be made a partner soon, and Linda's quiet brilliance meant that for her it was a foregone conclusion. Despite his feeling of Friday night well-being, John was hit by a pang of jealousy, their iridescent inner-circle glow being everything he wanted to have. It just wasn't fair. He had always been a passionate believer in the democracy of success which was there waiting for anybody who was prepared to make the necessary effort, so he had put his head down and gone full tilt, only to crash into a brick wall he had unwittingly built himself. Even now he was still in shock from the impact, and now these people were standing on the other side of it, simpering and preening while he could only crane his neck to see just how nice it must be for them.

Recognising the onset of self pity he was about to get back to Ron and another bottle, when he was surprised to see Rupert Davies come in to the bar and walk over to the Luke group with the easy confidence of someone who knows that they will be welcome. Rupert was an ex-member of the firm who had moved on to join Crowther-Van, one of the Golden Circle of top City firms with billion pound turnovers and senior partners reputed to be taking home something approaching a million a year. Tall and bespectacled, Rupert was effortlessly brilliant with a brain like oiled clockwork and a photographic memory. John had been suffering from pangs of inferiority before his arrival, but now it was almost beyond bearing. He suddenly felt grubby, a drunken second rate career failure exchanging schoolboy smut with a beery old has-been in an ash stained suit. Rupert somehow managed to look so relaxed and easy with these other high flyers, his lanky frame encased in a pale grey suit, and his longish hair falling in a silky curtain over his forehead. What must he be on now, £200,000? Easily, and he wasn't even a partner yet.

All that John wanted to do was to pretend that he wasn't there, but, it was like trying to pretend not to notice that the Queen has dropped in on your suburban living room, and without any conscious will he left Ron and drifted over.

"Rupert, dear boy. Nice to see you."

"And you, John." Rupert flashed a smile at John that would have fooled the average bystander that he was greeting an equal. "How's things?" He was younger than John, but already his voice was already taking on the practised bonhomie of someone used to eating at high table, but a slight deadness in his expression gave a hint that he was not over excited by this meeting. Democratic to the last, Luke and the rest of them said nothing and waited for John to finish whatever he wanted to say to Rupert before they could get on with their inner circle gossip.

"Shouldn't you be in one of the City bars?" John asked. "What brings you slumming to Chancery Lane?" This was more for the benefit of Luke who was always irritated at the suggestion that a Lincoln's Inn practice was inferior to one in the City.

"Thought it would be nice to look you all up. It can get a bit incestuous in the City sometimes."

"How's Alison?" This was Rupert's fragrant wife, a doctor already gaining a reputation in heart surgery.

"Bit stressed. We both are. We've just moved to a house in Holland Park and it's still all packing cases and confusion. It'll be months before the decorators have finished with it. Are you still in... where is it?"

"Belleville." The name turned to ashes on his tongue when he thought of Holland Park. Well done, Rupert! Straight into an old money postcode and not having any truck with those nasty middle men like Islington and Notting Hill. He could have wept. Rupert was scarcely thirty, and he had left him at the starting blocks already.

Shrieks of laughter from a group of girls took his attention, and he could see they were all pulling their tops out and comparing bras, wetting themselves with hilarity while Ron and a couple of other no-hopers were egging them on, and in another corner Chris and Julia, both married but who everybody knew had had something going on, were in their own separate huddle. He suddenly felt very alone. He knew he wasn't really wanted in this group of high achievers even if it was where he truly belonged but circumstances had closed the door in his face and that was that. Fair enough he was always welcome with the bims and the drunks, but it wasn't where he really wanted to be.

Pulling himself together he decided that there had to be worse things in life than mingling with a bunch of not quite pissed office girls comparing cleavage and uplift so he made his excuses to Rupert, then shambled over to join in the increasingly lurid exchanges of smut and innuendo as grain and grape had an ever more potent effect. Anaesthetised by his heavy intake, he was unaware of the passage of time, the wholly forgettable conversations melding into a haze of indistinguishable words. One by one people sloped off until he realised that the place had emptied out considerably and it was close to chucking out time. It seemed that the only survivors from Hart-Russell were him and Tracy in a one-to-one conversation which was moving from the general to the specific as they found themselves alone. Where had everybody gone? He didn't remember anybody saying goodbye, or if they had, he hadn't heard. Couldn't be helped. The two of them moved to an empty table and sat down, Tracy showing no desire to abandon ship even though it was now just her and John. He looked around him to make sure he wasn't dreaming, but it was right enough, he was alone with Young Tracy From Accounts in a smoky wine bar on a Friday night. This would normally have been beyond his wildest dreams, but he wasn't sure how he should deal with it. He had never actually had a conversation with her before, all previous exchanges having been no more than passing remarks. Suddenly he realised he might have to deal with her as if she were a real person with a life of her own rather than just being a pocket Venus with a taste for provocative clothes who had been created by God for the sole purpose of giving visual pleasure to him and the other men in the office. In the state he was in, he wondered if he would be able to manage it.

The edge was taken off things when he realised she was talking with some enthusiasm about her boyfriend, but what did he expect? He couldn't really be surprised by her having one. To his certain knowledge all the men in the office fancied her, and judging by the way most of the men in Drums had been looking at her, they did too, so as there was some reasonable possibility that every man in the world fancied her, in due course at least one of them must have made it through whatever recruitment process she insisted on. He wasn't that surprised to discover that his name was Nikos, that he was a waiter at a small restaurant on a Greek island called Zandos, and that she had met him on holiday the previous August and was saving up to go again as soon as possible.

How old was this girl? Twenty two, twenty four? Surely by now she must have learned that Greek waiters along with their Italian and Spanish counterparts considered English girls on package holidays to be part of their wages. Feeling positively middle aged he discretely suggested that she should prepare herself for the possibility that she may not be the only girl at whom Nikos had fluttered his long Greek eyelashes and that she might find that he had a dozen other romances on the go when she went back.

"No, really! It's not like that. He writes every week, sometimes twice. I've got them all, seventy-one. He's saving up to buy his own restaurant, and when he's got enough money together, I'm going out there to live with him. We've got it all worked out."

"Seventy-one?"

"Honest! He never misses. Sometimes I get two the same day."

Even through his drunken haze, John was impressed, if slightly appalled at the idea of any young man with whatever it takes to bed a girl like Tracy squandering his no doubt golden youth writing all those letters when he could be bedding all the other girls like Tracy who go on holiday to Greek islands for the sole purpose of being bedded by men like Nikos. At the same time he felt concerned for her, her smiling face so enthusiastic and innocent.

"You will be careful, won't you? No girl who looks like you can have any illusions what men can be like. If you burned your boats and found yourself stranded in Greece it wouldn't be funny."

"Look, I'm not just some stupid airhead you know! Can I let you in on a secret? This really is a secret, so I'll kill you if it leaks out."

John knew instinctively that anyone who promised to tell you something that was absolutely secret and known to no other soul on earth had already leaked it like a geyser to everyone else they knew, but was still gratified by this apparent show of confidence. "Course I won't tell."

"I've got two passports! One Greek and one English."

Well, she had impressed him. No doubt of that. "I'm staggered! How come?"

She looked pleased at his reaction. "My dad's Greek and I was born in Crete. My dad registered my birth there, but my parents had just split up and my mum brought me straight to England, and pretended I was born here and registered me here all over again. In Greece I'm Sophia Kostakis, and in England I'm Tracy Spooner."

"Well fuck me!"

"Thought you'd be surprised."

He digested this for a moment, more concerned now of her landing up in prison in one country or another rather than just having her heart broken. "Well do be careful anyway."

"I don't have to be careful. When you're really in love there's never any doubt about it, is there. You can fancy people rotten, but once you're in love, that's it. Aren't you in love with someone?"

"No I'm afraid I'm not." He wanted to add that he did fancy someone rotten, and that she was sitting opposite him right now, but thought that getting back to that level of conversation might be counter- productive.

He had not seen Tracy at such close quarters before and was trying to get the measure of her. She had large brown heavy lidded eyes with sooty eyelashes, and her shoulder length hair was dark and glossy. He already knew that her figure was amazing, but although he couldn't stop taking sneaky glances at it while he had this opportunity there was something he was trying to understand. She was gorgeous enough with her youthful optimism and brightness, but was she actually beautiful? He tried to work out if the hint of tiredness round the corners of her eyes was the temporary effect of a late Friday night, or that already too many girlie nights out fuelled by Bensons and Chardonnay were making their mark and that this was a clue to what she might look like when middle age and life's disappointments had had their way with her.

"But you must have been in love at some time. I mean, you must have!"

"I didn't say I hadn't ever been. Just that I wasn't right now."

"So tell me about it, who was she?"

He took a deep breath wondering if he really was going to go public about something so personal. "Her name was Diana. She was very sweet, very pretty and a truly lovely person. It was the one time I've ever been in love with anybody, and I agree that when it's the real thing there's no doubt about it."

Tracy's eyes were alive with interest. "So?"

"So?"

"So what happened? Don't stop there."

Could he deal with this? He knew he was probably way drunker than he realised and he was already regretting his momentary candour. This was not a story from which he would emerge with any credit if the full facts came out.

"Can I just leave it that she's now married to someone else. They've had a child, and I've no reason to believe they're not very happy together." This was the truth and nothing but the truth, but it was a long, long, way from being the whole truth. He wondered if even this limited information would give him away, but there was no reason why she should suspect.

"Oh no! What happened?" Tracy's face was a mask of anxiety, and pleasure at her concern for him won over the feeling of being a shit that he always experienced when dredging this up.

"Do you mind if I don't."

"No of course not. Oh, John, I'm so sorry!"

Tracy leaned forward and took his hands in hers, her eyes looking into his and brimming with sympathy. The evening was getting out of hand, and seemed to have a momentum of its own that he was powerless to control, but if this was fate he was happy to give in to it. After looking back at her for a moment, he let his eyes drop as if to collect his thoughts before speaking again, but whatever booze fuelled cliché he was about to come out with was interrupted by the barman banging on a large drum, the signal that the place was closing. Tracy pulled back and looked at her watch.

"Oh my God, is that the time! I didn't mean to stay this long."

She started to gather her things, and John found that he could just about manage to stand unaided. In an attempt to prolong their time together he offered to get her a taxi and his heart leapt when she said she lived in Tooting, which was the next borough along from him, so suggesting that they shared did not seem opportunistic. They were lucky to get one without much delay and, not sure if this was a dream or not, he climbed in beside her, and fell back into the seat pleased that his body seemed to be doing more or less what it was told. They didn't talk very much during the first part of the journey, but when the taxi cornered so she was pushed against him, a protective arm round her shoulders seemed appropriate and was clearly not unwelcome.

"You've been really nice to me tonight." She said after a while. "I've always liked you – you're different from all the others. Most of the guys are just money mad, and just think of me and the secretaries as stupid bimbos."

Well, God forbid! He gave her shoulder a squeeze and she nestled her head into him. Her skirt had ridden to the top of her thighs, and with his head nuzzled against hers he could scarcely believe that she was so relaxed with all this intimacy. It was a warm night, and in the dark interior he became aware of the cocktail of aromas she was giving off, talc and tobacco crossed with a hint of armpit and a touch of perfume. The feel and the look and the smell of her joined together to create an overwhelming erotic charge and it was taking all his self control to keep himself under control.

Sensing that she was being looked at, she looked up at him then reached up and kissed him. It was a nice kiss, soft and sensual, and whatever other signals it might have been giving it was full of affection. After a minute, he let nature take over and he moved his hand to take hold of her breast, and was gratified she did nothing to stop this, and if anything increased the pressure of her kiss. After a further minute, her own hand was on top of his keeping it in place on her breast while they kissed some more. At the end of a further minute however her hand gently pulled his away and she disentangled herself.

"This is very nice, but we know we shouldn't be doing this."

"Well, I agree this is very nice."

"And don't start getting any ideas that I kiss just anyone in taxis"

"Wouldn't cross my mind."

"You're a sweet guy, and I really like you, that's all. Just allow that I've had a few to drink."

"I promise not to tell Nikos."

"Bastard!" She smacked him on the hand, and the resulting tussle could just have turned into something interesting, but suddenly they were at her street and it was all coming to an end. Not knowing how to deal with the sudden void he struggled for words, but nothing intelligent emerged and he was wholly unprepared for the short but enthusiastic kiss she gave him before pushing him back into the seat and jumping out.

An hour later in his flat, he lay on his bed not quite asleep but in a drunken stupor. He had dropped his jacket on the floor, and in the act of taking it off was convinced he could see a badge pinned to the lapel saying *I have snogged Young Tracy From Accounts*. Was that true? Yes it was, it really was! Time and again he went over the taxi interval in his mind, a half smile on his lips, but each time he found himself dropping into sleep, the image was overtaken by thoughts of Rupert Davies and his house in Holland Park.

SEVEN

IF YOU DIDN'T COME INTO the office at weekends it looked as if you didn't have a proper work load, but it was important to pace it. A token visit every now and then suggested you were a bit of an amateur, but if you came in too often it looked as if you were a sad tosser with no private life. Much of the time a weekend visit was the only possible way to keep the work under control, but even so, coming in on Saturday night when any self respecting Cool Britannic should have been munching at Momo or carousing at the Met Bar was going to extremes. John couldn't quite believe he was here at this time, but temporarily he was without anyone he could formally classify as an actual girlfriend and tonight the couple of locums he could normally rely on were going out with their regular boyfriends. The hangover that had greeted him on waking this morning had put him off the idea of alcohol, but somehow an evening alone with Inspector Morse seemed even sadder than being in the office recording chargeable time at £175 per hour.

He looked at the heap of files on his desk wondering if he would cope with it all. He had two costs schedules to prepare for hearings next week, a skeleton argument for an application for judgment, witness statements to draft for a possible injunction, and a ton of unanswered letters. If he worked all night and came in Sunday as well, he might just catch up. Checking his screen showed nine emails since he had left the office on Friday, and three faxes waiting on the tray. Fuck it! He might just as well be on an assembly line. He picked up his copy of *The Lawyer* and thumbed through for the latest legal gossip. He read without any pleasure that Brakely-Spears in the City were now paying newly qualifieds the sort of salary that a senior partner in a small local firm would be thrilled to get, and that Charlsley&Hopkins were only just behind them. Brilliant! It wasn't so different from what he was getting. To rub it all in, there was a profile of Rupert Davies and the International Property department he was setting up with Crowther-Van and the anticipated fee income it was predicted to generate during the next financial year.

The badge on his lapel that had kept a smirk of self satisfaction on his face during the day had been replaced by two lead weights pulling down the corners of his mouth. He knew he should get stuck in, but suddenly the will wasn't there. The only thing that blipped John's adrenaline count at all was the contract that had to be drafted agreeing to sell the Gambols site to The Saul Liebling school. This was partly because he was terrified of getting anything wrong for George, and partly because he would have to negotiate the details with someone who intrigued the pants off him. Her business card was tucked in to the edge of his blotter and not for the first time he pulled it out and looked at it. *Wendy Vyne, Ormorod and Co.* She looked and sounded like City material, but he had looked up her firm in the directory and found it to be a very minor three partner outfit in Belleville, barely ten minutes from his own flat. More to the point, women in her position didn't normally dress themselves up like refugees from Greenham Common and go round waving banners. Even if none of this applied, her looks alone would be enough to have him interested.

He was no conveyancer, but the agreement would be an oddity and he would have to do the initial drafting himself and then get it vetted by Ron or Ingrid. Ron had put him on to a precedent on one of Adam Granger's directories that was the closest thing he would find as a working draft, so he called it up and had a look at it. It might be the best he was going to get, but it would need a ton of work. He made himself a cup of coffee and set about pulling it into shape, making a few false starts, but eventually getting into his stride. An hour and a half later, his brain foggy with concentration, he was reasonably pleased with what he had created, scrolling it down the screen a couple of times to ensure that subject to some possible fine tuning, it fitted the bill. He pressed the Print button, but as he did so, his screen blanked out and a message appeared: *"Your interface Ram Widget is temporarily disenabled. Press Crown Key to re- route."*

Oh Christ! He had no idea what the Crown Key was, but it brought home that he had not copied the precedent across before starting on it. Fuck it! This could be serious. He clicked on the X at the corner of the message hoping it would go away, but it was replaced with one that said *"Your programme is not responding to Server Command. Press   X to re-link to base directory. WARNING – YOU MAY LOSE UNSAVED MATERIAL IF YOU DO THIS."*

Please no! The thought of losing all this work made him feel weak; he was now tired and not able to cope with having to recreate it all, but if he didn't do what the computer said, he was doubly buggered as he had Adam Granger's precedent locked in to his system. OK. Go for it! He gingerly pressed the keys, and this time the message sent ice through his veins. *"Your computer has performed an illegal operation. Press any key to delete this programme, or F14 to close down."*

No! Please not this! He was perfectly happy with the computer in day to day terms, but when it did this sort of thing it terrified him. What did it mean by *"Delete programme"*, the reference to *"programme"* suggesting that he was not merely in danger of losing the work he had done, but the whole of the precedent file as well. Of course he should have copied the precedent across before starting to mess with it as then at least it would not have bogged up the whole system. It was all spelled out in the office manual that you should never alter anyone else's precedents, and to make matters worse if that was possible, the precedent he had borrowed and bowdlerised belonged to Adam Granger the head of conveyancing who was not known for taking prisoners.

The message flickered on the screen, bright with sadistic glee. There was something about the reference to *"Any key"* that fine tuned its menace. It might only call for John to nudge the screen for the forces behind it to erase great chunks of the firm's intellectual property in a single sweep. It was the end of any work this evening, or the rest of the weekend. He contemplated sleeping here next to his machine, guarding it from the danger of passing mice of the vibration of the cleaner's hoover, but decide that this was fate, and that if an electronic bug was determined to bring his career to an end then it would happen despite anything he could do. He gathered his things and crept out. If he was really lucky he might catch the tail end of Inspector Morse.

* * *

He had never been so pleased to see a Monday morning. He got in even earlier than usual, desperate to get himself out of the poo before anyone found out what he had done. Ashock the Systems Administrator was on holiday this week but he had remembered what Ron had said about Tracy being a wizard on the computer. His big concern that she would misinterpret a crack of dawn call following their interval in the taxi as being motivated by other things entirely, but the situation was too serious to worry about that. He forced himself to wait until nine thirty one before he called, but her internal phone was constantly engaged. Reluctant to send her an email as it would then be a public record, eventually after a number of failed attempts to make contact, he wandered upstairs into the account's office.

"Hi Bob."

"Oh yes. And a very good morning to you, John. Let's hope we all survive till the afternoon, eh?"

Bob the chief cashier answered John in his flat monotone voice, peering at him through his thick jam jar bottom glasses, before turning back to his own screen. Tracy was busy clacking away at her keyboard and talking into a telephone tucked under ear. Without pausing in either of her activities, she swivelled round in her seat to see who it was, but having done so failed to acknowledge his existence in any way so he hovered there feeling uncomfortable and unable to avoid talking to Bob. There was no harm in Bob which was probably much of the problem with him. He spent a great deal of his time in a rearguard attempt to prove that he actually existed, the walls of the accounts office being lined with posters along the lines of *"The floggings will continue until morale improves"* and even verging on the controversial with *"If God had meant us to be homosexuals, he would have put our bottoms in the front."* He backed these up with photographs of his extra-curricular glories, the centre piece being one of him with his bowls team when they were runners up in a local competition seven years ago. Rumour had it that he was a mean line dancer, but John had always managed to avoid the subject. He was efficient enough in day to day terms, and cheques were issued and petty cash allocated without any problem, but as for the bigger picture, he wasn't quite sure what that was. In his life he hadn't so much missed the boat as not realised there was one, so at least he wasn't disappointed. When God decided that it was the Meek who should inherit the earth, he had almost certainly put in some small print along the lines that, of course, that didn't include Bob.

"We don't often get to see you high flyers down here. What can I do you for?"

"It's actually Tracy I want. Bit of a problem with my computer." John tried to catch Tracy's attention, but her eyes were fixed on her screen.

"Tracy's the girl for that all right." Bob looked blankly in her direction, the thick lenses of his glasses distorting his eyes and making them look like shirt buttons. John wondered if having Tracy in his room all day had fried his brain and been responsible for his personality by-pass. "Her and Ashock, both of them. Wizard on that thing. I leave all the technical stuff to her. Shall I tell her?"

"Would you. Shouldn't take her a moment, just a bit of a jam up."

Tracy's call came to an end, and she turned round and looked at him, her face a frozen mask and her expression impossible to read. Suddenly he was going to have to ask her direct and it was going to be even more difficult than he had anticipated.

"Oh Hi Tracy. Look, erm, I've got a bit of a problem with the computer and it's urgent. Ron tells me you're really good with it. Could you help me out? It's quite important. Sorry and all that." He felt stupidly unsure of himself. They'd had a nice little interval together on Friday night, but he didn't want her to think he was the sort of saddo who considered that a drunken snog in a taxi was enough to make them an item. Looking back at him, her blank expression didn't change.

"OK. I'll pop down in a minute."

Back in his office he swivelled back and forth in his chair as he waited for her, but her eventual entrance did not encourage him. She came into his room cautiously, and though her eyes were now shining like two large and well polished conkers, her mouth had a firm set to it. She was doing dignified for all she was worth, and her movements were stiff and artificial. Her voice when she spoke to him after a short but uncomfortable silence was frosted with an unusual formality.

"What's the trouble then? I'm very busy you know."

Even as his brain went into overdrive trying to find a way to ease through this Arctic impasse, his eyes took in all the important information. Friday night she had been showing the effects of an alcohol- fuelled end of a long week, but now it was first thing Monday morning and she looked as fresh and bright as a newly minted coin with all her bimbo kit in perfect order:- black shoes with kitten heels and ankle straps, tight black skirt to mid thigh raising the possibility that the sheer graphite tights might just be stockings, off the shoulder maroon top making an exhibition of her white bra straps, a gold crucifix on a simple gold chain and her dark hair as loose and shiny as a curtain of silk. She was as fanciable as anything he had ever seen and although right now he felt like a complete tit, not only did he know, but he knew that she knew that he had a big badge welded to the lapel of his jacket and nothing she could do could prise it off.

"Look I'm really sorry, Tracy, but this really is serious. I'm all frozen up and likely to lose the firm's precedent system as well as a big chunk of important work. I'm afraid to touch a button in case I just screw up the whole system."

"Look you didn't have to do this you know."

"What, sorry…?"

"I'm embarrassed by Friday too you know. If you wanted to talk to me, I'm quite human. You didn't have to do all this."

"But I didn't……"

"You're not the first bloke who's made a grab at me in a taxi. I'm not going to tell anyone."

Outrage at the slant put on the event battled with the need to survive. At least her face was losing its look of frozen dignity. "Look, Tracy…. Of course I would have wanted to talk to you about Friday evening, but that's not why I asked you to help me. This is really serious. I was in the office on Saturday night and things suddenly screwed up. The worst thing is, it's one of Adam Granger's precedents I've locked in."

"You were in here on Saturday night!"

"We all come in at weekends when we're busy."

"But Saturday night's a bit sad isn't it?"

"Not as sad as losing my job."

"But," She looked at him like a disappointed parent dealing with a not very bright infant. "Shouldn't you have copied it across to your own file first before you started to change it? Isn't that in the office manual?"

Please don't tell me what I've been telling myself all weekend! "Yes, I *know* ! But the fact is I didn't."

To his horror she started to laugh. She was half sitting on his desk and malicious giggles came from her like bubbles from a sinking ship. "So who's a naughty boy then, John? You're going to owe me for this aren't you?"

The beginnings of a not wholly un-pleasurable panic started to set in. He knew she would do what was necessary to help him but she was clearly planning to extract maximum humiliation first. "Look *please*, Tracy. Anything you want."

Her glee increased at this role reversal and his naked dependence on her good will. "I'm a very expensive girl you know. Might cost a lot to stop me telling them all what you get up to!"

"*Please*, Trace!" Some men paid to be humiliated by sexy young girls in mini skirts, but John couldn't wait for all this to be over.

"I could just press the wrong keys by accident and make it even worse. Wouldn't that be terrible!"

"Tracy, I'm begging you. *Please!* "

Her obvious pleasure increased at his every word. "*Begging* are you! I could get to like this. You can get on your knees if you like." Laughing with her temporary power she finally decided it was time to relent. "Oh all right, John! Course I'll help you. Let's have a look." To John's surprise she sat herself down onto his lap and swivelled them both round to look at the screen. "Tell me, what happened to get you to this point?"

John talked her through it, his concentration impaired by having her on his lap, the pleasure mingled with concern that what he'd done was beyond help and panic in case anyone should suddenly come in. Her fingers flashed across the keys, screen overlaying screen in front of his eyes as she clicked and moused through the system.

Suddenly it was there in front of him, the contract he had done so much work on. With a burst of affection he squeezed her waist and kissed her on the shoulder.

"You're brilliant. You're fucking brilliant, Trace!"

"Let me copy it across and save it. What file do you want it in?"

He gave her the info, not removing his arm from around her waist, and while he was at it he cautiously investigated her thigh with his other hand till he could feel the tell tale knob of a suspender button through her skirt which he fiddled with like a worry bead while she did her stuff on the computer. She carried on as if unaware of what he was doing and he found himself overwhelmed with the urge to have another feel of her breasts but knew he could not take the risk. He really had no idea where this girl was coming from, and if she suddenly slapped his face and flounced out the room at this point it would ruin everything.

"There you go. All done!" She got up from his lap showing no more concern than had she been getting up from an office chair.

"Look, Tracy......I'm really in your debt."

"Aren't you now!" She looked down at him, a second wave of giggles starting to erupt. "There's not much I can't ask you for now is there, or I'll have to tell everyone what a naughty boy you are!"

Looking up at her, his loins were boiling with a potent cocktail of lust and affection, and unable to stop himself he made a rapid lunge in her direction but with practised ease she evaded him and was at his office door in a split second. She paused for an instant before slipping out, but with a backward smile at him he knew he would spend days trying to interpret.

EIGHT

"GEORGE? YES, IT'S JOHN. HI. Got a moment?"

Three days on, and after much re-working, John was ready to put the draft contract under George's nose. He had done the Land Registry searches, consulted colleagues, and had done everything possible to ensure that he had covered all his exits. George's instructions had been to prepare a watertight agreement that Dragoon would sell the Gambols site to the Saul Liebling School for seventy percent of its market value provide that the development of the Old Brewery site went ahead and the holding deposit was paid by Clarendon Properties. That was precisely what George had said. With any other client, John would have known that was what was meant, but with George, he was afraid that he had not been told something vital and that it was all part of a scam about which he would not want to know, or that George had intended John to realise that such uncharacteristic generosity was not what he had in mind at all, and that John should build in escape clauses invisible to the naked eye. Why did he have to have clients like George? Why couldn't his clients be outfits of the calibre of Clarendon, long established, up-market, and probably who gave clear written instructions rather than nudges and winks over lunch.

"How you doing, John? Very impressed with you at the meeting. Good crowd control."

"Yes, err thanks, George. Look I've got the contract drafted, the one you want with the Saul Liebling outfit. It's being sent round to you by courier now. I know you're going to say that if I'm happy with it, then you are, but I want you to read this one carefully. Not all the legalese, but the meaty bits that I've highlighted. I want to be really sure it says what you want it to say. Once both of you have signed it, you do realise you're stuck with it and you really will have to sell."

"*Yes, sure.*"

"I've done all the searches and the title seems OK, and there's no charges registered."

"*Well, there wouldn't be, would there?*"

Well there certainly shouldn't be. He wished he could see George's enormous blubbery face, but knew that even if he could, all that flesh was expert at masking any emotion and that he would have no better idea of what George was thinking than he could now. "It's just that I've drafted it as you said – it really is watertight. If the Old Brewery development goes ahead, then you really will have to sell the Gambols site to the Saul Liebling school."

"*Good lad.*"

There was no point in pushing it any further without sounding neurotic. It was all in his covering letter and there was nothing further he could do. "How's the arrangement with Clarendon coming on? It all depends on that doesn't it?"

"*Wankers are being sticky with the up-front payment. I've asked them to get their lawyers to give you a ring and you can take it over. Don't take any shit, John. Tell them it's five mill or they can go screw themselves.*"

Using those very words, or being more up front about it? "Right, George. Send me copies of all your stuff and I'll deal with it."

"*Will do. I'm relying on you, John.* "

He clicked off and the disengaged tone rang in John's ear.

* * *

"*Call for you, John. A Miss Vyne.*"

"Who?"

"Miss Vyne. Ormorod & Co."

His heart rate quickened slightly when he realised who it was telephoning him. OK, this was Harrods negotiating with a corner shop, but she had already managed to wrong foot him twice over.

"Oh right. Put her through will you. Yes, hi. John Foxton."

"Wendy Vyne, hope you remember. Ormorod and Co? Yes. How are you? Good. Calling about the Gambols site in Belleville and the old Brewery Development. That's right. You sent me a draft contract to look over."

She went on that it didn't look as if there were fundamental differences between them, but she thought that it was too cumbersome to keep blue pencilling and exchanging drafts. Why didn't they sit down together and try to knock something out? John's heart rate increased a fraction more as he agreed. It was just a case of her office or his. He wasn't keen to tell her that he actually lived in Belleville, probably less than half a mile from her offices, but said he would be in that part of the world on Thursday and suggested an appointment later in the afternoon. She agreed and the time was fixed. When he put down the phone he felt quietly pleased with himself.

NINE

ON THE THURSDAY MORNING OF the meeting he dressed with extra care and chose his bluest shirt and his soft Lanvin suit in pale grey. He thought about their meeting on and off through the day, and driving to her offices he even kept the car's hood up to avoid being too windblown by the journey; on arrival he found himself self consciously checking his appearance in the driving mirror before getting out. Could it be by any chance that he was trying to make a good impression? As he completed his parking manoeuvre outside her office the hollow boom of his TVR's exhaust had made its presence felt, and walking up to the front door he was embarrassed to see a number of faces vacantly staring through the window as he approached; with such an attention seeking car he wasn't that unused to this, but it was the window itself that was most off putting. He knew her office would not be Lincoln's Inn or the City, but still couldn't believe that members of his profession could practice in a place like this. The legal world like any other has its clear hierarchies. Undisputedly at the top are the big City firms, the Golden Circle with massive corporate clients, telephone number salaries, and hourly billing rates which would pay most people's monthly mortgage. This is where he wanted to be, considering himself to be in exile until he made it. A little way behind and where he was now were the long established Lincoln's Inn practices, just as competent, and certainly as academic, but with a more modest client base and producing an income that did not run to yachts and private aeroplanes; next along were the West End firms, just about keeping their end up, and finally there were the poor sods at the bottom, the pound shops of the profession operating from local high streets and struggling to make ends meet on legal aid rates. That's what this was. The premises had clearly once housed some depressing retail shop selling perhaps prams or hardware but now had the name Ormorod and Co in massive letters pasted across the window along with a notice that they did Domestic Injunctions, Landlord and Tenant, and Immigration. A twenty-four hour phone number for emergency police station work was prominently displayed. He would have cut and run, but the down market faces with their gloomy eyes pressed against the glass made it impossible.

John had never fooled himself that he liked the real world. Couldn't see the point of it if there was any possibility of being somewhere better, and he knew that when he passed through that miserable looking door he would have it smeared all over the soles of his polished black brogues. He took a deep breath and walked in, feeling dreadfully self conscious to find the reception desk empty but the waiting area full of depressed looking people in charity shop clothes staring at him with silent curiosity. This was his worst nightmare come true. He hated being in the company of poor people as they picked the scab of his fear of failure and reminded him of everything he hoped he had left behind. He was convinced that when they looked at him they could see through his veneer of superficial affluence and knew that underneath he was actually no different from them and that it was with them that he really belonged. When at last Wendy Vyne appeared and rescued him from this sea of inquisitive eyes, he almost threw himself through her office door with relief, breathing heavily as he sat down opposite her.

"You look a bit flushed. Do you want a glass of water?"

"No thanks. I'll be fine."

Coming too, he looked around her office and took in the details, Dickens crossed with MFI. Piles of papers and files in tottering heaps on the cheapest office- surplus furniture, an out of date dictating machine, a very Third World looking computer screen, and several discarded plastic cups. His expression must have given him away as she suddenly laughed out loud.

"It's not Grand Hotel, is it!"

He gained some composure "Remarkably unpretentious."

"Just about sums it up. I did my training in Stone Buildings so I know where you're coming from."

"Which firm?"

"Houghtons"

Would be! A small, but highly regarded firm giving a high quality and personal service to a small but wealthy clientele. A training with them would be a springboard to anywhere in the legal hierarchy, so what the devil was she doing here?

"You don't have to look quite so confused. Is it really that much of a culture shock?"

On reflection, no it wasn't, but she was. This time to further un-man him she was tidily dressed, but in a clearly well worn denim trouser suit with her hair pulled back in an elastic band. He had a feeling that the light jumper underneath the jacket might just be cashmere, but her watch with its plastic strap looked like something from Woolworths. To confuse the picture further there was a gold signet ring on her left little finger which was engraved with what could well be a family crest, and the pen on the table half hidden under a litter of paper was a Mont Blanc. Clearly there had been no attempt to glam herself up for meeting with him nor to tidy her office and all in all this wasn't playing fair! Was she so indifferent to his visit that she hadn't bothered to make any effort at all? Personally he had been excited at the thought of visiting her ever since the appointment had been made.

"Sorry I'm not wearing my posh suit." Was she able to read his mind as well as scrambling his brains? "I've only got a couple and I have to look after them. Clients here don't give a damn what you look like as long as you can sort them out. Do you want to talk about this contract?"

No, quite frankly he didn't. He just wanted just to look at her for a few minutes more. With swot glasses, token make- up and her hair scraped back she was still outstandingly attractive and presented an almost perfect blend of English Rose and Nordic goddess. Her looks were at the sort of level that made him wonder if there was any avoiding the word "Beautiful" and that was what he wasn't comfortable with. He had always tried to ensure that his world was crammed with polished professionals or toothsome bims, but the real thing like her was still a rare find and it was unnerving to find himself sharing a small scruffy room with her.

"By the way," she looked up at him, clearly a little embarrassed and her colour rising a fraction, "I think you and I got off to a bad start. I don't normally pull bags over people's heads, and I presume that you're not in the habit of screaming to other solicitors to shut the fuck up either. Shall we take a mutual apology for granted and start with a clean slate, or would you rather we never mentioned it and have it hover over us permanently like a black cloud?"

He began to see that he might just enjoy this. Her voice was straight classless English, but locked in a distant cupboard there was just a hint of hunt balls and Glyndebourne picnics and if he strained his ear he could just hear it calling through the keyhole. He gave her his best smile "I've no intention of apologising, and intend to bear a permanent grudge."

"Can we go off the record?"

"Be my guest."

"I could just say that you were behaving like an arrogant pig in that traffic jam, that I'd do it again if the same situation arose, and that as I was in the right throughout I wouldn't dream of apologising."

"And in reply," He paused and considered his words with care, "I could just say that you and your comrades were guilty of aggravated obstruction, and if there were any real justice, which we both know there isn't, I would have been in my right to run you all down." They stared at each other for a moment like two wrestlers wondering whether to attack or wait for the other to move. She was about to speak but he beat her to it. "But, perhaps on mature consideration, a mutual apology might be an excellent idea."

She laughed out loud. "I'm bursting to say I've changed my mind, but we'll never get this contract sorted. Let me show you what I'm concerned about."

Three quarters of an hour and much red penning later, they had made little progress. The safeguards she wanted to build in were way beyond anything John could possibly advise George to accept. Eventually she sat back and looked at him. "Look, can we go off the record again?"

"You've already asked that. I'm treating everything we say as off the record until either of us makes a formal proposal. Till then, this is just negotiation."

"No, I want more than that. I want this to be completely and totally off the record, Without Prejudice, and if you breathe a word of what I'm about to say outside this office I'll kill your children."

This clearly wasn't the moment to say that to the best of his knowledge he didn't have any. "If you're worried about defamation, I give you my personal undertaking to keep this all confidential until we agree we are on the record again."

"Good!" She was clearly composing her words carefully. "I think your client is a crook and I don't trust him an inch. I know that if it's for real, what he's offered in this contract is fantastically generous, so I have to go along with it, but judging from his record I suspect he plans to pull the rug out at some point before this comes to fruition, so please understand if I come across as neurotic and anxious about the small print." She warmed to her subject. "Have you any idea of the numbers of business failures and bankruptcies that man has behind him? Almost every small business that gets involved with him gets either swallowed up or goes bust. I've got an enquiry agent who's managed to get me some personal stuff as well which is strictly off the record, but he earned himself a pretty grisly criminal record before he went so-called legitimate." She paused to let him take this in. "While we're about it, he's physically disgusting and every time I think of that gross body of his, my toes curl like a railway sandwich."

"But apart from that, you've nothing against him."

"I'm sure you can't fault his Victoria Sponge."

John walked round the room so far as the limited space would let him, allowing his thought processes to settle into some sensible order before he spoke.

"Can I think out loud for a moment?"

"Of course."

"We want to find some means of seeing that both of our clients get what they want. Both the local community and the Saul Liebling school want to have a school built in Belleville. There's only two possible sites at the present time, the Old Brewery and the Gambols site. My clients own both of them. My clients want to develop the Brewery site, and as far as I can make out, even with local opposition, they will almost certainly get permission for it to go ahead." Wendy nodded her agreement. "It would be a waste of time and energy in real terms for your people to pin their hopes on blocking planning permission as they almost certainly won't be able to. My clients have offered to sell the Gambols site to yours for a bargain price provided the Old Brewery deal goes through. You've looked at the contract, and you have to accept that even without the changes you have suggested it looks water tight"

"A duck's arse could take lessons from it."

Her mouth was fighting a smile and he was tempted to say something even cruder but decided against it. "Exactly! Your concern is not really the small print, but that there might be something going on we neither of us know about. That being the case, if we fine tune the small print all night it still wouldn't make a scrap of difference. So why don't we just tinker with it a bit for the sake of form, and then just go ahead on that basis. Your clients have everything to gain, and if it turns out there's something nasty in the woodwork, you'll have to try and deal with it as best you can then."

Wendy stared at the ceiling for a few minutes. "I'll want to think about it, but that does seem to make sense."

John picked up the draft agreement and scanned it. "What changes do you want that you consider to be fundamental, that is, what changes if I they were left out would be deal breakers?"

"Oh I don't know," She pointed to a couple of additions she had made, "What about that one, and perhaps that one."

"They're not a problem. I'll try and sell them to him." John got up to leave, noticing that the office had an eerie silence to it. "Sorry to have kept you so long."

"No problem. I only live in Clapham so it doesn't take long to get home."

"Want a lift? My car's just outside." He visualised the journey and wondered what was the longest route he could take without arousing suspicion.

"Are you sure it's no problem?"

Of course it was no problem; he would be happy to drive a woman like her to the moon. She gathered herself up and let them out, raising an eyebrow at the sight of his car loitering with low-slung intent outside her office and he found himself feeling proud and slightly shame-faced all at the same time. His ambitions went way further than what he was currently driving but his TVR still had a certain sleek brutality about it that its more high-tech rivals lacked. The trouble was, like the girl with the curl, when his car was good it was very very good, but when it was bad it could be an absolute bastard and he had no idea how it was going to behave over the next hour. Wendy lowered herself into the leather lined interior, her face inscrutable, and he prayed that this would not be one of the times it decided not to start or otherwise show temperament, but he was pleased that it fired up at the first turn of the key, an aphrodisiac bellow coming from the twin exhausts.

After a second's pause she glanced across at him, her expression impossible to read. "So this is what the young Turks in the City and Lincolns Inn are driving then?"

He did his best not to sound defensive. "I take it you don't approve?"

"Of course I don't. It's a noisy anti-social gas guzzler, blocking the roads and polluting the atmosphere."

"Feel free to take a bus."

She laughed. "Not a chance! Just because I don't approve doesn't mean I don't like it." She put out an exploratory hand patting and feeling the knobs and buttons. "This is really exciting! I've always wanted to have a car like this!" She looked up and tapped the hood. "This comes off doesn't it?"

"Yes"

"Well, come on then, take it down. We can go home the long way if you like."

* * *

Friday night at The Drum again, a familiar and comforting scene. A few of the usuals in one corner, a bunch of the girls celebrating something in another and John and Ron in a huddle just starting on the second bottle. John was feeling that life was quite a nice place to be, but so far had kept his opinion on the subject to himself as there was something in particular he wanted to explore.

"Got a tough one for you, Ron. It'll probably need spread sheets, a couple of scientific calculators and access to a heavy duty computer."

"Will the back of a fag packet do?"

"That depends. Is it a ten or a twenty?"

"Twenty, John! Got to give your problems the attention they deserve."

A few yards away, the screams of hilarity from the secretary group grew louder, and the two men dutifully put other matters on hold for a second to look across and check out what was going on. Tracy was predominant amongst them in all her glory, and for whatever event they were planning to move on to he could see that under her tight top she was going there bra-less. Even for a Friday night she was very animated, and as she giggled and strutted, she kept sending covert glances in John's direction as if to remind him what he was missing. Ron stared at her in his usual hungry way, his eyes like hot coals.

"God, I'd love to jiggle her jugglies just once before I kick the bucket. That's not too much to ask is it?"

He had been bursting to tell Ron about the badge he had earned the previous Friday night, but felt that life had moved on since then. "You really are such a Dirty Old Man, Ron."

"And I hope I'm giving you a first class training, John. In another twenty years or so you'll be ready to take over from me."

Fond of Ron as he was, John was afraid of that this might be truer than Ron realised, and that unless his career made a rapid right angle turn, he was destined to become a beery old has-been who hadn't in fact been anything. He

~ 77 ~

had noticed that introspection was becoming something of a habit these days, but Ron suddenly brought him back to the here and now and stopped him from getting in any deeper. "OK. Let's get back to this problem of yours, John. If you don't get me when I'm sober it might be too late."

Pulling himself together, John reeled out all the information he had gleaned about Wendy during the drive the previous evening. "How would you score this one? Female solicitor, I'd guess about twenty six, seriously beautiful, and that's no exaggeration. Professional middle class parents with a fair bit of money; minor public school education. Got an MA and LLB at King's Cambridge, trained with Houghtons in Stone Buildings. All right so far?"

Ron, making a great pantomime of writing this down in an imaginary ledger, nodded and indicated that John should go on.

"Right! Was asked to stay on at Houghtons with hints that a partnership might be in the offing, but because she's got a social conscience chose to move to some two bit high street legal aid outfit, possibly earning about twenty five grand. Mostly cheap clothes, no memberships worth mentioning, and lives in a flat above a launderette in Clapham. What we've got here is race horse material pulling a milk float. OK, what score do we give her?"

"I think this calls for another bottle, John. I'll pay this time." They were well into this before Ron got back to the subject, taking a deep breath, and talking with exaggerated seriousness. "It will be necessary for me to ask you a highly personal but very pertinent question, which you will understand..."

"No. I haven't shagged her."

Ron glanced at his cigarette packet on which he had scribbled a few figures. "Then I give her a three. I would have just said two on the ground that anybody with all that going for them who chooses to work for a pound shop has to be a fruit cake, but as she has sense enough not to let you shag her, she may just have a few brain cells so I added a point."

But of course John hadn't tried to shag her. Even he had more sense than that. All he had done was drive her home and had a bit of a chat, and that was that. Asking Ron to work out a score was just an excuse to talk about her, hoping that Ron would want to know more so he could wallow in thinking about her again. It hadn't worked and Ron was now fully occupied watching the secretary group gather their things to go off to wherever they were going off to.

Never mind! The bottle in John's hand was already empty and he shambled to the bar to get another one. That's what Friday nights were for, getting wrecked. Looked like another hung over Saturday morning.

TEN

THE E-MAIL FROM TRACY ON Tuesday morning came as a complete surprise, the single word *"Well?"* questioning him from his screen. Puzzled and intrigued, but not a little nervous, he replied, *"Well what?"* and moments later her answer came, *"Is that all the thanks I get?"*

She had to be alone or she wouldn't be doing this, but he was nervous to continue an electronic dialogue as nothing that happened on the computer was ever completely erased, and this was not the sort of exchange he liked to have on the record. Checking that his office door was firmly closed, he dialled her internal number. When she answered, her voice had the clipped and dignified tones that he associated with the offended bim, and he knew that he would have to carefully tease and probe till the cause of his offence was made public. It took about ten minutes, but gradually it emerged that the very least she had expected after helping him out last week with the computer, was that by now he would have taken her out one evening as a thank you. She knew he was going to be at the wine bar on Friday evening so she had had made a particular effort to look attractive, but despite the previous week he hadn't even come over and spoken to her, and the way he and Ron were all hugger mugger together it looked as if they were laughing at her, and frankly she didn't think that was very nice.

Amazing as this was, it was not what he wanted to hear. It was unbelievable that Young Tracy From Accounts, the most covetable girl in the entire office, and something like ten years his junior, actually wanted him to take her out with whatever that might imply, but that wasn't the point. Being a man who knew exactly what he wanted from life, even if he had few illusions about his chances of actually getting it, he knew how the classic Tracy and John screenplay should go. He had run it through his mind so many times he knew it off by heart, and this wasn't it. Ideally there should be some celebration at the office, a birthday or something similar, and everyone, particularly him and Tracy, should get nicely drunk, then one thing would lead to another and by whatever means, teleportation if necessary, they would land up in her place or his where they would indulge in several hours of mutual pleasuring. The next morning he would wake up alone and without a hangover, and later that day at the office, they would shyly acknowledge to each other that they had got a bit carried away, that they shouldn't have done it, and that no offence was taken on either side. And that would be that.

To actually ask her out was another ball game entirely. That implied taking an interest in her as a human being and accepting a measure of moral responsibility. In addition, if he didn't get a good seeing too at the end he would feel short changed, and if he did, he wouldn't have a clue how to deal with the morning after.

As he tried to deal with this, blustering and stuttering down the telephone, his secretary came in desperately trying to mouth something he could not understand. He already had enough to cope with and waved her away, but she continued her efforts with a look of some urgency on her face. He managed to mutter to her that he was tied up before returning to his conversation with Tracy, and with a resigned shrug she left his room banging the door behind her.

"Sorry about that, Trace, Marge came in. Of course I would love to take you out one evening. Can't think of anything I'd rather do. I just thought you might think I was trying to take advantage of you rather that saying thank you. Yes, that's right, let me see….um….how about ….bit tied up this week…next Thursday? Great. I'll confirm the details nearer the time. Yes, yes .. ..And you."

Even as he put his phone down, his screen flashed up a further message, this time from his secretary. *"He wants to see you. Urgently!"* Desperately trying to drag himself back to the here and now he tapped out a reply, *"Who does?"* which was answered with, *"Luke. Who else?"*

This was *déjà vu* on stilts, and his heart was in his boots when he went into Luke's' office. Luke was not at his desk but pacing around when John walked in, his colour high and clearly in something of a state. John had not ever seen him anything else but icy calm, and his heart stopped when he saw the reason. On Marcus' otherwise clear desk was a copy of the Belleville Chronicle, the banner headline, *"Solicitor Tells Residents to Shut the F*** Up!"* in clear view.

It never once crossed his mind to take a local paper, and he had not seen this before, the implications of it all to clear. Luke was clearly beside himself, his breath no more than staccato gasps and there was something in his eyes like an animal about to attack. John had never seen anyone so angry, and for a second the look on his face made him physically afraid.

"What," Luke started, close on hyperventilating with the effort of forming words "What the FUCK......WHAT THE FUCK did you think you were doing?" He stomped round the room, grasping his head in both hands. "Are you completely crazy? Are you determined to drag this firm into bankruptcy? Don't you realise what you've done? They've got this firm's full name and have done a whole page on it as their main story. Can you imagine what will happen when *The Lawyer* gets hold of this?"

John closed his eyes, trying to will away this nightmare. He knew that when you were in a hole you stopped digging, and he also had no doubt that Luke's anger was justified and that there was absolutely nothing he could say in his defence. Because of the past events known only to him and Luke, his long term future could not be with this firm, but because of the same events, he had not been able to leave. This had suddenly crystallised matters, and now, whatever the future held, he had no choice.

"OK, Marcus. Let's cut right across this. To save you a lot of trouble, please accept my resignation. I can go right now, or can work a month's notice to clear things up. Whichever you prefer."

Luke continued his feral staring, the expression on his face not wholly sane."You can stay where you are, John Foxton, thank you very much." What? Was he hearing correctly? Surely this was the very opportunity Luke had been waiting for. "Let's get things clear. There's no love lost between you and me and we both know it, but unfortunately the firm needs you. There's a lot of good litigators out there who could take over your general case load, but then there's Dragoon. Nobody here likes them, and nobody here wants to deal with them, but they're a big player and they bring in a lot of fees. George will only deal with you, so if you go he may well decide to follow you, and I'm not kissing off that amount of revenue, so you can just stay put." He stared at John daring him to disagree with anything he had said. "On the other hand, George is the sort who could suddenly throw a wobbler and chuck you without notice or reason, so don't get any silly ideas about setting up on your own with him as your main client." He appeared to be calming down a fraction. "And if you were thinking of going elsewhere, we both know that you will need a reference, and I think you know the score on that. I think we're rather stuck with each other for a little longer."

John knew that very well, but it was the first time that Luke had come close to saying in as many words that he would pull the plug on John's legal career if he tried to get away. In a strange sort of way he felt liberated by Luke openly acknowledging the truth between them.

"Now just get out of my office and leave me to try and rescue as much as I can from this shambles. I want a blow by blow account of what happened at that meeting in writing so I can prepare a press release. Let me have it before three."

Light headed with emotional overload John staggered back to his office, his phone ringing even as he went through the door and without thinking he picked it up in a trance. "Yes? What is it?"

"Rupert Davies for you."

What the hell did he want? He was going to say that he was engaged when the call connected, and Rupert's chummy voice was on the other end of the line.

"John dear boy, how are you?"

"Oh, err, a bit pressed, Rupert. How can I help you?"

"The Old Brewery site at Belleville. We're acting for Clarendon Properties who are going to lease the site from Dragoon. You're acting for Dragoon I gather."

I can't cope with all this at once! Just bugger off and kill yourself in your expensive Old Money villa in Holland Park will you, Rupert. He took a deep breath and let the professional take over. "Well this is brilliant! You're acting are you!" And probably charging about a hundred pounds an hour more than I am. "I'm not fully up to speed with this side of things. Can you fill me in."

"We are off the record aren't we?"

What was the panic everyone had when talking about Dragoon to go off the record? "Course we are. Be as frank as you like."

He didn't expect him to be quite this frank. Clarendon were planning to lease the whole of the site from Dragoon. Dragoon were going to do all the building work necessary to create the large multi-use complex, and Clarendon would sublet the individual units to a whole series of different outlets. Legally it was not that complex, but the logistics were difficult as Clarendon didn't want to do all the necessary work to secure sub-lessees till they had entered into the head lease, but Dragoon wanted a five million holding deposit both for the head lease and the building works. Even for a company as large as Clarendon this was a lot of money, and they were keen to reduce their exposure by limiting the deposit to say two million.

"But what's the problem Rupert? You can't be saying Clarendon can't raise that sort of money, and provided we get the paperwork right between us, they'll get their lease."

"We are off the record aren't we?"

Here we go again! Why don't we all say Cross our Hearts, and Hope to Die? "I said we were. Your clients don't trust mine, that's what you're telling me isn't it."

"Frankly, I don't trust them either. Dealing with people like this makes me nervous, but Clarendon want this deal very much. They simply want to put a

smaller sum up front. As you say, provided we get the paper work right it's all going to go through so it's just a question of sharing the risk more equitably at the beginning."

What was it George said to tell them, it's five million or they can go screw themselves? Perhaps he would put it more subtly than that. "I don't think they'll move, Rupert. George Stavros isn't someone who changes his mind easily."

"But you can suggest it to him can't you."

"I could suggest he goes on a diet, but I don't think it would reduce his calorie intake."

"Listen John, Clarendon are keen on this deal but there's a point beyond which they won't be pushed. I'm not exaggerating when I say they might just pull the plug, and that's not in anybody's interest. Both of our clients are big people with fixed ideas, but when things get to this stage it's up to us to try and make things work." He paused as if wondering what to say next *"You don't think this might be a bit too big for you to handle? I'll quite understand if you want to pass it over to one of your partners."*

Fucking cheek! He saw the sense in what Rupert was saying, but bitterly resented being patronised. "George won't deal with anybody but me, Rupert. I'll try and talk him down, but I'm not making any promises."

* * *

The phone call from Sid was brief and to the point. George wanted to see him, and the car was on its way. Within fifteen minutes, John was sweeping out of the tree lined security of New Square to an unknown destination. He had assumed they were going to George's offices in Mayfair, so was surprised to find himself speeding down the M4. Sid had kept the window separating him from John closed, and when John pressed the button that opened it to enquire where they were going, nothing happened and the car continued on its journey. This was going too far but there was nothing he could do about it. George was now a legitimate business man so he needed a lawyer to get things right for him, but more than that, George was a client with a lot of clout so when he pulled the strings, everybody jumped. To compound the problem, the recent chat with Luke had made clear that George was John's lifeline with Hart-Russell. If George ever decided to take his business elsewhere, John would be selling the Big Issue in a doorway without enough money to fund a dog.

On the glaring TV screen in front of him a muscular stud strutted his throbbing tumescence for the benefit of a an eager female cohort, in due course producing the all too tangible evidence of how much he enjoyed his work. It made John even more aware of his own impotence, unmanned by a series of events beyond his control which now seemed to affect almost every aspect of his life. Any other lawyer could tell his client to take a running jump and to make an appointment in the usual way, but hog-tied by circumstances, John had to let George walk over him, just as he had wrong footed himself with Tracy and was currently at her beck and call. As far as he could see, currently he could just about deal on equal terms with Rupert Davies and Wendy Vyne, but he presumed that with both of them it would be just a matter of time before he was making their coffee and running their bath.

He tried to think what the reason for this summons could be. The main communications between him and George over the last few days had been his letter to George recommending minor changes to the contract with the Saul Liebling School and encouraging George to consider some flexibility as to the amount of the holding deposit. He had followed this with a phone call. He felt it very much in George's interest not to do anything that might risk the deal falling through and he had pressured George to see that showing flexibility would not weaken his position and could well avoid the whole deal collapsing. With hindsight he was pleased at the way he had dealt with it. He had put it to George that he might be so close to matters that he could not focus properly, and how much he would regret it if Clarendon pulled out. As always, George had given little away over the phone, but John thought he had taken his advice on board.

His mobile rang, and when he pressed the button to answer, the sea of writhing bodies on the screen was suddenly replaced by George's meaty face, huge and horrible in the confined space of the car's interior.

"Hi, Johnny boy. Thought a bit of country air would put some colour in your cheeks. A visit to the house will be good for you." The innocent words, as with everything that George said, carried an undertone of menace. Before John could reply, the connection was severed and George's face disappeared like the Cheshire cats to be replaced by images hardly less palatable.

John looked out of the window as they sped along. He vaguely knew this part of the world and recognised Amersham and Great Missenden after which they went through a maze of less familiar country lanes in the general area of Seer Green. The complete lack of control over where he was going made him feel insecure, and he carefully took in each landmark should it ever be necessary to find his way here again. In due course the car was making its imperious way through a large pair of iron gates which opened silently at the car's arrival. The gate pillars were topped with figures of George and the Dragon and the word "Georgian Manor" were spelled out in wrought iron on the gates. Well, it was George's money, he could spend it how he wanted. The house they were coming to was almost certainly less than twenty years old, but designed to look anything but, a mish-mash of architectural details thrown together to form a cross between a Mediterranean villa and an English Country house overlaid with a handful of gothic embellishments. In a strange way it was impressive, if ludicrous, but being practically dragged out of the car by Sid strangled any inclination to laugh he might have before it even started.

Sid opened the huge front door with a remote control, then led the way through the house, John following at his heels, their shoes clacking like a flamenco dancer's on an endless sea of wooden floors. The exterior architecture may have been Disney World with Al Capone overtones, but the interior was Versailles on acid. Angry and humiliated as he was by this treatment, John was fascinated by the vast art exhibition opening up before him as Sid hurried him through. It was as if George had bought paintings by the acre, Tiepolos and Gainsboroughs flashing past his eyes counter pointed with tantalising glimpses of Rubens and Titians, paintings as vast as hoardings and as florid as a monkey's bottom. If even half of these were real, there was enough money on these walls to buy out a couple of third world countries.

They finally came to rest in a separate wing. Sid who had been silent throughout escorted John through a door into a large sauna, and the heat hit John in the face like an oven door being opened. For a second he could see nothing, the blanket of steam attacking his eyes and obscuring everything in its fog, but after a moment his vision cleared and he could see George sitting on a wooden bench horribly naked, and overwhelmingly huge. Though John always tried to keep himself in shape he was always shy about stripping off in public in case he did not make the grade so found it unbelievable that anyone as grotesque as George could expose himself like this. He sat there like a vast Buddha sculpted from pitted lard, his usual cigar stuck in his face, its thick shaft wet with condensation and the end a glowing beacon in the swirling steam.

"Nice place you've got here, George."

George took a pull at the cigar and expelled the fumes. "Not bad. Not bad. I don't actually own it of course, but near enough as not to matter."

Of course he didn't own it. People like George never do own anything. All their assets are held by off-shore companies and obscure trusts, so that if ever the balloon goes up, no one could get their hands on anything; the lavish lifestyle goes on, and the poor creditors are out there crying impotently for their money.

"Get your kit off, John. We can have a chat, and Sid can give you a rub down."

On the whole John would have preferred to have root canal work done, but didn't know how it would be possible to make his excuses and leave. He looked George in the face, and could see that all debate on the subject was over before it started. Sid had already stripped to his vest, to reveal a body not by any means beautiful, but as functional as a machine. Underneath his vest was a frozen avalanche of bone and gristle, as unyielding as a rock face, and as friendly as a hammer. He indicated where John should lie down with a hint of a smile on his face, the first that John had ever seen there. Well, at least someone was enjoying the afternoon. John, determined to keep his bodily functions under control, reluctantly began to disrobe, trying to keep it all in proportion. George was a legitimate business man, John was his solicitor, and as a special thank you for services rendered, Sid was going to give him a rub down. In reality, it was no more than an elaborate form of corporate hospitality.

George waited till John was in position on the bench before producing what turned out to be John's recent letter, wilting in the sopping atmosphere. "Now look John, I've got to say I'm a bit disappointed in the way you're dealing with all this. I thought we understood each other." John naked and vulnerable in the steamy prison gritted his teeth and wondered what was coming. "I know you're dead good at the lawyering stuff which is why I use you, but it's the approach."

He paused and Sid started the 'Rub Down', his boot leather fists thumping a rhythm on John's back, their impact making John's ribs bounce on the wooden bench and forcing all the air out of him. From the corner of his eye he could see that George had got up and was pacing the tiled floor, still puffing at the huge cigar. As he walked, his stomach rolled down in endless folds and layers, and even from his vantage point, John could not see any sign of George's penis which he guessed must be hidden somewhere in its depths. When he took a piss he must have to reach up for it with long tongs; wiping his bottom must call for depth charges.

"When I give other people my terms, that's what they are." George pulled at his cigar making the tip glow like a hot coal. "If I start backing down, people might think I've lost it, and I don't want that." Struggling not to cry out with the pain of Sid's treatment, John tried to concentrate on what George was saying. "You see, we start with your telling me that the contract that you drafted was as tight as a nun's fanny and covered everything, but now you're saying that the blonde tart acting for that Funny Farm school wants to make changes to it. You see John, I don't give a fuck if she wants to change it. You're as good a lawyer as I've come across, so if you say it's fine, then it's fine, and if she doesn't like it, she can go and stuff her head up her arse. Do you get the picture?" John, dizzy with lack of oxygen and punch drunk with pain, certainly got the picture. "Now that's not so important, as just between ourselves I'm not too worried about that side of things, and a few changes won't make much difference. But then we get Clarendon throwing their weight about and saying that they don't want to put their money where their mouth is, and your telling me I should met them half way. Well!" He gave a little shrug of his shoulders creating a flesh tremor that rippled its way down the length of his body, "Well, that's the thing John. I don't meet people half way, I don't have to. The way I deal is to set up packages that people want very badly and can't get elsewhere. Like this one. Between me and the council I've got planning permissions in place that no one else could get, so this is a very attractive proposition for anybody. Once I've got someone on the hook, when it comes to the point where it needs a bit of common sense or it'll all collapse, then I leave it to them to show that bit of common sense." He took another pull at his cigar. "Believe me, John, they always do. In this case I need all that cash up front as there's some finance going on behind all this, and it's got to be serviced, and if it's not, then I'm going to lose the site, and all this is just for nothing." He indicated to Sid to stop and came and sat close to John's head. "I know I didn't tell you that in as many words, but I shouldn't have to. I need to have the full five mill up front, and Clarendon have got it, and they're going to cough it up or I'll go elsewhere. Clarendon will pay up all right. Don't worry about that; they've got plans for the site and they won't risk losing it. Go back to your oppo and tell him it's five mill or Dragoon will go elsewhere. There's a good chap."

He moved away, and John, soporific with heat and relief that the ordeal was now over was catapulted back into full consciousness as a bucket of icy water was thrown over him. For a second he reflected that outsiders considered lawyer's fees to be outrageous. £175.00 per hour for this? It was cheap at the price!

ELEVEN

THE ONLY PLACE WHERE TRACY wanted John to take her as a thank you was La Fenice, a new restaurant recently opened in Belleville with a fanfare of publicity. She had been told it was really classy, and it would be convenient for both of them. John wanted their evening together to be anywhere else. Belleville might be up and coming, but it had never occurred to him to socialise there, preferring his usual haunts in the Fulham Road or Brompton Cross. More importantly, he was obsessed about staying anonymous in his own locality, and hanging out with a girl who looked like Tracy would inevitably draw whole floodlights of attention in his direction. If he was playing away it would be different. Then he would be quite happy to be seen as a lucky sod likely to be at the receiving end of a good seeing to from a bim ten years younger than him, but in a place where the adjoining table might turn out to be occupied by the man who sold him his morning newspaper, it wasn't on.

Tracy was immovable. This was his thanking her for helping him out, so it was her choice that mattered. He used up every excuse he could to try and talk her out of it, but as he couldn't go as far as saying that he would be embarrassed to be seen squiring someone who looked like a paid escort in his own locality he had to give in.

They agreed that rather than going straight from the office, he would pick her up from her flat so they would both be able to freshen up, and in the shower he had an anxiety attack about the way the evening might go. If she dressed the way she did to the office, what the hell would she wear when out on a date? However things might pan out between them he didn't want to end up with a reputation in Belville for being the sort of man who spent his evenings with girls who charged for their time by the hour. By the time he rang her door bell his imagination was running riot, but the sight of her was still enough to send him into shock. She answered her door wreathed with smiles, pausing in the doorway to give him an opportunity to take her in. There was no denying that even by Tracy standards she was giving a bravura performance. Instead of a skirt she was wearing leather hot pants looped round with an elaborately buckled leather belt, her legs were sheathed in sheer tights, and her stilettos were so high they should have been equipped with a fire escape. The hot pants were so skimpy and tight he suspected that most girls must wear bigger knickers, and it was a good bus ride from their waist band to the lower edge of her top, a soft wool garment showing off her silky shoulders. Her one accessory was a shoulder bag just big enough to take a small hanky, and the air about her was perfumed with a soft but definite hint of eastern spice.

As he stared at her in mute amazement, he knew that if he were her father he would telling her that no daughter of his would be allowed to leave the house dressed like that and to go and change at once. On the plus side it did occur to him that she could not possibly have dressed this way if she wasn't planning to do him proud when the meal was all over, but right now that was of little concern. All he could visualise was the attention they would get as they walked into the restaurant, and he was already flinching.

"Well?" She asked. "How do I look?"

He looked her up and down to take in every detail. "You look really amazing, Tracy." That at least was honest. "Quite unforgettable."

* * *

La Fenice was reassuring. It took the head waiter no more than a second or two to recover from the visual overkill of Tracy before showing them to their table, and looking round, all John's concerns that a local restaurant might not be able to hack it vanished. The interior walls were scoured brick hung with ornate gilt mirrors, silk drapes, and elaborate Venetian masks. The air was perfumed with garlic, and opera arias fought for attention against the buzz of conversation. He immediately felt at home. If the food matched the look and smell of the place, then this was the real thing. Following Tracy to the table however was not a happy experience. The impact her front view created as she strutted her way between the diners was upstaged by the sight of her rear, the lower swells of her buttocks cheekily peeping out from the hot pants and rippling lasciviously as she walked in front of him. He was not the only person to notice, and for a mercifully brief moment, the noisy buzz was replaced by a stunned silence as the diners temporarily lost all interest in their food and stared in disbelief. No longer fighting any competition, the music filled the room, and Tracy's bottom undulated to the rhythm of Riggoletto as she made her way to their table.

"The wine list, Sir." At last they were sitting down, and it wasn't quite so bad. Their waiter, a man in his forties with a swarthy complexion and dark hairy arms bowed from the waist. "I am Giovanni, and will look after you this evening." He consulted a list with practiced eyes checking who his customers were. ''Ah yes, table thirteen, you are Mr John Foxton. Good evening, Mr Foxton, and to the lovely lady.'' He pointed to a blackboard and listed the glories that went beyond the standard menu, and showed them for their inspection fresh pasta created by virgin nuns, lamb that had died of love listening to Puccini, and a huge fish he had killed with his own bare hands only minutes before they had sat down to their table. John knew the ritual from every other Italian restaurant he had ever been to, and was happy with the familiarity of it all. Tracy's pleasure was something else. She was festooned in smiles and innocent enthusiasm, and he found it refreshing to be with someone who did not glitter with sophistication and had seen it all a thousand times before. They made their choices and settled back. Sitting down, she was less of a spectacle, and now that he felt less conspicuous, John was suddenly overcome with a genuine affection for her. She was bubbling with the excitement of being here, and if she had a tail it would be wagging like an excited puppy's.

"A good choice, Tracy. I should listen to you more often."

"I told you, didn't I! You would have had us somewhere in the West End miles from anywhere." She looked round, thrilled with it all, her huge brown eyes shining with pleasure. "This place is really great isn't it."

He decided to show off. "La Fenice means *The Phoenix*. It's a bird that can rise from its own ashes after it has died, and can then live its life over again."

"I suppose it must be named after that opera house in Venice called La Fenice. That's always burning down and being rebuilt isn't it."

He was confused. Bims weren't supposed to know about things like that! At least it gave him an excuse for a compliment. "Very impressive! What other wonderful things do you know about?"

"Well I don't know how to rise from my ashes. That's a bit spooky isn't it. Must be funny walking home from the crematorium after everyone's been crying about you."

"Well at least you'd get a share of the ham sandwiches and fruit cup, instead of all the relatives getting it all. Most of them only care what's in the will, but they get to go to the party and the poor old stiff goes hungry"

She nibbled a bread stick, as happy as a toddler at a tea party. "At least you'd get to hear some nice things said about you. People are so shitty when you're alive, don't you think. It's only after you've gone they start saying how wonderful you are. It shouldn't be like that."

"You're absolutely right." He took hold of her hands and examined them. "In case you suddenly pop your clogs between courses, let me tell you right now how wonderful you are." To his great surprise, he meant it too, and he hadn't even had a drink yet. "Many many thanks for sorting me out last week."

"And you're a really nice guy, John. I wouldn't be here if you weren't. Look, why don't we cut the crap about this being just a thank you. It's just an excuse for us to go out together and we both know it."

As they were only here because of her having press-ganged him in to it that seemed to be putting a bit more responsibility on him than he wanted, but that apart this all seemed to be going pretty well. "OK, I'm really pleased that we've got an excuse to do this, but I'm still really grateful to you anyway. You're much better than Ashock, and he's supposed to be the technical expert."

"It's easy, honest. My brother is a real computer nerd, so I've picked up tons from him. He's one of these people who hacks into other people's systems and messes them about."

"Should you be telling me that?"

"Probably not, but it's a fact."

"Anyway, it doesn't matter how you learned, you're still brilliant."

"I'm much better on the accounting programmes. The computer frightens Bob to death and he leaves all the difficult stuff to me."

The waiter came with the wine and after the charade of tasting and sniffing he filled their glasses and left them alone again. They clinked glasses, looking at each other conspiratorially before taking a drink. "Look John, can I say something embarrassing and get it out of the way." She took a second gulp to give her courage. "I know what I'm like when I've had a few drinks, I'm going to say things I probably shouldn't, so can we just get a few things straight right now. I really do think you're a fabulous bloke, but I wasn't mucking about when I told you about Nikos. I really am in love with him, and when we've both got our act together, I'm going out there to live."

"That's fine."

"Yes, but I'm probably going to flirt with you a bit, and I don't want you to misunderstand."

"Tracy, that really is fine." He took her hands again and kissed them with genuine affection. This was panning out really nicely. Tracy had no illusions that sharing a meal was making them an item, but if nature, given a helping hand by a bottle or two of Pinot Grigio, took its course, then it was the *"Sorry we shouldn't have got carried away like that"* routine tomorrow at the office, and things could carry on as usual.

He took another swallow of his wine, feeling the customary surge of self confidence that a boost to his blood/alcohol level always gave him. This was all getting very good and he intended to enjoy it. "You do realise I'll be deeply insulted if you only flirt with me a bit. I intend to flirt with you a lot more than that." She said nothing, but looked happy enough at what he'd said, her eyes dancing with excitement as she waited for his next move. "As this is the moment to be frank with each other, there is something I've always wanted to ask you." He leaned forward and whispered in her ear, wondering if he'd gone too far, but the expression on her face when she slapped his hand told him everything he wanted to know. It only took a second before she inclined in his direction and whispered her reply. Their first courses arrived and briefly broke up this exchange but very soon they were back at the same level, alcohol and intimacy eventually creating a tunnel of darkness through which they could only see each other. Eventually, while John was finishing the last of his saltimbocca, Tracy sat back and looked round the restaurant.

"You know, although this place is brilliant, in a funny way I think it's sort of wrong the way places like this are opening all over South London." He was busy with his food and happy to let her talk. "Well, have you ever thought about it? We all know there's people pouring into London all the time and it's getting even more crowded, and at the same time there's hardly any bit of it that isn't being gentrified to oblivion." He was all in favour of this, but just nodded, not sure where this was leading. "But in fact, there's far more ordinary people than posh ones, aren't there."

"I suppose there are." He hoped she wasn't going to start anything that would involve his having to think or express a serious opinion.

"But if everywhere is going up-market all the time, I mean, where do all the ordinary people go? I don't just mean just to live, which is bad enough with the cost of flats and houses going up, but eating and drinking and, I don't know, just having a good time."

"I take your point."

"If I had lots of money, I think I'd build dog tracks and amusement arcades and places with cheap food. That sort of thing. It would do people a good turn and at the same time I'm sure you could make a fortune that way. What do you think?"

For a second his imagination was filled with the vision of hoards of *Homo Yobbus*, stumbling and shambling their way through a neon lit amusement Mecca, all wearing the baseball cap, earring, and tattoo combo that they must buy as a job lot in a blister pack from Woolworth's. He shook his head to dismiss it, keen to get back to Tracy and the trivial conversation they were having earlier.

"But I suppose you haven't got that sort of money to invest."

"If only! Come to think of it, if I had, I wouldn't do what I've just said, I'd just go to Greece straight away and buy Nikos his restaurant."

"What a nice girl you are, Tracy." He leaned forward and kissed her, happy with the way she responded.

"If I were that nice, I wouldn't be kissing a bloke I fancy rotten when I'm in love with someone else." She took a deep swallow of her wine. "I told you I'd say things I shouldn't."

The wine was making him feel nicely mellow, and this was all turning into his sort of evening. "*Do* you fancy me rotten?"

"You know damn well I do, but it won't make any difference." She looked at him across the table, her eyes hooded and inviting. "As we both know exactly where we stand with each other, do you know you haven't actually said you fancy me in as many words."

They grasped hands across the table and he leaned towards her, his voice a hoarse whisper, his head engorged with alcohol and his loins engorged with need. "I fancy you sick, Tracy." How nice for once to be totally honest. "I think you're absolutely edible, and if I were your boyfriend, I'd kiss you till your clothes melted off your body."

She said nothing, but pulled his right hand towards her, taking his fingers one by one into her mouth and sucking them suggestively.

"And if you were my boyfriend..."

"Does Sir have everything he needs?" Giovanni appeared from nowhere bringing him back to reality with a jerk. "Perhaps some coffee or maybe a cognac..?"

John asked Tracy a question with raised eyebrows, and with a simple nod she replied that coffee at his flat would be fine. Giovanni went to organise the bill and Tracy announced she was going to the ladies and gathered herself up.

On the whole John wished she hadn't. For the last hour or so he had lost all awareness that he was in a public place but a sudden drop in conversation as she stilettoed her way through the restaurant brought back to him that they had been making a modest exhibition of themselves. He could feel a sea of eyes looking in his direction, and with a rush of self consciousness, he buried his head in the menu to avoid meeting anybody's gaze. Eventually he risked a quiet look round just in case, God forbid, there might be a local face he recognised.

It was as bad as it could get. Sitting diagonally across the room from him was Wendy Vyne. The shock of meeting her eyes was enough to make him choke on the bread stick he was nibbling and to knock his wine glass spinning across the table. In a second Giovanni was at his side, mopping and clucking reassurance while John tried to gain some composure. By the time he was able to risk looking in her direction again, Wendy and her companion were in the process of leaving, her hand briefly raised in his direction the only acknowledgement of his presence and the expression on her face impossible to read. As discreetly as he could John strained to get a look at her escort and was not happy to see that he was the sort of man whose effortless good looks and easy relationship with himself and with life would make him irresistibly attractive to anybody who came near him. He was big in a totally unthreatening way with roughly combed blonde hair and wearing a Viyella shirt, brown cord trousers, and clumpy brown brogues. Only someone as good looking as him could wear clothes like this and still look good. He moved with a clumsy boyishness that suggested that he had a problem keeping excess energy under control, and the overall impression was of an overgrown puppy who was only restraining himself from running round because it had finally learned that you weren't allowed to do that indoors. At the door he exchanged jokes with the waiter, both of them laughing out loud, and the whole time he had a protective hand on Wendy shoulder with a look of easy familiarity.

Whatever might pan out between him and Tracy over the next few hours John felt a stab of irrational jealousy, vinegared with a feeling of unfamiliar shame. In his one meeting with Wendy he felt that they had established mutual respect and there was no avoiding that he was strongly attracted by her. Now she had seen that he spent his down time having his fingers sucked by a girl who looked like she performed such services for a living. He wondered if the Great Almighty had pre-programmed him so that he was doomed to wrong-foot himself with everyone with whom he made contact and to spend his entire life having to apologise and explain.

Tracy returned from the ladies, freshened up by whatever it is that ladies do there, her eyes glowing, her hair glossy, and her petite frame lithe with curvaceous invitation. At least it looked as if all this humiliation would be worth it. He left the restaurant with his arm round her shoulder, and with Giovanni's exhortation to *"Have a very good night, Sir"* in his ears. As an optimist, even if a battered one, he was in no doubt that whatever problems he might have otherwise, currently his glass was at the very least half full and indeed might even be in danger of spilling over.

* * *

On the short walk back to his flat Tracy had told John that he shouldn't get any wrong ideas and that there was something she ought to tell him, but her arms were so tightly clutched round his waist that he didn't bother to ask her what it was. On more than one occasion in the past the quiet elegance of his flat had been the final straw weighing the balance in his favour and turning a date into a conquest. It looked as if that might well be the case here. Once inside his flat she enthused at this wonderful place where he lived, dancing round his living room with pleasure, and marvelling at the big white space.

"This is really wonderful, John. You're so lucky!" She stood between the couch and the fireplace, staring at the pile of logs in the grate, her back to him and his arms round her waist. When he turned her round and kissed her she responded with such sweet enthusiasm that he quite forgot about offering coffee. This was all very well, but as a seasoned operator he knew that one wrong move and all could be lost and that he should subtly signal where things were going without being too hasty. He picked her up into his arms, but instead of walking to the stairs, stepped backwards and sat down on the couch. In a moment she was lying back across his lap, her arms round his neck and kissing him enthusiastically, alternately muttering *"Oh, John..."* and *"Look, John...."* as if there might be something she wanted to say. John carefully worked on the *"Oh, John!"* lobby, continuing to kiss her, and at the same time sliding a hand underneath her short top. This was now all going very much to plan and for a while he kept his hand busy travelling between her breast and the general run of her body as far as he could reach in the other direction, the *"Oh, Johns!"* now outnumbering the *"Look, Johns...!"* by about three to one.

Decision time was clearly close. He could raise the stakes here on the couch, and then hit the bedroom when consummation had become a foregone conclusion, or carry her to the bedroom now with risk that the tension might be broken and put things back a cog or two. By now the *"Oh Johns!"* and *"Look, Johns..."* had became little more than breathy gasps so he decided to go for broke here and now. Continuing with the kissing, he made his first preliminary attempt to undo the buckle of her belt.

Only days before, John had had a bucket of cold waster thrown over him, but familiarity did not make the experience any easier to bear. When drinking her in when he had picked her up, he had not taken in the precise detail of the complex looking buckle on her belt, so it was only now that he appreciated that its principal components were a hasp held in place by a small, but nevertheless real and functioning padlock. She had made herself impregnable with a three line defence of knickers, tights and leather shorts, all securely bolted into place! This was raising cock teasing to high art and he sat up as if his face had been slapped.

"Tracy, what on earth...?"

"Oh I'm sorry, John." She looked genuinely distressed. "I've been trying to tell you..."

"That you've locked yourself in! I don't believe it!"

"It was the only way….."

He shrugged her off him and stood up, what had previously been an erection that could have opened packing cases now little more than a moist pot noodle. "But you've been to the loo tonight! There must be a way out of them somehow!"

"Of course there is. Look, come here. Don't be cross with me." She took his hand and pulled him back on to the couch, manoeuvring so they lay side by side. "That's better. Can I explain?"

"I think you'd better."

"You already know I'm in love with Nikos, I've told you that. I'm determined not to be unfaithful to him, but we're a long time apart from each other and I'm only human. I really fancied having a kiss and a cuddle with you tonight, but I made up my mind it wouldn't go any further." She tried to kiss his unresponsive mouth. "I knew damn well what would happen if I went out with you and we had a few drinks, so I had do something to keep it all under control. We both know that if I'd been wearing a skirt so you could have got at me I'd never have stood a chance. That's why I dressed like this. I've got the key in my bag, but it's in an envelope wound round and round with sellotape. Of course I could get it out of my bag, unwrap it and then undo the lock, but that's not exactly me being overtaken by events is it? That's me saying, you know……"

"Come and have me, Big Boy!"

"Exactly! I couldn't live with myself if I did that with poor Nikos in Greece working all hours to buy a restaurant for us to run together. You do understand don't you? I like you a lot and I really do fancy you, but it's just not possible." She paused to see how he was taking it. "Please say you understand, John."

Yes, he understood, he understood all too well. Never in his life had there been so much gift wrap and so little present. He got to his feet and stumbled across the floor to the kitchen. "You'd better tell me how you like your coffee."

T W E L V E

THE NEXT MORNING, MILDLY HUNG over, and with no enthusiasm for the day ahead he dragged himself from his bed and went straight to a client's office for a meeting, leaving it just in time to make an 11.30 directions appointment in the High Court. That over, lugging a case bag heavy with files he went onto a conference with counsel that lasted for two hours. Leaving a lot of the files there, he wandered back through Middle Temple Lane to his offices in New Square.

The Temple, the enclave of barrister's chambers between the Thames and the Strand, is a gas lit time warp. Hidden behind its gates are cobbled squares, the gothic beauty of Temple Church, and Fountain Court with its ancient mulberry tree. Either side of him barristers in long black gowns and 18th Century wigs rushed to their afternoon hearings. For several years now this had been the stuff of life for him, the glamour of the court room and the adrenaline rush of a new case, but right now he couldn't give a damn. He felt completely burned out, but knew that at bottom he was just over tired. The farce with Tracy the previous night had not helped, but he never fooled himself that such evenings, even when successful were anything but acts of escapism. He knew his real problem was the cancer of knowing his career was stuck on a treadmill and that he couldn't see his way off it. Having a few clients he believed in would not do any harm either.

At his desk he unwrapped his Prêt-a-Manger sandwich and dispiritedly booted up his computer to find an E mail from Tracy. *"Thanks so much for a wonderful evening. I really did enjoy it. Sorry that it couldn't finish the way I know we both would have liked. I'm now in your debt big time."* Yeah, too right, Tracy! But what good does that do me? There was also one from Wendy Vyne. *"Would appreciate a call to discuss a few points of detail."*

He wouldn't ring her until he had eaten and had a coffee. He wasn't yet strong enough to cope with unexpressed contempt from someone who had seen him out on a misguided attempt to get his leg over with the office bim, particularly when his flat voice would give away that, as with everything else he seemed to touch at the moment, he had failed even to do that.

He leafed through his post, interested to find the result of a Land Registry search he had made against George's house in Buckinghamshire. He had only done it out of curiosity and had taken it for granted that it would be in a company name rather than George's own, but not one that was based in Liechtenstein. The freeholders were Reggeo Associates of Vaduz. It was hardly unexpected that George had interests that John didn't know about, but interesting to find this foreign connection.

Gagging for a cigarette he took the remains of his coffee and went to the front door facing out into the square. In the old days smokers had been tolerated and at worst merely frowned upon. Now they were untouchables who had to stand on the roof or hang upside down from their windowsills if they wanted a few puffs. On the doorstep he found Ron taking a last hungry draw from his Benson and offered him one from his packet. After the shortest moral tussle in history, Ron accepted, with a look of guilty pleasure on his face. For a moment or two they puffed away in silent complicity.

"Ron, I think I know the answer, but can you confirm – Liechtenstein companies, is it possible to do a search and get the same sort of information you could get on an English company, you know directors and shareholders? That sort of thing?"

"Liechtenstein! What's this connected to?"

"Georgy Porgy"

"Would be!" He sucked on his cigarette as if it were going to be his last, expelling the smoke in a great torrent. "If it's Liechtenstein, it's dodgy from the foundations up. You won't be able to find out anything that matters. Not much more than the date the company was registered."

"OK. Why would someone register a company there?"

"Come on, John! Why do you think? Hiding assets, tax dodging, anything you like. If you've got a scam on the go, I don't know, you can pretend that a company that's nothing to do with you is shafting you when you own it all the time. Want me to set one up for you, cover your tracks?" He stubbed his cigarette out on the stone step.

"If only! Thanks anyway. See you at the Drum tonight?"

"Can't. Partner's meeting."

"But it's Friday! What's this one about?"

"Making up the new partners."

It would be. It was that time of year, but of course it wouldn't affect him. Other fast tracked favourites would overtake him as usual, leaving him to watch them pass the winning tape. God he was heart sick! He didn't despise successful people, far from it. He just wanted to be one of them, wanted some of that self satisfied sleekness that comes with knowing that you've made it and that the world knows it as well. All he had was duff clients, a crap love life and his career in the deep freeze. Yes, he was feeling sorry for himself, but so fucking what?

Back in his office, he looked at the message to ring Wendy realising that the thought of speaking to her made him feel a little better, even if she took the piss out of him about last night, or worse still just despised him silently. Since his painful meeting in Buckinghamshire, the terms of the contract had been agreed and signed by George and largely agreed with Wendy. Finalising things should now just be a matter of form. With a fluttering stomach he dialled her number.

"Hullo? Wendy Vyne."

"Hi, it's John – John Foxton. You left a message for me to phone." Should he mention their seeing each other in the restaurant or not? He didn't have to.

"Oh Hi. Nice to hear from you. Funny our choosing the same restaurant last night."

"Yes, wasn't it? I owed someone a meal. It was just a thank you."

"So I saw!"

John, just shut up for once and don't make it worse. "I'd best not say anything. You wanted me to ring."

"Oh Yes. I've got the contract signed, so whenever you want to exchange copies we can."

He couldn't risk it, could he? "Err, how shall we deal with it – I can send a trainee round with it, or…"

"As you live so close, why don't you just drop it in on your way home? I'll be here fairly late so it's not a problem."

"Yes why not? I don't suppose…." What had he got to lose? "I don't suppose you'd fancy sharing a meal afterwards…. I don't know, to celebrate the contract being finalised…. but…of course, if you're busy…." What's this? He was stuttering like a schoolboy, and even in the privacy of his office he could feel himself blushing.

"Are you sure it would be much of a celebration with someone as boring as me? I think I left my hot pants in the laundry."

"Oh please..!"

"If we do, I'll expect more to eat than your fingers!"

"Look, I'm sorry………"

"I'm teasing! Sorry! I'll understand if you change your mind after all this. Look, it really is very nice of you to suggest it, and yes, I'd really like to. This is really cheeky, but is there any chance that we could go to the same place? I thought it was really fabulous."

He felt his heart lift and for a moment he did not trust himself to speak. For all he knew she could be living with the man he saw her with the previous night, might be a lesbian, or have ten children, but that was fine. Why should he expect anything else?

"I'll ring for a table right now."

"Mr Foxton. An extraordinary pleasure to see you again! If you come this way, you can have the same table as last night"

Giovanni had come close to genuflecting at John's arrival and strutted in front of him on the way to the table as if leading a papal procession. A man such as John who could command the favours of two such extraordinary women two nights in a row must be some sort of demi-god, and if he served him well, perhaps just a little of his power might rub off on to him.

Tormented by a strange mixture of pride at being seen this way, and mortification at how undeserved it was, John followed in his wake. He wanted to take Giovanni to one side and tell him that he didn't get to shag last night's and wouldn't be shagging tonight's, and that being so near yet so far was probably more painful and humiliating than not getting close at all.

His mind set was so different from the previous evenings as to make him virtually a different person. Last night he was incandescent with anticipation, but this time he was suffused the quiet calm of someone who expects nothing and therefore confident that there is no room for disappointment. His one cautious assumption was that, provided he exercised at least some minimal common sense he would have a pleasant time. If he didn't say anything too stupid or inflammatory, didn't express extreme opinions about lesbians or foreigners, kept a hold on his drinking, didn't jump on the table and sing Nelly Dean while pissing in her soup he might just survive the evening with his reputation in one piece, and in fact if she didn't actually empty her spaghetti over his head or stab him in the eye with her fork before storming off into the night, he would consider the evening to be a resounding success.

They took their time choosing and ordering, John finding it hard to concentrate with such luminous beauty sitting opposite him. She was wearing what looked like the same clothes she had on at the local meeting, a well tailored two piece with a discreetly short skirt and heels. She looked so gorgeous and expensive it was almost too much for him and he wondered if this really was such a good idea. With her hair scraped back and wearing her denims he could cope, but when she looked like this it was frying bacon in front of a starving man. It might not be so bad if he were not convinced that someone else would get the pleasure of licking the plate.

"John, is there something bothering you? For a second there you looked as if some great tragedy had struck."

He pulled himself together. "Sorry! Just thought of an office problem."

"Oh come on, it's Friday night! I know we won't be able to avoid talking shop to some extent, but sod the office for a bit." She looked at her surroundings with unselfconscious curiosity. "This is such a great place. I can't believe I'm eating here two nights in a row. You've no idea what a simple life I normally lead."

But you're beautiful! Staggeringly beautiful! And what about that horribly attractive man last night, and what about all the other men who must be in love with you? So much he wanted to say, and so much he was afraid to say in case he messed it all up before the first course arrived and another night was ruined forever, along with the rest of his accident prone life.

"I'm glad you like it."

"I think it's brilliant." She leaned forward conspiratorially. "Should we check to see if there's people we know here who are covertly watching to see if we misbehave?"

"Look, about last night…."

"Never apologise, never explain. Who was it who said that? Last night Guy was quite jealous of your lady friend. Went into great detail about what he would like to do to her if he had the chance. It was all I could do to stop him drawing a diagram on his napkin."

Was this for real or was she just teasing him again? "That was the chap with you last night? "

"Mm."

"Didn't you mind?"

She crunched on a bread stick. "Frankly there wasn't a lot I could do about it. You know what men are."

They had barely sat down, but for all his good intentions, he had to get some things clear. "Look, do you mind if I ask you a personal question?"

She sat back in her chair and gave him the strangest smile. "Look, John. It's the end of the week, we are in a restaurant, and I'm sure that after a few drinks we will be baring our souls like pole dancers on acid, so you don't have to be so cautious. Can I say your body language since you turned up tonight has been *Man on Best Behaviour?* I promise I'm not going to eat you."

He had rather taken that for granted. "And if I ask something you don't want to talk about?

"Naturally I'll slap your face and storm out in tears."

"So long as I know. I was just going to say, with all the tact I could muster, was that presumably as what your friend Guy said about my, err, companion last night didn't upset you that much, that you're not in love with him?"

"Oh yes, last night! Guy you mean? Yes, I love him I suppose. Everyone loves Guy. Sometimes I think it's impossible not to." The gush of cold water wasn't as bad as it could have been, he had expected it anyway. Ever since they arranged this meal he had protected himself by wearing a psychological wet suit, so it wasn't too much of a shock. He did find bits of him going numb though as if his circulation had stopped. "He's my brother." She went on. "I've got to love him I suppose."

"Your brother!"

Giovanni brought the wine at the precise moment she said this, and couldn't understand why its arrival should be such a cause of celebration. John rocked back and forth in his chair trying to suppress a fit of joyous laughter, thanking him effusively with such a vigorous pat on the shoulder he wondered if he might have done damage. Wendy looked confused. "While we're on personal questions, you're not an alky are you? I've never seen anyone so happy to see a bottle of wine."

"Not at all! No. Sorry! I suddenly agree with what you said a moment ago. It's Friday night and sod everything else. Let's enjoy ourselves; what shall we drink to?"

Wendy was not in any doubt. "A Saul Liebling school in Belleville."

Yes why not! He clinked glasses enthusiastically and threw down his first drink of the evening suddenly feeling ludicrously happy. OK, this was going nowhere, but she would be really good company so what did it matter if she was the most beautiful thing he had ever seen? He would just have to put up with that. "Look I've got a good idea. Why don't you slap my face now to save time, and then I can really start getting personal?"

She mimed a gentle slap, the palm of her hand just making contact with his cheek, and his own came up and held it in place for a fraction of a second before he released it, a shiver of electricity running through him. "Right. Now I'm in credit. Why is it that tonight you look like Ms City Solicitor, but the first time I saw you were in head to toe Greenham Common?"

He was pleased to see her blush. "Oh God! I'm a bit embarrassed by that. I wasn't actually in disguise but I just wanted to reduce the chances of being recognised. I know my firm doesn't have the sort of clients yours does, but even harassed South London housewives prefer their solicitors to be at one remove from real life. I felt I had to be part of the demonstration, but didn't want to make things too difficult for myself at work."

It answered his immediate question, but triggered a dozen others. "Look, I've got to ask you this, and there's no tactful way to do it. I mean, what are you doing working for a firm like yours? You've got a good degree from Kings and you trained with a decent outfit. You've got all it takes to get into the Golden Circle, and you're doing crappy landlord and tenant and legal aid stuff."

She fidgeted in her seat and looked slightly less sure of herself. "Oh dear, I hate talking about this as it makes me sound horribly earnest and I'm not really like that." Their first courses had arrived and Giovanni was getting busy with the pepper mill. They both paused, and John was pleased to see that she was doing the wine justice and that a second bottle would be needed before long.

"Go on. I'm hanging on your every word."

"OK, if you really want to know. I've been very fortunate in my life. I was brought up in a wonderful old house by lovely parents. I was happy at school, got into a decent university, and when I was twenty five a trust fund kicked in so I've got no money worries. I'm healthy and I'm not spectacularly ugly so what with one thing and another I've been an exceptionally lucky person. There are so many people out there who have the dice loaded against them from before they are born, and have lives so deprived and awful you couldn't possibly believe it. I felt that as I'd been blessed with so much that I had to give just a bit back." She looked up at him defiantly. "I sound so fucking priggish when say that that I hate myself. Can we get something straight?" She took another generous drink from her glass "Don't you dare start thinking of me as being saintly or even seriously left wing because I'm not. I'm no less selfish and trivial than anyone else. I like clothes, food, and booze, just like any other woman." She paused, checking out his reaction "I'm not beyond a joint or two either when work gets on top of me. You get the picture?"

He was getting the picture. She liked a drink and said "Fuck" if she needed to. Couldn't be that bad. "You don't sound priggish at all and I really respect what you've done. You've probably guessed that my sole reason for being in the legal profession is personal ambition."

"That's fine. If I hadn't had a financial safety net I would probably have been just the same. But you love it though don't you, I can tell. You'd hate anything else."

"God knows I love the buzz. When I've got a bit of serious litigation on the go there's nothing like it. I don't need food or sleep then."

"My work's just the same. Let's get basic shall we. When I get one over on some shit who's been battering his wife I know that life is worth living."

She'd just broken down the final barrier. Their backgrounds and primary motivations may be different, but underneath they were just the same. Giovanni brought them their food and a further bottle and he started to enjoy himself in earnest. He was surprised to find that before joining Ormorod and co she had done a spell with the legal department of Belleville Council, but had given it up after six months. The sheer inability to get anything done because of second rate staff and the usual petty in-fighting always found in such places became all too much for her. "They're all frustrated politicians with their own secret agendas.

The vast majority are either corrupt or incompetent or both. The one decent person was Martin Fletcher, you know, the guy who was attacked and left in that skip. He really was the one voice of common sense in the place. Until he gets back I dread to think what they'll all get up to."

"I've not really followed what's been happening. Is he going to get better?"

"Looks that way, but it'll be a while yet. The attack was probably because he was frustrating some lunatic scheme someone had cooked up. You should do a spell in a place like that. You wouldn't believe it."

"I think I can survive without."

She pointed out that so far the exchange of information had been one way and she wanted to know more about him. "I presume they'll make you a partner soon."

Oh no! Please don't spoil the evening! " I rather think not."

"OK. I won't ask why that is. I suppose you'll be moving on then."

He put down his knife and fork, wondering whether to get into all of this. "Oh dear....!"

She looked genuinely concerned. "There's a story here isn't there. You don't have to talk about it if you don't want to."

But he did want to. He hadn't talked about this for a couple of years and desperately needed to get it out of his system.

"Look, it's a long story, and I don't come out of it very well. Are you sure you want to know?"

"Can we understand one thing, there's no way I'm going to judge you. We're all human for God's sake. I've got things in my past I'm not especially proud of too."

No, she wouldn't judge him. He could tell she meant that. He leaned across and gave her a chaste kiss on the cheek. "That's me saying thank you for a really nice evening so far, just in case you decide to walk out."

To his surprise, she reached across and gave him a small kiss in exchange, then sat back. "I'm not going to walk out, and that was to thank you for suggesting we did this. Come on, I want to hear."

It took him a moment to get started as he marshalled the facts in his mind. "There's two stories, nothing that special with either of them, but then they link up. OK, after I'd been qualified for a couple of years I joined a firm called Russell Brookes & Keeling. I was as ambitious as hell and so fired up my energy never seemed to run out. I was happy to work the clock round and was doing really good work and as they were quite a modest outfit I was making quite an impression. I was handling a big work load, billing well and my salary was going up in leaps and bounds. It was all bloody brilliant." He paused."You can see where all this is going can't you?

"Possibly, but go on."

"Anyway, I was becoming the real young Turk, thought I was invincible and living on adrenaline, you know the scene. OK. A trainee joined the firm called Diana. Very sweet girl. Pretty in an un-dramatic sort of way. Perfectly bright and capable, but without any killer instinct. Sort of girl who was happy to have a career, but basically more interested in having a husband and a couple of kids. Anyway, we got on well, had the odd coffee together, then the odd dinner, and eventually we landed up in bed. Then we kept landing up in bed, and before I knew what was going on we were falling in love with each other. It was all pretty wonderful at first, but being the sort of person she was she thought this was heading for the altar and lots of babies. I really did love her as far as I was capable of, but domesticity just wasn't my scene. My career was going like a rocket and I was a cauldron of testosterone. I wanted all the rewards that went with the territory, money, models, travel, cars, the whole bit. Women didn't find me too repulsive and when the odd one threw herself at me I didn't make much of an effort to duck." He looked up at Wendy, unsure of himself. "You're getting the gist. Do you want me to go on?"

"Yes of course I do."

"OK." He took a deep breath and carried on. "After I'd been unfaithful the first time, I couldn't stop. I started making a pig of myself and bedding every girl I came across, and inevitably one of them threw a wobbler and sent Diana a letter telling her everything I was up to. Big scene. Lots of tears, and Diana left the firm and then joined another one. I don't know if it was because she was on the rebound, but she became involved with one of the partners in her new firm, married him and now has a child of about eighteen months."

"Oh John, I'm sorry. Did you really love her?"

"As it happens I did. Don't worry about that though. The way I behaved I don't expect any sympathy, and I'm now long over it. Anyway, life went on and I just carried on working the clock round, and then the inevitable happened. First I wrongly diarised an important court hearing, so the client and a whole bunch of expert witnesses went to the county court in Gillingham in Kent rather than Gillingham in Dorset causing a massive cock up which cost the firm a mint to sort out, and about the same time I failed to realise that there had been an important company law update so I badly misadvised a client"

"So you made some mistakes. So what? Everyone does that at least once during their early years. It's only when you learn that you're not invincible that you have any chance of becoming a half way decent lawyer."

"OK, I accept that completely." He finished his glass and called for another bottle. "But this is where it all links up. Just when the balloon went up with these two cock ups my firm was taken over by Hart-Stanley, and Luke Chaplin, the managing partner of what is now the combined firm, is the guy who married Diana. He knows all about how I'd behaved with her and he hates my guts. As managing partner he's got me under his complete control. I'm being starved of high quality work which is affecting my earnings, partnership is out of the question, and without saying so in as many words, he's made it plain that if I try and move on, using the two cock ups I mentioned as the excuse, he will ensure that any reference the firm gives is guaranteed to stop me getting another job." He looked round, his eyes desperate. "For God's sake, Wendy! Who was that woman in mythology chained to a rock so a sea monster could eat her liver day after day forever? That's how I feel. I'm completely fucked. If I stay on, I will just die of gradual suffocation, and if I try and get out, it's sudden death. Sorry about my language, but it's sodding slavery and I don't know what to do about it." Wendy looked disinclined to speak, so he went on. "Can I say that I don't expect any sympathy. I behaved like a complete shit and I deserved it, but I'm going mad with frustration."

"I'm sure you must be." She fiddled with her glass. "This Luke character, your managing partner, what sort of man is he. Is he capable of listening to reason?"

"I just don't know. I don't think he's a sadist if that's what you're getting at. He's a pretty ruthless lawyer, but most of us are, it comes with the territory. Otherwise, I think he's a man with a slightly over developed sense of right and wrong who loves his wife and wants to get back at someone who has hurt her. I can't really blame him for that."

"Time for my personal question. How much are you being paid?"

He wouldn't have told anyone else, but his defences were down and he gave her the figure. She pointed out that it was more than twice what she was on.

"But so what? You know the sort of money that can be earned at the top end of this game. Brian, a guy I used to work with has now got a house in Notting Hill, a property in Provence, and he's about to take up flying. Charles Ingrams who's head of corporate recovery at Crockford-Amery has got an estate in Scotland as well as a big London house. I could give you a dozen examples. But it's not just that. I want to succeed in life as a result of my own efforts and I want some of the recognition that goes with it. I'm ambitious and I'm good, and it's all being taken away from me.

She sat quietly for a few moments before speaking "How long since you have seen Diana?"

"I haven't since she left Russell-Brooks and Keeling."

"Do you know what I think? You should get in touch with her and meet up. You should tell her exactly what's going on, and see if she can persuade Luke that enough is enough."

He resisted the urge to ask if she were mad, but quietly debated with her all the reasons why it could never work, to have each point re-presented to him in a more positive light.

"Look, I'll need to think about this. Thanks for being so supportive. But don't you hate me for what I did?"

"Course I don't. We are all the victims of our emotional urges until we have reached a point where our bodies are no longer capable of following them up. You're not a bad person, John. You just wanted to live it all to the full. Frankly, I also think that you're a bit of a lost soul."

"Well that's a new one! No one's ever said that before." He looked her in the eye feeling one of his occasional rushes of sincerity. "I'm so glad we did this. I really like you, Wendy."

"For a womanising, money hungry solicitor with a history of cock ups behind him you're not so bad either. I'll even let you make me a cup of coffee if you promise it's not instant."

* * *

He let her in to his flat, his heart beating so fast it made him slightly dizzy. She quietly looked around and took it all in, but when he put his hand on her shoulder as she was admiring the fireplace she said that it was important that she made something very clear. He guessed what it would be, and tried to tell her so, but she insisted that she spelled it out. Accepting this he went and sat quietly on the couch while she remained standing a little apart from him.

"Listen, John, these situations can be so embarrassing so it's best to clear the air at the start. We've had a very nice evening and we've both had quite a lot to drink and here we are at your flat. It's just I don't want any misunderstandings to spoil things."

"I don't Wendy, really…"

"Let me say this anyway. I can guess what you think might happen; we sit and have coffee on the couch, we get a bit touchy, one thing leads to another…."

"Wendy, I don't expect…"

"It's just that, if that's what you have in mind, that's fine. But if you'd prefer, I'm quite happy if we go straight to bed right now."

It took a quite a few minutes before he could believe what he had heard, and longer again before he could trust himself to speak.

"Listen, Wendy, in my own way I'm an old fashioned boy at heart, so I quite like the idea of starting with a cup of coffee and seeing how things develop from there."

"That sounds really nice." She bent forward and kissed him, then straightened up. "I'll make the coffee if you like. I'm sure I can find everything."

Leaving him in the living room she went into the kitchen and he sat there on the couch, not sure if he was in a dream. He'd had the most wonderful evening he could remember, exquisite food in elegant surroundings and of course in the best possible company. He'd got something off his chest that had been festering like cancer and he hadn't been criticised for it, and even as he sat here the most beautiful girl he had ever met was making him coffee. Waves of calm wafted through him along with a strange feeling of peace and tranquillity that he had not experienced in years. By the time she came out with the coffee he had fallen into a dead sleep.

THIRTEEN

THE LAST FEW HUNDRED YARDS defeated him, so he stopped and tried to get his lungs functioning again, hanging onto the lamp post opposite the newsagents for dear life, gasping and coughing as if it were his last. He needed to buy his Sunday paper anyway so could pretend that this was the point where his run ended.

It was a brilliant morning, the sun high and the few clouds tinged with red. If this was his last moment on earth, then at least it was up-beat. Since Friday night he had been wearing rose coloured spectacles, and he was enjoying how it felt. With any luck he would never have to take them off. Even when he looked at his circumstances with dispassionate eyes, things didn't seem so bad any more. Wendy's suggestion that he had a word with Diana no longer seemed so lunatic, and he was beginning to think it might prove to be workable. It would call for a lot of tact and careful handling, but provided it did not backfire in his face, he had little to lose. In the meantime, his lifestyle was hardly a torment. He had a more than decent income, an elegant and spacious flat, and a car that at the very least was not short of character. In Belleville too, things were bucking up at a rate. During the last stages of his run he had noticed the tables outside the new French café were full of affluent looking thirty-somethings, gossiping over their newspapers and baguettes, a fine food shop selling fresh pasta and virgin olive oil had just opened, and two new wine bars were in the process of being built.

As for his love life, he would have good think about that after his shower. OK, he had been thinking about it seamlessly the whole weekend, but before going into the office for a couple of hours he wanted to just lie on his couch for some big time self indulgent wallowing. Following his impromptu snooze Friday night, Wendy had woken him with coffee, and as it had already been made clear that she was staying the night, there was no need to hurry. They sat together on the couch getting to know each other until, having reached a point of no return, they went to bed. Saturday morning they had taken their time both waking up and getting to know each other even better, and after a lingering breakfast she had finally left.

During all this, the sort of things that people said when making love for the first time were exchanged, but nothing that need frighten the horses. When she departed nothing specific was said, but the air was pregnant with the fact that they would see each other again. They had made love a total of four times, and hanging onto the lamp post John was aware that whatever his emotional state, there was a strange and unusual void in the middle of his body as if his sexual organs were simply no longer there. Every time he thought about her however, his brain was glowingly tumescent and that was what mattered.

He risked letting go of the lamp post and hobbled unsteadily into the newsagents.

* * *

"I know it's always the same in here, but I can still never quite believe it."

John looked round the decadent gloom of Ron's office and took it all in. Unlike the rest of the building which had been progressively modernized over the years, Ron's office had barely changed since the firm was founded at the beginning of the century. Ron had moved in to it in the late 1960's following the death of one of the original partners who in his life time had seen no reason to change the furniture or the William Morris wallpaper. When he had first taken it over, Ron had been too busy to care about his surroundings, and once he had reached a point where he had time on his hands, he couldn't be bothered to do anything about it. Other than the compulsory computer screen, the room was a piece of history. The single window was hung with heavy velvet curtains which the cleaners refused to touch in case they fell apart or disgorged teeming life, there were dark mahogany bookcases, a large desk with a fading leather cover, and a grandiose armchair sagging with exhaustion. Very little natural light managed to gain admittance which helped to hide the level of dust, but the glow of the red shaded lamps dotted round the room made the place very cozy. Although the no smoking rule had been in force for a couple of years, the fabric of the room was impregnated with thirty years of Bensons and cheroots.

"Anyway, what's this all about, Ron?" Ron had sent John an e mail asking him to pop in when he had a moment. "Is it the new partners? I bet I can give you two definites and one possible." The weekend's optimism was not gone, but was tinged with an un-blinkered understanding of his circumstances. Knowing there wasn't a chance that he would be on the list meant he could discuss it without feeling too much pain. Ron gave him the names, and he had been right with two but the third was a rank outsider. They discussed his qualities for a few minutes, but Ron seemed distracted.

"Ron what is it? Is there something else?"

"Fraid so. I've been expecting it for a couple of years, but it still came as a bit of a shock"

"They haven't!"

"Yes they bloody have. It's all been dressed up as being for my own good, you know the sort of bollocks, but the bottom line is compulsory retirement. I'm out.

It took a while to sink in. Over time the firm had become a strange mixture of the traditional and cutting edge modern, and Ron, like his office, was one of the disparate elements that made it that way. It just wouldn't be the same without him. "How long have you got?"

"Oh there's no massive hurry. I've got up to three months to wind things up, but I might go earlier. I can't blame them. If it was twenty years ago and I was in charge, I'd have sacked a passenger like me. My pension is well stocked up so it's not a problem financially, it's just the thought of being home all day with Clarissa and just not being here where all the action is." He laughed, "I've been thinking I might not tell her, perhaps get myself a flat somewhere and just pretend to be at the office. I just need to find a way to get young Tracy to come and do a bit of filing for me. Having her leaning into the bottom drawer once a week would make it all worthwhile."

John had still not told Ron about him and Tracy and this definitely wasn't the moment. "Is it full retirement or will you become a consultant?"

"Clean break. That way I can do the odd bit of freelancing and pocket some fees." He poked John in the ribs. "If I've got a little love-nest to keep up, I'll need the odd bit of pocket money."

"Look, Ron....."

"I know! I know! You don't know what to say." He paused and looked unusually unsure of himself. "Look John, can I ask you something.....? You and Luke..."

"Yes?"

"Is there something between the two of you?"

Even with Ron leaving, John did not want to make anything public. "What do you mean?"

"Thought so! I've never wanted to mention it, but at partner's meetings it's like you're the skid mark on his underpants. You should have been given a partnership a year or so back, certainly before this bunch, but every time your name comes up he just brushes it aside. Won't even discuss it. I know we're supposed to operate as a committee but in reality he makes all the decisions and there's no moving him. I've tried to push it, but it's like trying to nail custard to the wall."

"You've never mentioned this before"

"Well you know..."

"It's good of you to have tried....Thanks."

"But if there was anything I could do, you would have mentioned it already."

"Something like that."

Ron plonked himself down in his chair. "At least you've got the rest of your life to sort things out. Looks like this is the end of mine."

"Come on, Ron" John clapped him on the shoulder. "There's plenty of life left in you yet."

"We'll see won't we? He took out a cigarette and lit it. "I'm not offering you one as there might be a public flogging." He expelled two thick jets of smoke from his nostrils with a look of deep pleasure. "Not much they can do about me smoking now though is there!"

* * *

"Yes? Who is it?"

Hardly anybody bothered to knock on his door before coming in, so who was this? Tracy put her head round and came in, nervously shutting the door behind her and looking very un-Tracy like. It was an unexpectedly cool day and she was wearing a woollen jumper and slacks, and had none of the strut and thrust he associated with. Her eyes had none of their usual sparkle, and her body language was dejected.

"Do you mind if I put the engaged sign on?"

"Err .... Is that a good idea?"

If she was about to award him another badge, he was not sure he would be man enough to turn it down, but his career was precarious enough without being caught hot-desking it with the accounts junior.

"No, nothing like that. I just want to talk. Have you got a minute?"

"Of course."

She sat on the chair opposite his desk, fiddling with her nails like someone about to ask for a rise and wondering if it was such a good idea. "Did you know, John?"

"Sorry..?"

"Did you know what they were going to do?"

"Tracy, I've no idea what you're going to ask me."

She looked a fraction more relaxed. "I thought you wouldn't, or you'd have told me. I just wanted to find out."

It was clear something was wrong and he took a chair and sat close to her. "What is it?"

Her eyes filled with tears. "They've made me redundant."

"Oh Tracy...I'm so sorry!"

"Luke told me this morning. Ever since the take-over there's been one person too many in our department, but it was OK at first as there was lots of extra work to get all the accounts amalgamated. That's all been done for ages now, but now the financial year is coming to an end they decided one of us had to go, and it was me."

He put his arms round her and hugged her quietly. If someone came in he'd find a way to deal with it. "I had no idea, honestly. I really am sorry. I don't really know what goes on out there with staffing and the like. Is there any argument that it should have been someone else?"

"Not really. Even I know it has to be me. Luke said it's all part of a bigger reorganisation. "

"Oh, Tracy, you poor kid." He thought for a moment. "Will you get much of a redundancy payment?"

"Sod all really. They explained how these payments are calculated and 'cos I'm not very old and I haven't been here that long it's a pittance."

She disentangled herself and went to the small mirror on his wall and dabbed round her eyes with a balled tissue, carefully trying to avoid a mascara run. "It's all right in one sense, I mean, I shouldn't have a problem getting another job. It's just that it hurts. All I wanted to do was just hang on here for another year or so as then I could go to Greece for good. This job's now my only reason for staying here, but I can't go yet because I haven't got enough money together." She turned and looked him in the eye. "You know I'll miss you too. It's probably just as well I'm going as even I know I shouldn't like someone as much as I like you when I'm going to marry someone else."

He well understood the problem. Wendy or not, the old urge to throw her across the desk and hang the consequences was beginning to creep up on him again. He shook the image from his mind

"Look, if you find you need any money...."

"Oh John, you are sweet. No I don't, but I really appreciate you offering." She gave him a peck on the cheek and left him on his own.

* * *

First Ron, and now Tracy. It was ridiculous. He had been poised for the chop for a couple of years, and now from left field two others went down in front of him. He had been living on this precipice for so long he sometimes took it for granted and didn't think through just how serious it might become. The difference between his circumstances and theirs was all too plain. Ron had a fat pension, and it would only take someone with Tracy's skills a couple of weeks to get a better job than the one she had just lost. He on the other hand would be straight into the wilderness, a quick overnight journey from an enviable lifestyle to the dole queue.

With fear for his situation concentrating his mind he rummaged round his desk for his address book and looked out Diana's number.

FOURTEEN

"JUST A COFFEE, THANKS. I shouldn't be here at all and I don't want to be a minute longer than necessary. Sarah's overdue her lunch and I don't want her to start getting fractious. Can you hold this jar for me?"

It wasn't a brilliant start, but at least she was here. When Diana had answered his call she had at first been so angry that he should contact her at all that it took a while before she would agree to even hear what he had to say. Once she had accepted that he had a serious reason for needing to talk to her, with great reluctance she finally agreed to have a brief meeting. Making the arrangements had not been easy. The whole concept of meeting in secret worried her, and she had insisted on it being a place where there was absolutely no chance of being seen by anyone who knew her. They had finally agreed on a small cafe in Richmond they both knew from their days together.

He arrived well before her having invented a fictitious client meeting, and sat in a distant corner and waited. He had not thought through the implications of her now being a mum and didn't immediately realise that the woman coming in with a toddler welded round her neck was her. But of course she would have Sarah with her. What else? There was no way that someone like Diana would even consider leaving her eighteen month old child in the care of anyone else, even for a few hours. She manoeuvred herself to his table, dragging with her all the paraphernalia of motherhood and started to get organised. John was a single man and travelling light was all he knew.

Sometimes even having to carry a briefcase irritated him. He could not believe the elaborate three wheeled buggy she was pushing or the number of bags and objects strung round it and even hanging round Diana's neck. More of a shock was the change in Diana herself. Nearly three years had passed since he had last seen her, but subject to a little wear and tear he was pretty well the same person he had been then. She had changed almost beyond recognition. There was just a hint of the eager and innocent girl she had been when they had been together, but that was the smaller part. She had turned into a competent and able mum, very much in control of both herself, and what as he started to realise was this unexploded bomb of a child. Arriving at his table, using what looked like sleight of hand Diana disentangled herself from Sarah and folded up the buggy, then unpacked bags and shoehorned Sarah on to a chair, all the while removing one object after another from prying fingers. He had not appreciated what dangers lurk for a toddler in glass ash trays and pepper pots, and was treated to a crash course in damage limitation as Diana rearranged all the potential land-mines in reach.

For ten or fifteen minutes he felt like someone who has turned up uninvited on anther couple's special date and it was an odd feeling. It used to be that Diana treated everything he said as if it were carved on stone tablets. Now he felt he was just in her way. It was time for Sarah's lunch, and that took priority over talking about his problems or anything else. Diana fed Sarah from a jar of something that had all the consistency and appeal of fresh vomit that had been livened up with bright orange highlights. It was apparently organic and completely GM free which did nothing to make it any more appealing to him or apparently to Sarah. Each mouthful had to be coaxed into her with subterfuges and tricks, a labour intensive exercise which, even though he was not directly involved, exhausted him after five minutes. To add to his discomfort, although Sarah was as beautiful and beguiling as a siren, she was the image of Luke, his every dint and feature deconstructed and reformed in her, but now overlaid with an angelic perfection. It made him feel uncomfortable, as if Luke were here in person and spying on their meeting. The upside however was that her being here was helping to ease the tension with Diana clearly edgy and reluctant to be there at all. In an attempt to lighten the atmosphere and with Diana's cautious consent John took Sarah on his lap and attempted to establish a bond. After an initial show of shyness she started to exchange gurgles and growls, but the timing was all wrong, and suddenly and without warning, her peaches and cream complexion turned an unhealthy grey and she spewed a whole jar's worth of GM free food over what until then had been a favourite suit.

"Oh my God!" Diana let out a squeal. "Take that off, and I'll wipe it down." With effortless competence she had taken back Sarah who appeared to have made an instant recovery, and at the same time opened one of her many bags and got out a damp cloth, but her attempt not to laugh was a failure. At least this was the first sign of the old Diana he had seen since her arrival. "Orange suits you! You should wear it more often!" She suddenly lost control in an explosion of laughter, initially confusing Sarah but who then joined in. For a few minutes they were both helpless, their laughter feeding off each other, while John sat there reluctantly playing the role of straight man. Eventually she pulled herself together.

"John, I'm so sorry. I shouldn't laugh. You looked so surprised"

"That's a good word for it." He looked at the partially digested orange glop sliding down his lapels, wondering if the colour would ever come out. "Don't worry it can be cleaned." He wasn't that thrilled, but if the cost of her co-operation was a ruined suit, on balance it was worth it. They did what they could with the damp cloth, and then he hung his wet jacket on the back of a chair. As Diana settled herself, he looked at her as if seeing her for the first time. He had been in love with her once, but it all seemed so long ago and he could barely remember how it felt. Even so, now all the pain was behind them, it was good to re-establish contact. "Dare I say, it's good to see you again?"

"In a funny sort of way, it's good to see you. You always did make me laugh." For a second their eyes met but they instantly looked away, reluctant to acknowledge to each other just how much there had once been between them when now it was as if it had never been. "Look, before you start," Her face resumed its previous seriousness, but she now looked more like her old self. "Can I do a bit of air clearing? I don't want you to think that I'm hostile to you because of the past, because I'm not. That's too long ago now. If I'm looking strained and unfriendly it's because I'm nervous being here. Obviously Luke doesn't know that I'm meeting with you, and I'm terrified of any chance that he should find out. I'm not going to let anything put a strain on our marriage."

"I understand that. I really am grateful to you for seeing me."

"Other than that, it's fine. You sounded so portentous on the phone I knew it had to be something serious, so thought I should see you."

After her earlier efforts Sarah's eyes were now beginning to close, and Diana settled her in her lap before going on. "While I am here, I do need to say a few things quickly. I've wanted to for the last year or so but it just wasn't appropriate. Whatever happened in the past is now all behind us. I know you didn't mean to hurt me, you just couldn't help yourself."

"Look Diana….."

"Let me finish. I just want you to know that it's all healed now, and if it's been gnawing at you, it's all right. I have a really good marriage with Luke and I have Sarah. I simply don't want anything else, and there aren't many people who can say that. Whatever else is going on in your life now you can enjoy it with a clear conscience." Sarah was now sleeping, and she kissed her forehead and tucked her closer in to her. "OK. I've said my piece. You'd better tell me now why we're here."

"Damn you, Diana! Look I didn't mean that nastily" He fiddled with his coffee cup, not sure what to say. "I come here for a favour, and very much against your wishes you go out of your way to meet with me, and then you give me an absolution I don't deserve. I can barely see you up there on your moral high ground."

"It's a very good place to be sick over people."

"*Touché!* Look, let me tell you what's going on. You may know all of it or some of it, I don't know. This is the situation." He gave her the story as best he could. "I'm not saying any of this to criticise Luke. It's simply that I don't know how much longer I can go on with this over my head. It's killing me slowly."

"I see!" Diana sat silently for several minutes, periodically checking that Sarah was comfortable. "Luke is not a sadist you know. He's actually a very kind and loving father and I'm very happy with him."

"I'm sure he is. As I said, I'm not here to have a go at him. I just want to bring it to an end."

"You know I can't possibly tell him that we have met up. That would make it even worse."

"I don't expect you to. I just thought, I don't know, that at the right moment you could find a way to bring the conversation round to me in some way and get him to tell you what's going on. Then you could tell him that it's past history now and that he should give me a chance to move on. Damn it, Diana, he and I have to see each other every bloody day. Surely even he would be happier if he never had to hear my name again."

She took a deep breath. "I do understand what you must be going through. You know, the two of you are very alike in many ways. You're both driven by ambition."

"Well? Will you try and help me."

"It won't be easy. You know that I'm not going to do anything that might alert him to our having made contact."

"That's fine. Thanks, I really appreciate this."

"That's OK. I'll do what I can. How's work otherwise, what are you up to?"

He told her about the work for Dragoon and she laughed. "I can remember big George. I did a couple of jobs for him when I was in Greg's department just before he left."

"What was that?"

"Oh, what was it, drafting a Legal Charge document for him against that land near where you live, you know the old Gambols building."

His ears pricked up. "That can't be right. There's no charge on that property. I've done a search."

"Maybe it's been paid off, then. I can remember all about it. It was to secure money he was borrowing from some Liechtenstein company. It was a few million, quite a lot of money."

"Hang on!" His brain was racing, but he didn't want to undo all the good will they had now established. "I don't suppose you can remember its name after all this time?"

"I don't know, Regina Associates, Roger Associates. Something like that."

"Reggeo! I thought so. Didn't you do anything about getting it registered? There's no record of it at all."

"I didn't need to. Reggeo were the lenders. They would do that."

"Not if they had a reason to hide it they wouldn't! Look, apart from recording it with the Land Registry, you know that under the Companies Act, Dragoon also had to register the charge at Companies House."

"I can still remember my company law, thank you John! It wasn't that long ago. George said that all he wanted us to do was to draft it, and that once it was all signed up he would get the registration done in-house."

John took his head in his hands and was saying "Fuck" over and over quietly to himself, as he tried to piece this jigsaw together.

"Please, John, try not to use that word in front of Sarah. If she wakes up it might be the next word she decides to shout out at her toddler group. Anyway, what's the problem? I don't understand."

"Look, I know you want to get away, but can I just talk this over with you. It might help me clear things in my own mind."

"I'll stay till she wakes up, but I really must go then."

"Fine! Fine! Listen, in Belleville a lot of interested people want a Saul Liebling School to be built, but there were only two places they might be able to it. It turns out that both are owned by Dragoon, and one of them is the Gambols site. Dragoon want to put a major complex on the other one, and they bought off local opposition by contracting to sell the Gambols site to the Saul Liebling outfit for less than its full market value once the other development got going. The contract to sell is fool proof on the face of it, but that's on the basis that the site is free of any charges. But now you tell me it's not. Reggeo Associates is clearly George's company – it's only just hit me, but it's an anagram for

George. That means that George was lending George money but keeping it secret, or even more likely no money ever changed hands. What I'm prepared to bet is that the loan was a paper transaction only and when it suits him, George can have his Liechtenstein company claim repayment, and in default they can take possession, that way the contract to sell it to the school won't be able to go ahead. George will have got his planning permission on the other site, and under the umbrella of his Liechtenstein Company he will be able to do what he wants with the Gambols site."

"But won't that expose him as a crook."

"Even if it did, he wouldn't give a toss. In any event, there's no way of proving that he has any connection with Reggeo."

"But, even so, wearing his Dragoon hat he would have known about the Legal Charge."

"He could say he forgot, or more likely that it was his solicitor's responsibility to register it and they cocked up. That would give him a stick to beat us with if he needed to."

Sarah started to stir, and Diana began to gather up her things. "Look, I've got to go. I'm going to do what I can for you, John, but as I said, no promises. Don't come to the doorway, I'll feel much safer leaving on my own." She hauled Sarah into the chair and strapped her in. "I don't know why you're worried about this George business. It sounds like the sort of thing you used to thrive on." She let out a dry cynical laugh. ''I'm so glad the law is behind me now; let's be honest, it's all so meaningless. *'Was there a quorum at a meeting? Was this somebody's domicile at a particular time? Was a document properly served or registered?'* What the hell does it matter, it's never about the actual rights or wrongs of any situation. It's all smoke and mirrors and you're welcome to it." She leaned down and kissed her daughter on the forehead with undisguised affection. ''This is reality, John. Everything else is paltry in comparison.''

* * *

"John, it's Wendy. Can you talk?"

"Sure. Hi, I was going to ring you anyway. Are you OK? You sound very serious."

"I'm worried about something, and I want a promise from you. This is very serious. You really have been completely straight with me, haven't you?"

"I'm sorry, I don't understand?"

"I didn't put that very well. I don't mean going to bed with me, I mean taking advantage of getting closer to me to pull the wool over my eyes about what's happening locally. I'm not going to go into detail on the phone, but just tell me you've been absolutely up front, and I'll believe you."

"I don't like the sound of this. Listen, I promise that I've been absolutely straight but I'm beginning to suspect that things are going on that neither of us know about. I think we need to talk, but I need to decide how much I can tell you at this stage without talking to George again." He drummed his fingers on the desk, annoyed with being in this position. He had knowingly walked into a situation where there was a conflict between personal and professional loyalties. "I suppose if we meet up we can talk off the record."

"You promise you've been totally honest so far."

"I promise."

"Then maybe we should meet at your flat. It will guarantee complete privacy, and I don't see why we can't combine business with pleasure."

His heart lifted at her words. "Well I'm sure that's OK. I'm never against a little pleasure, but you realise that as you opposing solicitor I might be having to ask you some very penetrating questions?"

He heard what sounded like a low giggle in his earpiece before she spoke again, her voice slightly hoarse.

"OK, let's stop this right now or I'll be done for! I'm due in the local magistrate's court in an hour and I'm having enough of a problem concentrating as it is!" He could almost hear her brain gathering itself together. *"Look, back to the real world for a second. I'm stuck till the weekend as I have to go and see the family. Are you free to meet up then?"*

"I'll make sure I am."

"Let me just give you a quick run-down of what I've heard. Vijay Bhagati who runs the shop on the corner of the site has heard that the development will stretch beyond the boundary of his shop, and further more that it's going to include an indoor dog track, of all things. All sorts of rumours are going round as to what will be going on there."

"What!"

"Exactly! As I'm off to the country for a couple of days, do you think you could find out what's going on."

"I'll try. Cross my heart I know nothing about this."

"It's OK, I believe you."

"Oh, and Wendy, before you get off the line...."

"Yes?"

"Oh, never mind! Another time." Marge had walked into his room with an armful of files.

"Not alone anymore?"

"Exactly!."

"OK .See you at the weekend then."

"I'll look forward to it, Miss Vyne."

"I hope you've got a full agenda."

"It's bursting!"

FIFTEEN

WAITING TO SEE RUPERT IN the reception area of Crowther-Van was as much of a culture shock as when he had visited Wendy's firm, but this time seen from the other end of the telescope. The public areas of his own offices were wood panelled and furnished with leather bound books and good quality Regency furniture. Copies of Country Life, The Economist and The Times were on the tables, and the parquet floors were scattered with Turkish carpets. Luke had plans for a radical change to something more cutting edge, but for the time being the premises announced solidarity and permanence, and a place where people had been doing business in complete safety for a century or so. This building was another world entirely, a huge atrium of pale stone and glass flying up to the stratosphere and possibly beyond. The limestone floor was as wide as a desert, and the massive coffee tables with their thick green glass tops were scattered with a selection of international finance magazines. Electronic screens displayed information about share prices and fluctuating markets, and a series of digital clocks told the time in the major financial capitals of the world.

This space said Money with a capital M, it said international power and privilege, and it said that if God had the odd legal problem, this was the place he would pop in to get it sorted, provided he came suitably recommended and could afford the hourly rate. Looking round at this temple to high finance, John was convinced that at any moment security guards would sniff out an untouchable amongst them and he would find himself being taken outside to be dunked in a bath of hot Dettol before being reluctantly allowed back in.

"John, good to see you." Rupert appeared and extended a long bony hand.

"And you Rupert."

"We don't have to go upstairs if you don't want to. We can use one of the tables down here."

"We won't be too crowded will we?"

"Ha Ha! Yes, it is a big space isn't it. Nice thing is, you can be as private as you want just by sitting a couple of miles from the nearest person. If we need to refer to any papers in any detail we can go to a proper meeting room or to my office."

No thank you, Rupert. I don't want to see your office which will probably be ten times as big as mine and full of priceless artworks plus a couple of obliging secretaries ready to do your every bidding. "I'm only here for an exchange of info. This is fine."

"Let's sit down here. I've ordered coffee."

Rupert sat down and wound his long angular legs round each other and sat back in the sofa like a beautifully tailored praying mantis. John wondered if commanding such a job gave you this appearance of benign and studious brilliance. If John could get himself a position in an outfit like this, would he too eventually start to look like someone who was born wearing half glasses, and who read Beowulf for light relief? At least John had scored a small victory over Rupert. George had been quite right that if they were immovable about the size of the initial deposit, Clarendon would cave in. Rupert had tutted over the phone about Dragoon's intransigence when John had told him it was fiver million or no deal, but in due course had come back and said his clients agreed.

The coffee appeared and was poured from a gleaming chrome Alessi pot by a supermodel in a designer uniform. She gave John a brief look that suggested that if he needed any other service from her, no matter what it might be, the mere dropping of a million pound note on the tray would be sufficient to secure it. Trying to act as if being in situations like this was an everyday occurrence John took a swallow of arguably the most perfect coffee he had ever tasted before starting.

"It's the Old Brewery development, Rupert. Your client's sub-leases. I always thought Clarendon only operated at the prestige end of the market."

Rupert took of his glasses, peered through them at the sky high above them, then polished them on a spotted silk handkerchief. "That's what they have tended to do in the past. Like all companies they have to be flexible and go where the money is."

John turned over his notes. "I've got a list of proposed lessees here. Listen, indoor dog track, amusement arcade, karaoke bar, five or six fast food outlets, two or three bar applications from outfits who normally employ topless waitresses. What is all this?"

Rupert looked genuinely confused. "Isn't it self-explanatory? As everybody always knew, it's going to be a mixed leisure complex. That's what everyone has been saying."

"But Rupert, I just don't understand. This just isn't the sort of business that Clarendon deal with. The mere fact that Clarendon were involved made everyone make assumptions what the development would be."

"Yes." Rupert looked at John as if realising that he wasn't really very bright after all, and things would have to be explained slowly and carefully. "As you said, Clarendon normally deal with prestige property in prime central London sites. To make money from properties of that calibre they have to be sub-let to high profit organisations such as major international companies, finance houses, that sort of thing. But that's a limited market with a finite number of potential lessees and prime sites. But there are other profitable markets out there. You know what I mean when I say socio/economic Cs, Ds and Es?"

Of course he did. His parents eking out their retirement years in a bungalow in Clacton, him when he was a boy and through all his schooldays in an embarrassingly second hand uniform, and indeed struggling through his first few years at university. He decided to make it easy for Rupert. "You mean people whose lips move when they read the Sun."

A pained expression appeared on Rupert's face. "Colourfully put, John, but you've got the point. Anyway, individually they may not have much financial clout, but there are massive numbers of them, far more of them than As and Bs. The whole concept of this development is to create the definitive leisure complex in South London which will bring in these people in huge numbers. It's a massive market with a very high profit potential."

John stared round the temple to high finance that surrounded him unable to believe what he was hearing, his primary concern suddenly how this was all going to affect him personally. He saw the value of his flat tumbling to nothing and all the incremental gentrification of the last few years destroyed overnight.

"But, Rupert, it'll ruin the area. You'll never get the permissions"

"Come on John, the permissions are all in place! Clarendon wouldn't have even got going on this if they weren't confident how it would turn out. There were a whole series of discussions with Dragoon and the council before all this got started. The council are all in favour as it will bring in so much money. But I don't see what your concern is. Clarendon is going ahead with the Head Lease and your clients will get all their money. Surely they don't give a damn if we build a concentration camp on it provided they get paid"

John had a problem controlling his voice. "Rupert, I don't think you understand. I *live* in Belleville. Overnight I could go into negative equity. I could be ruined by this! How would you feel if you were told that an all night boogie bar was going to be built bang next to your lovely Holland Park villa?"

Rupert continued to look as if John were an alien from another planet who simply did not understand how things happened down here on earth. "But it wouldn't happen in Kensington and Chelsea, would it? That's the whole point of living there. I don't want to patronise, John, but it sounds to me as if you're getting a bit emotionally involved in this. If you think that personally you have a conflict of interest, shouldn't you stop acting?"

This was the way John had talked to countless people over the years, his advice dispassionate as he explained the cold lucid inevitability of a logical progression. Please don't get excited because it interrupts the process of rational thinking. He of all people should know better by now than to let his emotions get in the way of calmly watching his life collapse in front of him. He suddenly thought about his meeting with Diana, and realised with icy certainty that there couldn't possibly be any chance of her covertly getting Luke to talk about the messy little problem of John Foxton and persuading him to instantly write out a reference that glowed in the dark. He paused to wonder if his job or his flat would go first. It would give him something to think about when he went home tonight.

"Are you all right John? You went into another world then."

"Yes of course. Sorry. You're right, Rupert. Provided that Dragoon's position is still safe, that's the only thing, isn't it. When is the first cash transfer due?"

"A few weeks. By the way, I've got a couple of letters here, one addressed directly to Dragoon and a copy for you. It's on something quite separate."

In a dream John took the letters and opened his copy. It was a letter from Crowther–Van on behalf of Reggeo Associates of Vaduz, Liechtenstein referring to the loan of £3.5 M charged on the Gambols building. It said that neither the interest nor the capitol sum had been repaid, and that under the terms of the loan they were therefore now entitled to take possession of the site. If payment was not made in 7 days then an action for possession would be started. John was now on automatic pilot, and merely raised his eyebrows. "I see! You act for this company, Reggeo Associates do you?"

"Only for any work that needs to be done for them in this country. They obviously have separate lawyers acting for them in Liechtenstein."

"Of course they do. Any idea who's behind Reggeo?"

"Haven't a clue, but that's not my concern. Reggeo is the client and that's all we need to know. If we wanted to investigate we couldn't – you know what these Liechtenstein companies are."

"Yes, I should have thought. Have you noticed that Reggeo is an anagram for George?"

"Oh so it is! I didn't know you were into crosswords. Anyway, I presume that there won't be any problem with Dragoon paying up. They've got £5m coming from Clarendon shortly. The thing is…"

John's mobile trilled in his pocket and, still not sure what planet he was on, he put it to his ear. "John Foxton."

The voice at the other end was tense with panic. *"It's Alfie, John. I need you. It's urgent."*

For Christ's sake! Could he switch to another dimension just like that? "Hang on! Hang on!" He looked up from the phone "We've finished haven't we, Rupert?"

"Think so. If we need to, we can speak on the phone."

"Fine! Fine! I'll be off then." Briefly shaking hands, he strode out with his phone to his ear, no longer sure that he really was cut out for this business after all. "OK. What is it Alfie?"

"I'm at the cop shop, they've got me in for questioning again. It's really urgent this time. For Christ's sake get here as soon as you can."

"Which one?"

"Bow Street."

Well at least it was close. "I'll be there."

He jumped in cab, chewing at his fingers with tension all the way. This didn't sound like Alfie who was a veteran of police interviews and knew probably better than John what the police could and could not do. They knew him too well to be knocking him about, so what was all this? And anyway, how the hell could he, John, really be of help to Alfie when his brain was on fire with all the information he needed to absorb following his meeting with Rupert. All he wanted to do was to throw his head back and howl but he forced himself to block it out and think about the job in hand. He could cry himself to sleep later.

A succession of road works delayed the journey, so nearly half an hour had passed before he threw himself out of the cab at the other end to find Alfie pacing up and down outside the police station, his coat collar as always turned up as if shielding himself from prying eyes, and a battered old leather satchel hanging over his shoulder.

He practically threw himself at John, his face an unhealthy colour and a coating of sweat over his face. "John! Thank God you're here! It's all OK now though. Jesus Christ!"

`"What is it? What's happening?"

"It's OK, John. They've let me go." He held his hand to his heart to check if it was still doing its job. "Can we go for a coffee? A strong one with lots of sugar."

"Sure! Sure!" There was a Costa close by and after getting what they wanted at the counter that sat at an outside table, Alfie's breathing coming back to normal. He slurped down some of the coffee, clutching the satchel in his lap.

"OK, Alfie. In your own time."

"God, John! I thought this was going to be the big one, the long stretch." He took a deep breath. "They suddenly came at me in a patrol car and took me in. Told me they were close to eliminating me from their enquiries about the stolen painting, but wanted to clear up a few bits of detail. All very polite this time, and it didn't take very long. I don't know whether to believe them or not. Could be they want me to drop my guard so I'll lead them to it."

"Is that it? You brought me flying down here just for a routine interview?"

"John," Alfie paused as if considering something portentous. "Have you ever had a patch in your life when events crowd onto events till you get to start thinking that it's all out of control?"

John considered his answer carefully. "Solicitors don't have problems, Alfie. They just sort out other people's problems."

"Well lucky you! Look, John, you know what my career's been. I'm a breaking and entering man. That's it. Don't do violence and I don't do drugs. Fine! Then I go out on an ego trip and do that sodding Vermeer which is coming back to haunt me, but at least I had myself to blame for that. OK. But someone owes me for a big job I did a while ago, and I've been nagging for payment, and he's been pleading poverty. I don't believe him, but never mind. So I nag a bit more, and he says he'll try and pay me in kind. Do you know what the little shit's done?" He looked around him carefully in case he was being overheard. "He's paid me in a sodding great bag of cocaine! Couple of hours ago. Just appeared out of nowhere in the street and shoved it in my hand."

"Christ, Alfie! What have you done with it?"

"I haven't done anything with it! Haven't had the chance." He shook the satchel in his lap. "It's in this bag. Why do you think I was shitting myself in there? I've been interviewed in Bow Street for half an hour with a great bagful of coke on my lap. Between that and that sodding Vermeer I'm a walking life sentence just waiting to begin."

* * *

Sitting in his office the next morning, John looked his usual self in a Thomas Pink shirt and a loosely knotted Balenciaga tie an inch or so adrift from his collar, but hanging on the back of his chair like a bad joke was his flannel jacket with the hint of an orange stain, and on the chair opposite him was a battered leather satchel. He wondered if he would ever need to sleep again. Common sense told him that he was brain-dead through being awake so long, but he was still amazingly alert. He had barely slept the previous night, his brain racing almost too fast to keep up with. He swivelled in his seat considering the plan that, suddenly and without warning, had come to him the previous day. He had yet to complete the details, but the general shape was there. If any one piece of the jig-saw he was gradually creating in his mind did not fit then he might find that the whole thing would simply not work, but he now had so little to lose and so much to gain that he owed it to himself to at least make a stab at it. And this first thing could stand on its own. Even if he did not get round to lighting the fuse, he could at least plant the bomb.

He picked up the phone and dialled George's number.

* * *

On the way down to George's office in the back of the stretch Merc he looked dressier than usual with a silk scarf thrown round his neck and his hands encased in fine leather gloves, but his heart was racing and his brain on fire. He sat back in the far right corner where it was hard for Sid to either turn in his direction or see him in the mirror, his hands covertly exploring for gaps or apertures in the upholstery till he found what might fit the bill. When Sid was heavily involved with negotiating a tight junction he eased the plastic bag of white powder out of the satchel he was carrying and then squeezed it down through the gap at the edge of the seat, then right underneath into the hollow below. He had done it! He was sweating with tension, but this at least had been easier than he had expected. Stage two might prove impossible, but a start had been made. He took off the gloves and scarf and shoved them into the satchel.

* * *

"George, good to see you."

"And you Johnny boy. Hope you're not bringing me bad news. Fancy a sandwich?" He pointed to a huge plate piled with sandwiches on the corner of his desk, taking two himself and throwing them more or less whole down his throat before reaching for another couple. "Ham and mustard. Nothing like it."

Any appetite John may have had vanished at the site of so much sliced white leaping like manic depressive lemmings down the black hole of George's throat. By the time he drew breath to answer, another three had followed the first couple. How could he do that without choking himself?

"Thanks, but no, George. What I've got to tell you doesn't sound wonderful, but perhaps you can tell me I'm worrying about nothing."

He looked at his surroundings, a typical Mayfair interior. Not a brash statement like Rupert's money palace, but the elegant panelling and expensive fittings discreetly smelling of old money and respectability which in John's eyes made George look even more of a crooked sleaze-ball than he normally did. More the point, and what he had correctly remembered, there was a shaggy white carpet covering the dark wood floor in front of George's desk, and over to one side a couple of cream coloured easy chairs. Even better than he could have hoped, George's vast camel hair overcoat was thrown over the back of one of them. He fished out the letter that Rupert had given him and passed it over, curious to see what the expression on George's face would be when he read it. He was impressed.

"What the fuck's this?" George's rubbery features gave no clue that he had instigated the letter himself.

"A good question, George. I did all the standard searches before doing the contract, and there was no record of any charge. I got in early this morning and fished around and discovered we've got a file from about three years ago drafting a charge for you, but it's in store and it will take a few days to get out. Can you tell me if you completed it? I mean did you borrow three and a bit million, and is there such a charge?"

George looked for all the world like someone vainly trying to remember a distant event, then suddenly seeing daylight."

"D'you know, I can remember it now! Young bit of totty in your office did it for us. That's right, we did do it."

"You borrowed three million from this," He looked as if he were having a problem pronouncing the name "Reggeo Associates, and charged the Gambol's property with repayment?"

"Yeah, we did. I remember now."

John suddenly felt the urge to laugh, and tried to suppress it. Two grown men were unconvincingly lying their heads off to each other like kids in a playground. If they were auditioning for RADA they would have both been firmly told to hang on to their day jobs. The difference was that he knew that George was lying, but he hoped against hope that George would be so wrapped up in his own story telling that it would not even cross his mind that John was.

"But George, this could be serious. Is this still outstanding?"

"S'pose it must be. We've certainly not paid it back"

Of course you haven't as you didn't borrow it in the first place, you lying ugly blubber mountain. "But are you able to pay it back? You can see where I'm coming from. If you can't, then depending on the wording of the Legal Charge, I don't how we can stop them taking possession."

George put on his thinking act again, his eyes vacant as he stared at the ceiling in mock concentration."

"Fuck me, John. I don't think we can! Three mill's a lot of dosh even for us. Tell me, where do we stand with that contract we've got with that school. We'd promised to sell it to them hadn't we?"

"Hate to tell you, George," He really couldn't keep this up much longer, before his face gave him away. "If Dragoon lose the property to these Reggeo people, the contract will be what's known as "Frustrated". In simple terms, if Dragoon no longer own it, then they can't sell it. That's the end of it."

"What about damages claims?"

"Provided it can be shown that the contract was frustrated because of events beyond your control, then there's no liability."

"Well John!" George got up from behind his desk and paced his vast bulk round the floor. "This is a bit of a turn up."

Could he risk it? "You'd just forgotten all about it, had you?"

"You know how it is. Pressure of business, things get put to one side and then slip under the floor boards."

Here comes the big one "What terms are you on with Reggeo? Would they give you a bit of time to pay it back? We can try that on."

George's expression did not falter "Not a chance. You know what these foreign garlic munchers are like. Cut their own mother's throat."

Time to move in. "Look George, it's just possible there might be some get-out clause we can rely on. It will take a day or so to get our old file out of store, but if you've got your copy of the Legal Charge in the office now, I can check it. I might be able to find some loophole."

"Hang on." George lumbered through a door behind his desk into an ante-room, and John could just see him opening a filing cabinet drawer. It was his one chance. He took a tiny twist of cellophane from the satchel and swiftly emptied a little of the fine white powder into the carpet and the creases of the chairs then, checking to see that George was still occupied, took the ultimate risk and tipped the final few grains into one of the pockets of his overcoat. He brushed the residue from his hands, satisfied that to all intents and purposes it was invisible. It was a warm day, but tonight he would be having a big fire at home and the suit he was now wearing would be on it.

George came back with a file, out of breath from his unaccustomed bending, and passed a sealed document to John who made a great show of reading it.

"George I've got to say this, it doesn't look good. I'd like to consider it back at my office, but as far as I can see, if you can't pay up, then they've got you bang to rights" He'd never said that to anyone before, and was happy that it had a nice ring to it.

George was now back at his desk, and there might just as well have a sign round his neck saying that his brain was earning its living. "John," He paused for maximum effect. "You tell me that you had searches done, and you couldn't find any trace of this."

"That's right."

"Whose responsibility is it to register a charge?"

Ah, so this was going to be the game was it! "Well normally the lender would register at the Land Registry to protect their own interests, so that was down to Reggeo. As well as that, when a limited company has its property charged to a lender, then there's a legal responsibility on them to register it at Company's House. That's so anyone who wants to do business with the company can do a company search and know what charges there are against the company's assets."

"Yes, I get you. So Dragoon should have had it registered on its company file."

"That's right."

"But it's not."

"Definitely isn't."

He could guess what was coming, and sat there with a straight face.

"Well, I don't like to say this to you John as personally you've always done me proud, but wasn't it down to your firm to have done that as part of the service? I mean, if we'd have seen it registered there, then we wouldn't have forgotten about it and got ourselves into this mess." George put on the concerned expression of an anxious parent reluctantly telling a child that punishment might just be unavoidable. "If there's trouble because if this, we may just have to find ourselves holding your firm responsible."

"Best I don't comment at this stage, George, don't you think? Perhaps I should dig out the old file first. Could be for example that you were going to do it in-house?"

For the first time a flash of suspicion crossed George's face, then vanished again just as quickly. "Well, we wouldn't have, would we? What facilities have we got for doing things like that in-house?"

"Didn't think of that. Anyway George, never underestimate what a good lawyer can do for you." He indicated the charge document. "I'll take this with me if that's OK. I can fine tooth comb it overnight. I haven't given up on finding some escape mechanism."

"Good lad. I'll get Sid to fetch the car round for you."

"Don't worry, George. It's a lovely day. I think I'll walk."

"Walk! You sure?"

Course I'm sure, George. Nothing is going to get me into that dreadful car of yours ever again.

SIXTEEN

"MORE COFFEE?"

"Thanks. Just a spot. I suppose we can't put it off any longer, can we?"

"Fraid not."

It was late Saturday morning and John and Wendy were in their dressing gowns on John's couch. On Friday, John had done the unthinkable and called in sick to the office as he had needed time to think and to get everything clear in his mind. It wasn't the detail that bothered him. What he really wanted to get clear was whether he was prepared to embark on a plan that was so fraught with risks and which, however it turned out would almost certainly change the pattern of his life for good. Rather than just entomb himself in his flat, in the afternoon he had gone walking to help him think. Wandering down Sloane Street did nothing to help him take a dispassionate approach. Following one after the other like sheets of toilet paper were Chanel, Maxmara, Yves St Laurent, and Cartier and a whole succession of similar outlets, each more expensively seductive than the last, and he could have room fulls of their fripperies if he were able to make his plan happen. Frankly that was not a significant consideration as it was quality of life that mattered to him rather than having a house full of expensive possessions, but even so, it was still a siren call. But then of course, supposing his plan failed? In his career he had always played with a straight bat on the basis that no opposing lawyer could find even the ghost of a skeleton in his legal cupboard. As a result he had been able to savage opponents over procedural irregularities or questionable conduct knowing that no matter how deep they mined for any dirt on him, they would not even be able to find so much as an overdue library book. Now he seemed to be considering a course of action which could not merely result in his pleasuring Her Majesty for the next twenty odd years, but possibly a contract being taken out on him by the sort of people who always carried a violin case but couldn't play a note.

When Wendy had arrived on Friday night he had told her that he had things to say which would likely ruin their weekend together. He felt it only fair to tell her that once she knew what he had in mind she might never want to know him again let alone sleep with him. She said that on that basis they had better keep it all to himself for the time being and they had gone straight to bed. Mid evening they got up and cooked, and after sharing a meal they watched an old film on TV before going back to bed for the night. Saturday morning John slept late, waking to find Wendy preparing breakfast from a bag of goodies she had brought with her. After enjoying this, they no longer had any excuse not to get down to business.

"Look Wendy, you know you're not going to like this don't you."

"You've given me enough warnings. I'm a big girl now."

"Don't feed me lines like that!"

"Enough of that! Just get on with it."

"OK. Whatever you were thinking about George Stavros was even closer to the truth than we both realised. He's a dyed in the wool crook and he's lied to everyone throughout including me. He has never had any intention of selling the Gambols site to the Saul Liebling school. Entering in to the contract was just a device to remove opposition to planning permission on the Old Brewery development."

"But there's still a contract in place. He can't get round that."

"I'm coming to that. Most of what I'm going to say is fact and a bit of it guesswork. What is fact is that the Gambols site is subject to a Legal Charge to secure an apparent loan of three and a half million. The loan which is probably only a paper transaction is from a Liechtenstein company called

Reggeo Associates, and although it's impossible to get any solid information about Liechtenstein companies, it's beyond doubt that it's owned by George Stavros. Think about the names for a second – Reggeo, George. You've got it. OK. Reggeo is now going through the motions of calling in the loan – you can see where this is leading?

Wendy looked very calm as she digested what she was being told. "Reggeo will take possession, and George will say, 'Sorry guys, I wish I could sell you this site, but I can't as the contract has been frustrated by its being repossessed.'"

"Exactly. We both know that legally there's a lot of shit that can be stirred up, but the bottom line is still that Dragoon can't sell a property they no longer have title to. If your clients make a damages claim, George will probably just have Dragoon pay off a lot off bogus debts to companies he controls to clear off all its cash and then let it liquidate. He's got a separate construction company that will continue with the contract to build the complex for Clarendon, and for what it's worth, George will almost certainly pretend that the problem was failure by my firm to advise him properly about registering the legal charge, and will probably make his own damages claim against them. If we went the legal route, it could take years, cost a fortune and probably at the end of it, no one would be any better off. "

"It's funny, as a safeguard I carried out my own searches rather than just relying on yours. Fat lot of good that was." She sat back in the couch looking at the ceiling. "Is there any hope for the human race John? At my level of work they're doing benefit fraud and beating their wives, and further up market it's exactly the same thing except that more money is involved. I really do despair sometimes"

"I'm afraid it gets worse. This probably doesn't bother you quite so much, but it looks as if instead of a prestigious development that will enhance the area, it's going to be a down market amusement centre for all the Neanderthals in South London to flock to, so that they can all have the time of their lives before lurching through the streets smashing windows and throwing up." He saw that she was about to protest and jumped in. "I know! I know!

Just because people are working class doesn't mean that they're yobs, but I'm too wound up by all this to be PC about it. What's beyond argument is that the price of every property in the area will drop like a stone." He waved his arms round to indicate his flat. "Including this one. What will bother you is that it will mean re-possessions of a lot of small businesses, the very thing nobody wanted."

"But surely we can challenge the permissions!"

"I'm not so sure. I might be wrong, but the feed- back I'm getting is that the current decision makers on the local council are in bed with the Dragoon /Clarendon camp. And this brings me to speculation, but I bet I'm right. You described your friend Martin Fletcher as the single voice of reason on the council, and the one person who had the ability to stop it seizing up with loony ideas. What happened to him? Just when all this becomes the subject of discussion, he gets beaten up and so badly injured that he's out of action for months. I've no doubt that one of the parties with a vested interest organised it, and the most likely candidate is George. The people on the council may be loony and possibly corrupt, but I doubt if they're into organised violence. And I might be wrong, but somehow I don't think it was Clarendon."

Wendy digested this for some minutes before she spoke. "I think I'm going to need a fair bit of time to think what can be done. You said I might not want to know you after we had discussed this, but I can't see that you've done anything wrong."

"That's right, so far I haven't. But as I said, I have a plan."

"It's more than I have, my brain's still numb. I didn't miss what you said earlier though. It's not going to be legal is it?"

"Not remotely. Do you still want to hear?"

"Of course I do. I'm not so poor that I can't afford a taxi home if I feel like storming off."

"OK, but I wouldn't be surprised if that's what you decided to do." He felt a huge surge of affection for her but was determined to keep the conversation cool and practical. "The good side is, that if my plan works, the new development is unlikely to go ahead, the school will get enough of a cash donation to chose any site they wish, and all going well, George Stavros will be put inside for a good spell."

She looked concerned. "Just how fishy is this?"

He laughed. "It'll put Billingsgate in the shade! Don't have any illusions about this, it's heavy duty crooked. If you like, I can stop here and we can just pretend I hadn't said anything. What I will say is that no one who doesn't deserve it will come to any harm. If we try to sort this mess out by the book it might reduce the damage, but I don't think anything else will get the school built. I can also say that you won't have to be directly involved, but you'll have to trust me, as the chances are I'll need to borrow some of your trust fund money from you to get it set up. The final thing is that there will be substantial cash left over and I have every intention of sharing it between us."

"My God! This is going way beyond anything I thought you were going to say!" She got up from the couch and walked about the room. John watched her, thinking just how lucky he was that someone like her could be in his life, even if only temporarily, and what a shame that this brief interval in paradise might have to be brought to an early close because of outside events crowding in on him. If she didn't want to know, then he would probably try and go through with it anyway, but would have to find some other source of working capital. "You'd better tell me what you've got in mind."

John summarised as best he could, after which she looked at him for what seemed like an eternity. "When were you planning on kicking me out?"

"I wasn't. You can stay through till Monday morning if you want."

"Thanks, but I'm a girl who needs her own space. I'll stay till early afternoon on Sunday if that's OK. I'll give you my decision before I go."

* * *

John knew that Alfie wouldn't be a problem. A short phone call and then a brief meeting to discuss the concept, was all that was needed. Alfie had seen too much of human nature in the raw to be surprised at what John was asking him. The logistics would have to be dealt with later, but there would be time enough.

Ron and Tracy would need more careful handling. Ron was pleased when John's suggested that they had lunch together, but called him a mean bastard when he realised that what he had in mind was sandwiches in the park. Knowing what Ron was like when food and wine were on the agenda, John decided to keep it low key. Time enough for the fatted calf when it was all over. At half past twelve they sat on a bench in Lincoln's Inn Fields with a selection of Prêt-a-Manger sandwiches between them and quietly watched the world go by. Ron twisted round in his seat and pointed at Sir John Soane's Museum in the square behind them.

"Have you ever been in there?"

"Fraid I haven't."

"I pop in every now and then. Weird place, very spooky. Few years ago it incorporated what used to be the office next door which was part of the original house. That's where I started my legal career, in number twelve. I was there for about five years and never once visited. After I moved on to another firm I paid a visit within a month and realised what a great place it was. You never value what you've got until it's taken away."

"You're sounding very philosophical today, Ron."

"It's the forced retirement. Makes me realise that a chapter is coming to an end and that in fact it wasn't so bad after all. I'll miss all you lot, even the couple of shits in the place. Even Luke in a weird sort of way. He's only doing what I would have done in his place. There's no room for passengers in a business. Slows it down."

"Stop it, Ron. You'll have me in tears. Wouldn't you rather talk about girls in skimpy knickers and wet blouses? More your line of country."

"Don't seem to have the inclination. The old love sausage seems to have lost the will to live since I was given the news. Turned into a bit of coprolite over night. Even if I felt like a bit of naughty I'd be afraid bits might fall off."

"Come on, Ron. What about your plans for a secret love nest then?"

"You didn't take that seriously did you? It's the potting shed from now on and an occasional visit to the library when I want some real excitement. My shag-by date expired a long time ago, but I hadn't realised it. "

"Ron, for Christ's sake!" John stood up and brushed the crumbs from his lap knowing that a completely different approach was called for. "I'm going to buy you a drink. You need cheering up."

In the cellar bar of Drums, John waited till a few glasses had put a glow back to Ron's cheeks before stalking the subject he needed to discuss. "Ron, you're not giving up completely are you. You said that you would do some freelance work to keep your hand in. You're going to do that at least."

"Possibly. Lot depends if I can get enough clients to make it worthwhile."

"Well here's one now."

"Sorry…?"

"I'd like to be your first client."

Ron peered into John's glass. "Are you drinking something I don't know about, or did you have a funny sandwich? I've heard shellfish can be very bad for you."

"I'm serious. I'd like to offer you some work, but it's a bit naughty as I want you to take me on now, before your retirement bites."

"If you're going to throw up, could I ask you to face in the other direction."

"Ron, be serious for God's sake!"

Ron examined John with care, trying to see if this was a massive piss take, or something was going on that he didn't understand. "At the risk of my dignity I'll take you seriously for a second. What is it you want me to do that you can't do for yourself, or someone in the firm won't have better facilities to deal with?"

John topped up Ron's glass before answering. "You've got all the company and corporate experience which I haven't, and a ton of foreign contacts. You can charge full partner rates for it, and I can give money up front. You must be at least potentially interested."

Ron's face brightened up. "I'll need proof of identity before I take you on."

"That's better. One thing, if I'm your client, then the usual rules of client confidentiality must apply."

"Course they will. What is it?"

John took a deep breath. "I want you to set up at least one company and a bank account for me in Liechtenstein, and possibly the same in Switzerland as well. I'll probably need someone out there to act as local agent, but it must be someone I can trust absolutely. Would that be possible?"

Ron's face took on the controlled neutrality of a Madame discussing whether a client would prefer to be thrashed with birch or willow. "Is timing important? It will take a few weeks."

"That should be all right. Sooner the better though."

"I'll make some enquiries this afternoon. Want to give me the details now or when I've made a contact?"

"Later will do."

"Right then!" Ron took a deep breath and threw back his shoulders. "I think this calls for another bottle." He indicated two girls in animated conversation at the bar. "Don't know what you think, John, but the one on the left could have me if she tried really hard!"

* * *

Please! Please! Just for once let her not be dressed like an advert for a porn mag. John stood at the downstairs door of Tracy's flat waiting for her to come down. Two days before he had suggested that they meet up as he wanted to call in the favour she said she owed him, hinting that he might be able to do her one in return. Her enthusiastic agreement made him nervous so he stressed that this really was business. To avoid any confusion as to what the evening was about he had suggested that they go for a drive somewhere and that she should wear sensible warm clothes though it did occur to him afterwards that being Tracy she might be wearing little more than a woolly hat and wellies.

"I'm here. Sorry to keep you waiting. Had a problem with the padlock."

"Tracy….!"

"I'm teasing, that's not what tonight's about is it? Do I look *Girl Next Door* enough for you?" She looked very wholesome in jeans and a woollen jumper, but this was very much the old Tracy with a bewitching smile on her face and glowing with enthusiasm. He was so pleased to see her looking like this that he kissed her more enthusiastically than he intended, pulling away suddenly in case he was giving wrong signals.

"Are you happy with a bit of a drive before we chat?"

"Great! I didn't get much of a ride last time. Where are we going?"

They agreed on the river at Chiswick. After putting the South London traffic behind them, he couldn't stop himself showing off for a few minutes and bellowed up the A4 for a moment of lunatic speed before turning off at the Burlington roundabout and burbling quietly into the Chiswick Mall. He came to a halt and she looked around her, unable to believe the grand ornate houses that faced the river and the peace and silence only moments from a dual carriageway.

"Oh, John! This is really beautiful!"

"Haven't you been here before?"

"Never. I had no idea it existed."

"Come and have a look."

They walked hand in hand from the St Peter's Church end down to The Doves where they had a drink looking out over the river, then came back again, pausing to look at individual houses and the moon reflected in the river.

"This is so nice, John. Fancy living here! Must be wonderful."

Yes it must be. Different, but at least as desirable as Holland Park, better in some ways. If it all came off, could he aspire to one of these? Shame they so rarely came on the market. But that was counting chickens, and at this stage he couldn't even be sure of any eggs.

"Let's sit in the car and have a ciggie"

He had parked the car just round the corner from Burlington Lane, and they settled themselves inside and lit up. From time to time the occasional dog walker or couple went past. Otherwise it was silent.

"You've not told any of the girls we're seeing each other tonight, have you?"

"No. I've been dying to let on to make them jealous as a couple of them fancy you, but I thought it best not to though."

That was nice to know at least. "Good. I think its best we keep this quiet. So no one knows you're here with me tonight."

She looked at him with an odd expression on her face. "You're not going to strangle me are you, John?" She giggled flirtatiously. "I shouldn't say it, but I find the thought of that quite exciting."

He laughed. "Not unless you misbehave."

"That's right. Shatter a girl's dreams! OK, what about kissing me instead then."

He would have to nip this in the bud. This was not what the evening was about. "Look Tracy, you know I'm very fond of you, but I just don't think..."

"Relax, I don't mean getting our kit off or anything. I'm feeling very lonely and just need a hug, that's all. You don't mind do you?"

"Well, how can I resist a request like that?" After a few minutes he pulled away. "OK. So what's the problem?"

"Oh I don't know. Yes I do. It's a bit of everything."

His heart skipped a beat. "Everything's all right in Greece isn't it?"

"Oh yes, if I can ever get there."

"Want to tell me about it."

"Yes. I'd like to." She snuggled into him and he put his arm round her. "It's just that all I want to do is get out there, but it all depends on getting enough money together, and now I've got all the fuss of finding another job and my heart's not in it. It's just, I don't know.... I don't feel I belong here anymore, but it's such fag to organise getting away. I get on with the girls I share a flat with, and the girls at the office are great, but I haven't got anyone really close. My Mum's dead, my Dad's in Greece, and my brother's gone to Australia. You get the picture."

Without even asking he was being told all he wanted to know, but what he had in mind was still asking a lot. "Tracy, can I ask you something odd?"

"Course you can."

"How do you feel about the idea of living in Greece for good and all? Never coming back, or at least not as Tracy Spooner but only using your Greek name?"

"Haven't really thought about that, but frankly it wouldn't be a problem. I really do love it out there and I wouldn't be thinking of marrying Nikos if I didn't want to live there as well. I've thought it all through." She turned in her seat and gave him an enquiring look. "I must say that was a funny question. Can't you wait to get rid of me?"

"Definitely not. I'll really miss you when you go." He suddenly realised how true this was, but the current business just had to be dealt with.. "You know I told you I needed to discuss something with you. I just need to understand what your future plans are before I even begin. You really *really* want to go to Greece and marry Nikos?"

"Definitely."

"And you've no doubt at all that is what he wants you to do?"

"I'll show you his last few letters if you like."

"And its only lack of money stopping you from going right now?"

This time she turned to face him full on. "What is this John, some Third Degree? Are you going to shine a light in my face in a minute?"

"Sorry! Sorry! I didn't mean to come on so strong." He tried to lighten the atmosphere. "We can have another kiss if you like."

She looked petulant and pretended she no longer wanted to but within a moment they were having an amorous hug. When the hug turned into a lengthy kiss, he knew it had to stop.

"Look, Tracy...I just don't know how to start this. I'm going to suggest something to you that you might not like the sound of, and it may be that if you don't approve you might lose any respect you've got for me."

She stared at him for a few moments her face troubled. "Look, John, I know I'm a bit vulnerable at the moment, but ...."

"Oh Tracy, for God's sake.....nothing like that. This is business."

She visibly relaxed. "Look, can you stop talking around this all night and tell me what this is all about? You know I've got a lot of respect for you, and if it's something a bit dodgy, I'm sure you have a very good reason for it." She looked at her watch. "If you haven't started to tell me what it is in one minute I'm going to get out of this car and call a cab."

"OK. OK. Here we go." He was here to tell her, so he had to do it. "I'm handling something which I thought was legitimate business for a very dodgy client. I now learn that it's one sodding great scam, and if he pulls it off a lot of people are going to be hurt by it. I want to sabotage what he's up to, which will see justice done in a lot of different directions, but what I have in mind will also liberate a big chunk of money. Exactly what's going to happen to that money has still to be decided, but I don't want you to be in any doubt that I have every intention of taking a decent chunk of it for myself." He paused to see how she was taking this, but her face was set and she gave nothing away. "What you need to know is that I haven't a chance of pulling it off without your help."

"Me, John! Oh come on!"

"Honest, quite literally nobody else will do. Before I go any further, can I ask you a couple more questions? You told me a while ago that you had a second passport, a Greek one. Is that really the case? Do you really have the ability to leave the country as, what was it, Sophia something or other…?"

"Sophia Kostakis. Yes, that's right."

"And there's no way of connecting her with Tracy Spooner?"

"That's right, John. I told you."

"I'm sorry to go on about it, but I've got to know that if we do try this, that there is no possible way you can ever be detected afterwards. OK. How much money do you think that you and Nikos need to start this restaurant?"

"Oh, that's hard. He mostly talks about it in Drachmas."

"£100,000?"

"Oh, for God's sake, John! Nothing like as much as that."

"So £500,000 would be well enough."

Her eyes turned into huge brown saucers. "What!"

Well at least he had her interest. "Shall I explain then? Might you be interested?"

"Course I'm interested! Christ, how could I not be? I've not agreed anything yet, but of course I want you to tell me."

"OK. The simple facts are that within a few weeks, five million will be transferred into the firm's bank account for the benefit of Dragoon Properties, I'm sure you must have come across them before in the office. They will then expect us to transfer it into a couple of their accounts. In fact, by then I will have at least one bank account set up in Liechtenstein, possibly a couple of others. This is where you and your computer skills come in. If I give you all the details, would you be able to send electronic instructions to the firm's bank to transfer the money into one of these Liechtenstein accounts, and then programme our system to cover up the instructions so at our end everything looks completely kosher, or at the very least looks as if the system has gone haywire. You won't have to make it completely bomb proof, just enough confusion on the system to hide what has happened for a few days. That will give enough time for me to get the money out of the Liechtenstein account and laundered into oblivion."

He could feel her change of energy and suddenly she was so concentrated she could be giving off an electric current; he was sure that if he put his hand on her it would sizzle. When she spoke her voice was so tight and controlled it would have served as a violin string.

"Why are you planning on doing this, John? I know that nobody's what they seem these days but you're not a crook. This is just not what you're about."

He was afraid of this. How much to say, how much to keep to himself? "Oh God, Tracy! It's all such a mess. Look, I don't want to go into too much detail, but it's a mixture of things. I can tell you honestly that I would rather not have to do this, but I don't see that I have any choice. Dragoon are total crooks and have got to be stopped and this seems to be the only way we can do it. If you need to know, I have some other plans running in tandem to this that should put George Stavros out of action for a while. Quite separately, I have career problems that I needn't go into save to say that for personal reasons Luke Chaplin hates my guts, and has organised things so that sooner or later I will not only be out of a job, but unable to get another one. If I don't go through with this, sooner or later I will end up on the streets selling The Big Issue."

"John, surely not!"

"I'm afraid so. Anyway, if stopping George Stavros has the effect of putting some money in circulation, then I have every intention of treating at least a bit of it as compensation for a lost career."

Tracy stared at the sky for a few minutes. "I need to think about the detail, but I'm sure it can be done. It'll have to be done directly from the accounts computer as that has a direct link to the bank's and has built in passwords and everything. Covering it up is more of a problem, but I'm sure I can programme in a virus to obliterate the evidence." She fiddled with her nails not looking at John. "I can see now why you were asking me all those questions. If I do this, I'm going to have to fly straight off to Greece as Sophia Kostakis aren't I? Tracy Spooner will just have disappeared off the face of the earth. Once it's been discovered how it was done, and that I'm not here anymore, I'll probably be the prime suspect won't I."

John suddenly felt sick, riddled with guilt that he could even be discussing this with her. She may come across as a street-wise sex bomb, but underneath she was just a young girl who wanted to live a normal life and marry the man she was in love with.

"Tracy, I should never have asked you his. I'm really sorry. I'll drive you back and we can pretend I'd never mentioned it."

"No way!" Her voice was thoughtful. "You said that if you had any choice in the matter you wouldn't do this as you would rather just get on with your career. I believe you. With me it's different. I *want* to leave the country and start a restaurant with Nikos. I was getting really depressed because I was wondering if I would ever be able to. If this works, then I can." She slid across onto his lap, and buried her face in his chest. "It's such a shame that I'll have to go as soon as we've done it, and I won't have a chance to celebrate with you."

SEVENTEEN

FOR THE NEXT FEW DAYS John was like a robot going through the motions of his ordinary life but barely connecting with it. Suddenly it didn't have anything to do with him anymore. He put in the same long hours as before, but all on automatic pilot. In a few weeks he could be sinking quietly in the Thames with a pair of ducky concrete boots on his feet or, if he was really lucky, merely sharing a cell with a twenty stone homosexual psychopath with a hatred of young professionals. On the other hand, if it all worked, he would be one of the idle rich eating a peeled grape prepared for him by one of his housemaids. Whatever happened, nothing would ever be the same again. The practice of the law, once the epicentre of his existence was now an irritating irrelevance that got in the way of his thinking. He could not find the off switch for his brain which was on a permanent fast forward. He had bouts of panic when he knew that he must just abandon the whole stupid idea, mixed with a strange euphoria that he had got back into the driving seat of his life, and that if he crashed at least he would go on a high note.

The share out of the cash had yet to be decided, but it looked as if he would be getting at least a few million. Wendy had taken a while to weigh up the moral considerations of John's plan against the benefits, but eventually agreed that they had little choice and it had to be done. John wanted her to share the proceeds, but she refused. All she wanted was the school to have the donation of one million that John had promised. Provided he did that, it was up to him what he did with the rest. Taking that at face value, and even allowing for some major present for her, plus an additional bonus to Tracy, he couldn't see that he could come out with less than two and a half million.

Years of conducting court actions had taught him to never take results for granted no matter how encouraging the signals might be, but even so, woven in with his other thoughts were his spending plans, seductive hallucinations that mainlined into his brain cells like ghostly sirens stroking his most sensitive parts against his will. Should he go for a particularly wonderful town house and slum it with a Porsche Boxter, or limit his new dwelling to an East London loft, and then even things out with a Ferrari? Then again, should he just go for an Alpha Spyder and throw in a villa in the south of France, or damn it, what about a simple London base and have lots of foreign travel? The possibilities went round and round his head like laundry in a spin dryer, leaving him too dizzy for rational thought. He had never been so in need of sleep, but never less able to get it. He would switch on late night TV to help him wind down, but within seconds the flickering images on the screen were superimposed by his plans and fantasies. He poured vats of hot chocolate down his throat, but it made no difference to his sleep patterns other than that he had to get up for a pee more often.

It was worrying that it all seemed a bit too easy, and that bothered him in case there was something he had overlooked. Ron had no idea what was happening and had been happy to do what was necessary, and indeed it had kicked him out of the doldrums he had been drifting in to. The questionable nature of John's instructions had only added a little spice to it all. To John's surprise, Tracy appeared to have no problem with her role in it and most of the time was as high as a kite. He had given her the general picture of what George had been up to, and she seemed almost as excited by the idea of doing him down as by the profit she would make. There was an added fizz to her step when she sashayed round the office and a new light in her eyes. She would pop into John's office to drop things on his desk, and if people were there make kissing gestures behind their back, and if he were alone, kiss him hurriedly then pirouette out of the door leaving behind a whiff of perfume and the lingering image of a flying hem. He was still concerned that although her dual identity meant that the risk of her being caught was remote, the shape of her life would still have to change forever. He continued to press her on that till she told him to stop nagging on about it, and he salved his conscience by promising her an additional £100,000 that she must pay into a private bank account so that, God forbid, if anything happened between her and Nikos she would have enough to start an independent life.

The Wendy question was something else for his brain to work on along with everything else. She was a class act and the most remarkable and special woman he had ever known. She was exceptionally beautiful but much of the time took little trouble with her appearance. Possibly because she had nothing to prove, she tended to dress for convenience and practicality during the day, and when she was working was happy to have her hair pulled back in an elastic band. When she did choose to make an effort she was catwalk material. Professionally she was the same conundrum, her academic pedigree qualifying her for the city and all its glittering accoutrements, but she had chosen the sort of job normally taken by those who had no other choice. She had a deep rooted commitment to her disadvantaged clients, but she never preached or moralised, and avoided discussing her crusades against crooked landlords and violent husbands. On top of all this, she was a relaxed and easy companion, had a self depreciating sense of humour and healthy physical appetites. Whatever score Ron may have given her, she was a clear ten plus in every category. All too aware that even the briefest summary of his own shortcomings would make Don Giovanni's list look like a note for the milkman, John's one big worry was her embarrassment of riches. He had always worked on the basis that the secret of happiness was to live out one's fantasies, but it had never occurred to him that it would ever be possible to live out all of them all at once. The L word had never been used by either of them, but if things did go in a certain direction, he would find himself a man with quite literally everything, including a woman like Wendy in his life. This was all very fine, but if at bottom, as he often wondered and worried over in the small hours, he was not really a class act himself and did not really deserve a woman like her or all the rest of it, then would he be the rotten egg stopping all the other ingredients becoming an edible cake? Would putting a cheap wine into an expensive bottle only draw attention to the poverty of its vintage?

Sitting at his desk it was all churning through his mind when his brain suddenly and without warning closed up shop and pulled the blinds down over his eyes. In one clean movement his body slumped forward in the deepest sleep and he came to a halt with his head resting on the keyboard of his computer sending a succession of "B"s lining up across his screen, page after page of them scrolling down, until a modest keeling over made his right ear catch the L which then did its best to outnumber the previous letter. After ten minutes of this, when the two letters were neck and neck and a token shift of position brought P into the race as a fresh young outsider, his door opened and Luke walked in.

John was not aware how long Luke had been standing there ostentatiously clearing his throat, but the repeat calling of his name brought him to a reluctant and bleary consciousness, staring stupidly in front of him for a moment or two, not really there, and unable to focus on the two men in his room.

"Oh shit!" Were his first words as reality came into sharp focus.

"Been over doing it, John?" Luke asked him, for once without any hint of sarcasm in his voice. "It catches up on all of us eventually. Shall I ask your secretary to get you a coffee?" This was said with a pleasant smile on his face and John felt a massive stab of insecurity. A few years before when he had been putting himself about even more than usual he decided out of caution to have an Aids test. When he had gone in for the result, the female doctor had been so solicitous and her voice so kind and gentle that John had immediately feared the worst and became convinced that he was unlikely to last the afternoon. A smiling Luke had the same effect on him. What did he want, and who was this person with him?

"John, let me introduce Dan Kleinwort. He's going to be our new financial controller. Dan, this is John Foxton, one of our litigation solicitors."

"Good to meet you, John." Dan put out a large hand and took John's, his grip causing a bolt of pain to shriek up John's arm like an electric shock. "Guess you've been putting in the hours by the look of you. The main reason I stopped doing law and switched to accountancy was so I could get to bed occasionally."

He was tall and rangy with dark hair cut into a crop and sounded American. He looked ludicrously wholesome and healthy, as if he'd never smoked or drank in his life and the one time he'd had sex he'd been careful not to inhale. His eyes were clear and friendly and his whole demeanour was open and candid. John disliked him on sight. The shock of what he had just been told brought him to full wakefulness, but he could think of little to say. "So you're our new financial controller, eh? Well, well! When do you start?"

Luke answered for him. "Officially it's next month, but Dan's current people are letting him phase out gradually so he will be able to get familiar with our system over time rather than just having to jump in the deep end." For once he was sounding slightly self conscious like someone seen driving a Roller by a work colleague, keen to show it off, but not sure if they could do it with sufficient panache. "Dan is a graduate of Harvard and a computer expert. We need someone like him in the driving seat to help the firm develop." He was interrupted by his bleeper going off, and he went outside to answer it leaving John alone with Dan. On the whole he would have been happier being left alone with George.

"So when does Bob retire? I thought he was with us for at least a couple more years."

"Well, I suppose he felt it was all getting too much for him. Some people just don't feel comfortable with new technology."

John wondered what Bob's reaction had been when they'd told him that that he wasn't comfortable with new technology and it was time for him to bog off and make room for the next generation to muscle in. Knowing Bob, he was still thinking about it, but that wasn't John's problem. Dan continued. "But I think accounting goes way beyond just making figures balance these days. Once I've got settled in here I want to look at the bigger picture, you know take a more holistic approach to the business. Don't you think that in the modern world, firms like this need to take a more active role in the community? Sponsorships, arts festivals, charity work? That sort of thing."

John looked at him with a new interest. Was this guy a nutter? He could imagine the partners here being told that a chunk of their profit was going to be spent on cardboard boxes for winos and poetry readings for ex-cons. "Have you discussed these ideas with the partners here?"

"Not yet. Right now everyone's more concerned with credit control and overhead rationalisation and that sort of thing." He laughed making his Adam's apple go up and down "Don't want to give people too much of a shock to start with. I'll tell you what my big thing is though, Zero Tolerance."

"What?"

"Zero Tolerance. Do you realise just how much a firm can lose each year just by cheques being paid in a day late, or cash transfers not being affected on the dot? It may be only a pound or two per transaction, but it really mounts up, and it's profit down the drain." His face lit up with evangelical fervour. "I'll be on every one's tail from day one, whoever they are."

Yes, well you can leave me out of that, you over zealous twat. Why don't you say, *Yes, Siree,* and slap your thigh and be done with it? Luke reappeared, and Dan patted him on the shoulder. "That even includes Luke here doesn't it? I was just telling John about Zero Tolerance."

Luke gave a nervous laugh. "I'm all in favour. You can nag me all you want, Dan if it means a tight ship. By the way, John, we'll be giving a cocktail party soon to welcome Dan and the new partners and to mark Bob and Ron's leaving us. There'll be a few VIPs coming, that sort of thing. Probably the 14th of next month, it's a Friday. Hope you'll come."

"Yes, it would be good to see you there, John." Dan shook John's hand again, clearly keen to turn a simple fracture into permanent disablement. The second both of them had gone and his door was closed, John picked up his phone with his remaining good hand.

"Tracy?"

"*Yes?*"

"Can you pop in? It's really urgent."

He almost resented her bright eyed optimism as she slipped into his room looking happy and normal. "Tracy, for fuck's sake! What's this with Bob being replaced by a proper financial controller?"

"I've only found out this morning myself. I think he's quite cute."

Cute! He could kill her! "Never mind that. He's a buggering computer expert. Is this going to screw everything up?"

"Shouldn't do, not if I can get a private half hour or so in accounts on my own. That's all I'll need. The problem will be if he's hanging around when I want to do it. Bob does nine to five whatever's going on, but this guy is likely to put in the hours and it'll be harder to find the right moment. I'm more worried about when we're supposed to be doing it. You know I've only got a couple of weeks left. I can't do anything after that."

"Christ!" John pressed his fingers hard against his forehead to relieve the tension. "Clarendon haven't told me yet when the monies are coming through and the Liechtenstein Company isn't set up."

"John, John! It's going to be all right, I know it is." She took his face in her hands and kissed him, something he preferred her not to do in the office, but for once he appreciated it. She fixed his eyes with her large brown ones "And don't worry about what I said about Dan. He's not as cute as you!"

EIGHTEEN

ALFIE INSISTED ON A DRY run, or a rehearsal as he called it. He was emphatic that it was not casing the joint; that was for the lower end of the business. This was positively his last job before retirement and he felt he had now reached a point in his career where he could call himself a gentleman burglar, and if this was his Swan Song it was going to be done in style. John didn't mind what he did, so long as it was done professionally and without a hint of his involvement.

The job was for their mutual benefit, but Alfie considered himself so deeply in John's debt for relieving him of the cocaine that he would have been happy to do it anyway. Without leaving any signs of entry, John wanted him to find a way into George's house in Buckinghamshire and plant the Vermeer. Alfie would then pass info to one of his informer friends that George Stavros was behind the theft and was also dealing in cocaine. Alfie would not only get rid of the picture that was plaguing his existence and at last get the police off his back, but he would also get a modest rake-off from the informer. The informer would get his back-hander from the police, and all going well George would get a long holiday at her majesty's pleasure and not be in the best position to investigate what had happened to his five million. This was an integral part of the plan. The police investigation would involve forensic accountants and computer experts which John could cope with, but if George was around to make enquiries, it would probably mean baseball bats and bovver boots. The timing was crucial, and the tip-off had to coincide with the transfer of the funds. If George was collared too soon, Clarendon might sit on their cash pending things being sorted out. If it was too late, John could already be in intensive care.

The dry run was tonight. John was going to drive Alfie to the house so he could check the place out. Now so close to getting rid of the painting which had been plaguing his life for so long, Alfie was in an up-beat mood. He told John that when he came to do the job for real he wished he could do it in style and wear a dinner jacket but as with all modern jobs he would have to wear an outfit so kinky, you couldn't get one in a sex shop. He explained that the curse of the modern criminal was DNA.

"Once upon a time you only needed a pair of thin leather gloves so you didn't leave fingerprints. All the police need to find these days is a fleck of dandruff or a bogie, and they know your mum's maiden name and when you last had a crap. I bet if you farted on a job now they'd bag it up, and five minutes later a trained sniffer dog would be knocking on your back door with an invitation to Wormwood Scrubs between its teeth." A few years ago, Alfie had what he called a DNA suit made for him, an all enveloping plastic garment with a narrow letter box for the eyes, and that's what he would be using. It was folded up now in a plastic bag inside a whole suitcase full of implements he needed to bring with him.

Alfie was paranoid in case he was still being watched, but felt that if there was still a tail on him, they'd clear off once they saw he was just meeting with his solicitor. The meeting place was Wendy's office. When John had told her what was planned she insisted on coming along for the ride. He tried to put her off as they were going in his car which was strictly a two seater, but she insisted that they could all squeeze in. Alfie was about to place an embargo on the idea, when the penny dropped that for the entire journey he would be having a twenty six year old blonde sitting on his lap. When he realised that she was also a solicitor, he positively insisted on it as he could then have two of them to defend his corner.

Leaving Alfie outside in his car, John went into Wendy's office to collect her but something about her confused him. She looked different somehow, her cheeks were flushed and she had an air of suppressed excitement. She was wearing her City suit, the dark blue tailored one with the straight skirt that today looked shorter than usual. Her legs which were now lightly tanned by the sun were bare, but her makeup was more emphatic than usual, and she looked if not more beautiful, certainly more dramatic and glamorous. The overall effect of well groomed sexuality mixed with her obvious adrenaline charge was almost too potent for him to cope with. He realised that he was happier when she was unrealised potential waiting for him to bring her out, rather than this full in-your-face explosion of feminine empowerment. She ran forward and kissed him enthusiastically, and not having had a drop himself, he could instantly smell alcohol on her breath. She pulled away far too quickly, clearly excited about something.

"I got the bastard! I got him at last!"

"Sorry….?"

"Ashock Patel, you know, the husband of my client Nabilla. I've been lining it up for a couple of days now. We were in court this afternoon and I got an order kicking him out of the house, an injunction stopping him from going within a mile of where she lives or where she works. On top of that I've got a freezing injunction locking up his bank accounts until we sort out what her share should be." She bunched her fist and punched the air with masculine vigour, whooping with triumph.

She threw herself at John and kissed him, but he had a problem responding with any enthusiasm. He was a passionate believer in sexual equality and treated male and female lawyers purely on their merits, but he was still a prisoner of his ego, and that demanded that he was the one who came home from the hunt with the mammoth over his shoulder while the story tellers made up new ballads about him. His place was not in the audience but centre stage, and he did not want to share it with his womenfolk who should be smearing themselves with their most fetching shade of wode ready to pleasure their conquering lordship's latest triumph. For a few moments common sense and emotion grappled inside his head until emotion, without actually releasing its strangle hold, allowed common sense to get a word in. "Well done. I'm proud of you." Then, unable to stop himself just had to add "You've been drinking."

"Just a couple. Nabilla took me to the wine bar afterwards to celebrate. "

He indicated her tailored suit. "Will you be OK in the car dressed like that? It's going to be a hell of a squeeze."

"I'll be fine. I feel a bit wild tonight." She gave him a look of smouldering promise. "Would it help if I took my skirt off?"

Thank God it was only Alfie! "No it bloody wouldn't! Behave, will you. We'd better get going it's going to be quite a long night."

Alfie couldn't believe her. He had expected a solicitor in mufti, not a goddess in a short skirt. At first he was too choked up to speak properly, but once he had recovered went into dashing old roué mode, flirting and joking with her. The two men got in the car first, then Wendy, still on a high, arranged herself on Alfie's lap, but with her legs stretched across onto John's, her knees up to reduce their length. Alfie continued to make silly jokes as if this were the most natural thing in the world, but there was a perma-smile on his face and periodically he emitted half strangled groans that suggested he was subject to some hidden emotion he could not quite control. To John's great annoyance, within a few moments he found himself horribly aroused and cross with her at the same time. That she was his lover did nothing to dispel the voyeuristic pleasure of her sleek legs spread across him at a fetching angle, not helped by the fact that each time he changed gear he could not help making the sort of contact with her which was best left for more private moments. It took a while for him to realise that irritation was overtaking arousal. This behaviour was for bims, not for a class act like Wendy. Something had got into her tonight and he wasn't happy with it. For her part, she could see the effect she was having on the two of them and was positively playing up to it with her arms round Alfie's neck, laughing and giggling with him while she stretched and posed her legs for their joint benefit. John couldn't actually be jealous of an old tosser like Alfie, but the realisation of how he would be feeling if this wasn't Alfie but someone young and attractive made him nearly boil over. He needed to demonstrate his dominance over her, but knew of no way of doing it, so just drove like a lunatic in a sulky silence.

George's house was way off the beaten track. When they got close, at Alfie's suggestion John crawled the car past it so he could have a quiet look, and then pulled in and stopped a mile or so away. Alfie had brought an Ordinance Survey map with him and examined it for footpaths and other possible avenues of approach. He then had John drive round certain lanes till he had got a clear enough picture to risk an approach on foot. It was necessary to adjust the seating arrangements so at the right moment Alfie could slip out quickly and John could move straight off. Rather than making Wendy get out of the car and leaving her alone in the wilds, for a short period she managed to cram herself into the small space on the back shelf. John drove past the point Alfie had indicated, slowed down to a crawl, and Alfie slipped out with his bag of tools and disappeared down a tiny lane. A rendezvous point had been agreed and mobiles checked for reception. All they could do now was wait.

"He's a sweetie isn't he." Wendy now sitting in the passenger seat for the first time pushed it back to its furthest point and stretched out her legs. "Gosh, it's nice to have a bit of room. You were right. There really wasn't really room for me, but I wouldn't have missed this for anything." She looked across at John who was quietly nursing his resentment. "My legs are a bit stiff. You would to like to give them a bit of a massage would you?"

His libido jumped up a further notch, but he wasn't ready to give up his petulance. "You know you're behaving like a tart don't you!"

"I promise it was all for your benefit. You're not annoyed with me are you?"

"Furious."

"Oh come on, you're not jealous of Alfie are you. He's about a hundred!"

"Of course I'm not!"

"What is it then?"

"It doesn't matter." He could feel his lower lip sticking out like a spare tyre and hated himself for it.

"Look, I'm sorry! I'm not like this very often, it's just that when I've had a good day in court I find I'm swimming in testosterone. I just want to get wrecked and pick a fight with the biggest bloke in the pub, and then go home and get laid." She looked across at him. "You're not seriously complaining are you? I thought most men like tarts." She leaned across and gave him a small kiss. "You didn't look, that unhappy with your dinner companion those weeks ago, you know, Miss Hot Pants. That's a point, you've never actually told me anything about her have you."

Shit! He'd have to change the subject. So far he had not gone into any detail about his 'friend in accounts' who was working with them on the scam, most certainly had not said that she and the girl sucking his fingers in La Fenice were one and the same. This was clearly not the moment to talk about that and feeling horribly guilty he hurriedly changed the subject. "I'm sorry. I'm being an old misery." He reached out a hand and stroked the inside of her thigh. "Do you still want your legs massaged?

She gave a little sigh of pleasure. "God that's nice! OK. Who's being a tart now?"

Outside it was pitch dark and silent, all civilisation being a good distance away. Every now and then an unidentifiable bird called out and sometimes there was an answering whistle, but that was it. It was light years away from John's day to day life in a bustling city and cocooned in the cars snug interior it was as if the two of them were isolated from the entire world.

"Look John," Wendy twisted herself to get even closer. "Alfie said he'd be at least an hour...."

"Wendy, no.....I'm not sure this is quite the time and place..."

"Come on, I've not done it in a car since my student days....he'll be ages yet. God, I feel really wicked tonight."

"Wendy stop that! You can't.....!"

He protested, but weakly. Twenty minutes later they were both reclining in their seats waiting for Alfie's return, all tension gone and a whisper of Mozart from the stereo the only sound. Had he really felt annoyed with her earlier? He must have imagined it. She was perfect, utterly without fault. How could someone as wonderful as her be in his life? God he was lucky! He stretched his limbs till they cracked in a spasm of pleasure. He was the luckiest man in the world.

NINETEEN

THIS TIME THE SUMMONS FROM Luke came to him direct, a curt request on the telephone to come in immediately. John picked up a thick green file from his desk and went in, wholly failing to keep at bay the feeling of smug self satisfaction. He felt a bit guilty because of divide loyalties, but that couldn't be helped. It wasn't fair on Luke of course, but if he was determined to shoot himself in the foot, it wasn't for John to push the gun out of the way.

"You've had your own copy of this I suppose." Luke was holding a letter John recognised. Reggeo had started an action for possession of the Gambol's site, and George had written to Luke as managing partner saying that much as he regretted it, if he should find his company liable to the Saul Libelling school for damages because he would no longer be able to sell to them, he would have to hold Hart-Stanley responsible as they had neither registered the Legal Charge nor advised him of the need to do so. Had the charge been properly registered, it would not have been overlooked and this problem would not have arisen.

"Yes, I've seen it. He sent a copy to me as well." He could see the piston of Luke's anger gaining momentum and waited for the anticipated eruption.

"For CHRIST'S sake!" Luke's breathing became irregular and his face turned an unhealthy white. "For once I know this won't be down to you personally, but I despair..." He hesitated, trying to find words sufficient to convey the depth of his feelings. "I despair of the constant incompetence I keep coming across with Russell Brooks. I thought I was taking over a firm that was well managed and professional, but the legal staff seem to have no idea how to monitor their work load. How you managed to keep a decent client base is beyond me with the constant cock-ups. Is that the file there?"

"Yes I got it out of store to check if what he said was right."

"Well? As we clearly didn't register the charge, is there any letter or record on the file advising him that he should do it in-house, or what the implications could be if he didn't?"

"I'm afraid there isn't."

"Jesus!" Luke shook his head, his eyes tight closed trying to obliterate what he was being told. "We're talking about a potential claim in millions here. Which one of your firm's dick-heads has landed us with this?"

John opened the file as if to check that the information he was about to give was accurate, wondering if he could do this with a straight face. "The reference on all the letters are D.M.F.. That's Diana isn't it, Luke?"

TWENTY

THE SOUND OF GEORGE'S VOICE on the phone used to make him nervous. Now being told he was on the line created primal fear. There was no reason why the cocaine should have been discovered, or that George should have any inkling that his own solicitor was planning to shaft him, but that made no difference. John felt the authentic ripple of his insides turning liquid. When the call turned out to be no more than the usual insidious threat with the undertone of disappointment in the voice that no one, and John in particular, ever came up to his expectations, he felt his body regaining a degree of self control.

"The Clarendon money, John. When's it coming? Not too much to ask I would have thought."

"It's all…"

"Listen to me, John. I pay you lots of money. I don't mind that, I know you lawyers cost. It's just I don't expect to have to do the lawyering myself if you get me. Get on the phone to Clarendon's lawyers and find out when it's coming will you. Get it across to them that if there's no deposit, there's no business, and if it's not soon, I might change my mind. I'm in Spain most of the next two weeks. You needn't bother me while I'm out there, but I'll expect something solid when I get back. "

"I've been trying to get them all morning, George. I'll come back to you shortly."

That was certainly true. No conflict of interest here. John was at least as keen as George to get the transfer set up. Ron had set up everything in Liechtenstein, and had already given John a not insignificant bill on his new notepaper. The missing piece of the jigsaw was knowing exactly when the money was coming from Clarendon so everything could be put in place. The delay was worrying. Without Tracy it simply could not be done, and she was due to leave on the 30th which was getting dangerously soon. Try as he could to remain cool, John was as tense as a piano wire. He knew that putting too much pressure on Clarendon could be counter-productive, but each day got closer to the possibility of his own deadline being missed. He had always hated clients with hidden agendas, and hated having one of his own even more. Telephoning Rupert and screaming that the transfer had to be within a week or he would not be able to embezzle a few million from his client would be unlikely to go down well. Taking a deep breath, he dialled the number.

"Rupert, it's John, John Foxton. How are you? Good." Why was it he could not get this plummy bonhomie out of his voice when he spoke to him? "Just wondered when we could expect the deposit monies. Dragoon are getting a bit edgy and keen to complete." Not as keen as I am though! *Please, Rupert, I'm running out of underpants.*

"You must be a mind reader, John. The arrangements with the bank have just been set up. It looks like the 13th."

"July!"

"Of course July. Couldn't be this month could it? We've past the 13th. That's really quite good isn't it?"

Stay calm, John! Just stay calm, and whatever you do, sound calm. "Look, Rupert." Even to himself his voice sounded strangled. "Dragoon were expecting it to be sooner than that, a lot sooner in fact. They just have to have it before the end of this month. If they don't get it, all their plans will go haywire. Surely Clarendon have enough clout with their bank to speed it up."

"Yes, but why should they, even if they could? It's within a perfectly reasonable time scale."

As panic set in, he regained control of his voice. "As I said, Rupert, it really will make things very difficult for Dragoon, maybe even impossible, is there nothing….?"

"You didn't say impossible did you, John? Dragoon aren't considering breaching the contract are they?"

"Of course they're not…"

"Look, John, your clients showed no flexibility whatsoever over the deposit figure, so I can't see Clarendon busting a gut to help them out. They'll produce the deposit within the time scale envisaged, exactly by the book. I'll confirm it, of course, but you can safely assume the 13th. There's nothing really more to be said is there."

Marge came in and threw an envelope on his desk as he put down the phone, a new coldness shivering through his blood stream. Tracy was leaving on the 30th June, and the money would not be here for nearly two weeks after that. There was just no way round it. He dialled Tracy's number, and keen to limit the number of times she was seen in his office, suggested that she went to the front door for a cigarette break. Picking up the envelope he wandered outside in a trance, desperate for a cigarette to calm his nerves. He lit up and inhaled deeply, waiting for the hit as the smoke flooded his lungs. It wasn't enough and he seriously considered smoking two at once to see if that would have the necessary effect, but decided that it would look too stupid if any one saw him. At this rate, it was touch and go if his nerves got him before lung cancer.

Waiting for Tracy he opened the heavy cream envelope and found an engraved invitation to him and a guest for the office cocktail party Luke had already mentioned. Just what he wanted! In all cultures no matter how primitive or advanced, parties are for the same purpose and have the same basic elements. People put on their finery, drink alcohol and eat food. Listening to, or dancing to, music is an optional extra. Their function is either to give those so inclined a chance to eye up a selection of people they might want to copulate and/or breed with, or to show off a victory or achievement. If you aren't a victor, or for any reason not in taking part in the copulation stakes, then you are just the audience, there to admire those taking part and to witness their achievement. That role is for the elderly, the impotent, or the failures, and as he would rather eat his own poo than be seen that way, this would be one party he would not be going to. With his cigarette clamped between tight lips he tore the invitation in two.

"What's that?" Tracy appeared in the doorway, and he instantly offered her a cigarette as her cover.

"Doesn't matter. I think we're fucked, Trace. In fact we *are* fucked. Sorry, but I think you're going to have to forget Greece."

She looked concerned but her voice was surprisingly calm. "OK, you'd better tell me."

"The monies not coming till the 13th, that's way after you leave. There's simply no way we can do it."

She smoked silently for a few minutes, her face concentrated. "I'm sure there'll be an answer if we work at it. I'm only going to need about half an hour in there. Can't you find some way of getting me into the office at night or something? You've got a key haven't you?"

"I've thought of that. It's not just the question of the key, there's a security code to be keyed in as well. We've each got our own separate code, so if any of us come in after hours there's a record of which of us it was and the time of entry and leaving." He desperately racked his brain for some solution. Is there nothing you can do to extend your time here beyond the end of this month? We only need a couple more weeks."

"I've already tried that. Before all this blew up I asked for a bit more as I was unlikely to get work straight away, but they turned me down flat."

He gave way in a sudden explosion of frustration, dashing the torn pieces of the invitation to the ground and clutching his hair. "It's just not fair! We were so sodding close!"

"But you've only just discovered this, John. Come on, we've neither of us had any time to think it through."

"What's there to think about?"

"I don't know, but it's too early to give up without giving it our best shot." Grinding her cigarette but into the paving she bent down and picked up the pieces of torn paper. "And if we simply can't do it, life will still go on. Let's look on the bright side, we'll both be around for a bit longer."

Her calm acceptance disarmed him. What a sweet girl she was. He wanted to hug her but couldn't risk it. "Oh Tracy! I know that life goes on, but I'm just wondering what sort of life it's going to be."

She was holding the torn pieces of the invitation together and looking at it with some concentration. "John, don't get your hopes up, but what day did you say the money was coming in?"

"The 13th July".

"Well what about this party? It's the day after. When the firm have had evening do's in the past they've sometimes asked some of the girls to do waitress duties, I've done two or three of them. I can ask if I can waitress this one, you know, pretend that now I'm redundant I'll need some pin money."

He couldn't risk speaking for few minutes, his brain taking in what she had said and sifting it for flaws. The party would be in the evening, and the accounts office would be empty. If she could slip away at any stage then she could do it. He felt some tentative hope coming alive inside him followed by a sudden rush of optimism and had to stop himself from throwing himself at her.

"You are amazing, Tracy. You are just too sodding wonderful!"

"Hang on, John. There's no guarantee they'll let me do it. It might all be outside caterers, or they may not like having someone there who's no longer on the staff."

"But it's a chance! Who would you ask about this? Tom I suppose".

"You know, that might make it OK, he's always had a soft spot for me."

Oh, and so have I Tracy, and a great big hard one as well you perfect little temptress! He'd been out here talking to her for ten minutes but only now took in what she looked like, the dyed in the wool Tracyness of her in her chain-store miniskirt and Boots cosmetics and the whole delicious package bound together by her complete lack of pretence at being anything but herself. "Tracy, I daren't come near you in case we're spotted, but consider yourself kissed till you swoon."

She giggled, her face lighting up in a big smile. "I might just hold you to that." She passed the torn remains of the invitation back to him. "You'd better get busy with the sellotape or they might not let you in!"

TWENTY-ONE

IT HAD NEVER ONCE OCCURRED to John that Alfie would want him to help out on the job itself. Casing the joint had been a bit of fun, but doing it for real was all too serious. John had a lot of respect for Alfie's professionalism, but there was no pretending this was not something with a high risk factor. Apart from not fancying a diet rich in porridge for the next ten years, even with George away in Spain, the thought of wandering round his house in the small hours was as about as appealing as jumping into a lion's cage and poking it with a sharp stick.

Alfie's rationale had been that John could provide general support, but there was more to it than that. The permanent police tail may be long gone, but they were still keeping an eye on him, and if he was seen leaving the warehouse where he had stored the Vermeer carrying an oblong parcel wrapped in brown paper, the entire local force would land on him like a swarm of bees. As John had been allotted the job of collecting it from the warehouse and covertly handing it over to Alfie, he might as well stick with it and come along.

The collection and rendezvous went without hitch and at 2.30 a.m. they were driving down the M4. The car's payload now consisted of one Solicitor of the Supreme Court with a lot of sweat under his armpits, one gentleman of a certain age with an impressive police record, one stolen Vermeer generally considered to be priceless, a bag of suspicious looking tools, two all-enveloping plastic suits, and a cellophane bag with the last of the cocaine in it. John wondered why they had not gone the whole hog with black masks and a bag marked "Swag", but perhaps that would be overdoing it. He could feel the sweat on the palms of his hands as he gripped the steering wheel and he limited his speed to a stately sixty MPH convinced that the merest whisper over the speed limit and the entire Thames Valley police would be subjecting them to an intimate body search and reducing the car to its component nuts and bolts.

Alfie was in good form, determined to do this last job in the style it called for. He was wearing a double breasted dinner jacket with a red carnation in his button hole and his hair was slicked down with some evil smelling Brilliantine. The Dinner jacket was at least as old as he was and there was a greenish tinge to the shiny black cloth. He looked both wonderful and ridiculous at the same time, and was chortling on about his career and the jobs he had done, regretting that he had not gone the gentleman burglar route years before, and even suggested that he might come out of retirement from time to time for the odd special job. No longer distracted by having Wendy sitting on his lap, he could fully appreciate the car and periodically ran his fingers over the leather and walnut trim.

"Very nice this, John I must say. Very stylish. I've got a fair bit stashed away so I might just treat myself." He patted the dashboard. "Can't you see it, *'Alfie the notorious gentlemen thief burbled off into the night in his fine motor car, no one, suspecting that the boot was piled with a ton of tiaras from a Mayfair mansion...'* "

"The thing is," John decided that a bit of man to man honesty might be called for. "Yes this is one of the most beautifully fitted sports cars on the road and it is immensely powerful, but being hand- made the build quality could be a lot better and......."

As if it had been listening and was put out by John's comments, without warning the car started to cough and misfire, and then after a series of kangaroo leaps and jerks it gave up the ghost altogether. John coasted it on to the hard shoulder gritting his teeth in frustration. It was Alfie who spoke first.

"I think on second thoughts I'll stick to the white van. At least I'll get home in time for breakfast. Hand-made you said this car was, did you."

"All right! All right! I'll call the AA."

"Fucking brilliant! I warn you, if the police take any interest I'm saying I'm John Foxton and a solicitor. You can be Alfie Matthews the well known ex-con."

John fished out his AA card and telephoned the emergency number, and after taking details, they said they would be there within the hour.

"I don't like this!" Alfie looked very put out. "I saw this as a stylish job, you know, the chromium tools in the leather briefcase and the electric stethoscope; *'Alfie Matthew's the Criminal Mastermind executes another daring escapade with as little trace as a black shadow.'* " He drummed his fingers on his knee. "I suppose if the AA can't fix it, they can drop us off at the house." He gave a humourless laugh. "There's a form you have to fill in with your name and destination when they do that for you. That would be a really slick way of doing an undercover job wouldn't it, leaving a written record of what we were up to. Shall we ask them to wait till we're finished so they can give us a lift back – *'We're just doing over a house. Shouldn't be too long'.*"

"Alfie!" John's voice was strained. "There's a flashing blue light, and it's drawing up behind us."

"Oh bloody hell!"

"For Christ's sake, try and act natural."

"OK. I'll shit myself!"

John opened the door to the approaching officer, the traffic passing at what seemed to be manic speed and the slipstream making his car door shudder. "We're broken down, I'm afraid. Waiting for the AA."

"Your car is it, Sir?" He had the usual traffic police voice, a hint of authority underneath the parental tolerance, still surprised that his evening drive should have to be spoiled by these motorists who just insisted on taking their cars out on the road. His companion just limited himself to walking round the car to see if anything was falling off it.

"That's right."

With the regulation glazed eyes, the officer made a call from his phone, and then asked John to confirm his identity. He looked at John's driving licence which unusually he had with him. "Well, Mr Foxton, do you know that your nearside hazard light isn't working? I'd get that fixed if I were you." His companion looked at his watch. "Bit late to be so far away from home. Do you mind telling me where you're going?" His accent had a strong hint of Scottish.

Alfie leaned across with one arm round John's shoulder, a grotesque figure with his slicked hair and antique suit. "We've been in town and my friend is just taking me home." Giving them his best yellow toothed smile he patted John's thigh. "You understand."

The two policemen glanced at each other, the Scott suddenly looking as if he'd just found a month old sliver of meat between his teeth. He turned his back on the car apparently to check something in his notebook, but used this as a cover to make a pantomime limp wristed gesture at his colleague before turning back to John. "Just a routine check, Sir. Do you mind just showing me what's in the boot?"

John could already taste the porridge and smell the latrine, but with his heart beating like castanets made a last desperate attempt to save things. "Listen, officer, I'm a solicitor. You're not entitled just to snoop through personal property unless you have a specific reason to suspect a crime has been committed – *Police and Criminal Evidence Act, section....*"

"Open the boot, John." Alfie hissed at him through his teeth and got out of the car.

"But…"

"Open the sodding boot will you!"

Praying that Alfie knew what he was doing, John pulled the release and Alfie opened it. He delved inside and pulled out a length of rope and waved it under the officer's nose, then pulled out one of the plastic suits and dangled it full length for inspection. John was now standing next to him, frozen with apprehension.

"Not sure if this sort of thing is to your taste, officer." Alfie said, an unwholesome leer on his face. "Young John here's not too used to it yet either, that's why he didn't want you to see." To John's horror he put his arm round his shoulder and gave him a kiss on the cheek. "He's still a bit shy about it all. Rather sweet that."

It was enough. "Solicitor are you, Sir? Well, well, well! Seems the two of you'll have no problem finding something to do till the AA arrives."

With a faces set with distaste they walked back to the patrol car and drove off and immediately John rubbed the remains of Alfie's kiss from his cheek as if it was burning him. "For Christ's sake, did you really have to go that far?"

"I was only trying to be authentic. If it would have kept us out of prison I'd have rogered you across the bonnet."

Half an hour later the AA arrived and sorted out what turned out to be a minor blockage in the fuel line and at about 3.45 John and Alfie pulled into a clearing close to George's house. Alfie looked around approvingly. "I must say, I like a proper country house. No one to see what's going on. London's got too many windows, and no one goes to bed at a respectable hour. A brass band could march through here tossing themselves off and no one would notice."

They both got out of the car and Alfie handed John one of the obscene looking plastic outfits. With work to be done, the professional in Alfie took over. Without a trace of self-consciousness he stripped to a baggy vest and pants and then slipped on his plastic suit, and John followed his example seeing that Alfie had everything under control.

"We'll have to go in over that wall to the left. Very clever your Mr Stavros, he's doing a double bluff. See that camera there on the top of that pillar, it's a dummy, but see those ribbed glass bricks either side of the brass plate, *they're* cameras, so we'll have to crawl across that bit of ground keeping our heads right down, then keep tight to the left before we go over the wall." He indicted a narrow section of wall. "Provided we keep within that we won't trigger the alarm sensors. You hold the picture and stay this side. I'll climb the wall first, then you hand the picture up to me. When I've dropped down, you follow me, but when you are on the other side, don't move an inch. There's a bit of electric cable in the ground I've got to short circuit so we don't set off anything between the wall and the house."

John's breathing was faster than usual, but keyed to the limit with their escapade he felt capable of anything. The brown paper had been taken off the Vermeer, and through the tight cellophane wrapped round it he could just make out the outlines of a small courtyard and a woman sweeping it.

Despite his years Alfie scaled the wall with the agility of someone who had been doing it all his life. John passed up the picture, then as Alfie disappeared over the side, leapt up the wall and rested on the top. The short leap raised his body temperature and although half-naked underneath the plastic suit, he felt himself begin to sweat. Sitting high on the wall he felt very visible. The space between the wall and the house was relatively modest but from his exposed position it seemed vast and open, but it was too late to go back now. He dropped to the spot indicated by Alfie and stayed there. Alfie was doing something with a length of electric cable but once finished indicated that John should follow and like two strange aliens from outer space, they ran silently across the lawn.

"Which way are we going in?" John whispered

"Front door like civilised people. Windows and back doors are for tradesmen." He produced a strange looking electronic device and pressed it against the door just below the lock and threw a switch. A series of red numbers flashed across the display, then came to a sudden halt, and from within the door came a quiet click. He repeated the process roughly a foot below the lock until a second click could be heard and miraculously the door opened.

Alfie looked pleased with himself. "You always have to be one step ahead of the opposition, John. When they use crude locks, we use crude tools. When they go electronic, so do we. It's a shame I'm retiring as soon we'll be able to fax ourselves in."

They entered and crept through the house, the two alien creatures tiptoeing through the dark gothic hallway creating a living horror tableau. The house may be empty and miles from the nearest eye or ear, but the two of them instinctively kept their voices to a whisper and used their pencil lights to see by. Alfie knew where he wanted to leave the Vermeer, a small basement room he had found during his first visit with a lot of canvases and frames stacked against a wall waiting for hanging or other attention. It meant traversing a good bit of the house first, and even by their limited torch light John was riveted by what he could see, an art collection which, if the real thing, must be worth a couple of fortunes. It may not be John's taste, but it was not possible to ignore the scale of it. Even Alfie had his mouth open.

"Not much minimalism here, John. Does that mean he couldn't afford it, or hadn't anyone told him that all this art gallery over-kill is old hat now? God look at that one!" He indicated a vast canvass that suggested Rubens, a pastoral scene with a whole football crowd of gods and shepherdesses frolicking and flirting without any apparent shame for either their nudity or their cellulite. The depiction of all that flesh suddenly brought back the memory of George in the sauna, and the implication of where they were and what they were doing stabbed John in the stomach. It was as if George was in the next room waiting to jump out on them, and he wanted out as quickly as possible.

"For Christ's sake let's just do it and go." He pushed open the next door and was blinded by the sudden light, the room illuminated by a large chandelier and a couple of small table lamps. To the right of the room was a vast TV, a porn channel displaying two generously proportioned girls doing their stuff as if the renewal of their contract depended on it. Opposite the screen was a small side table with a large plate of sandwiches, and next to this a vast Regency armchair ornately brocaded and swagged. Slumped in the chair in a massive velvet dressing gown was George, his face contorted with lack of oxygen, his mouth half open and the remains of the partly masticated sandwich that had choked him horribly on display. Confident that the house was empty John and Alfie had thrown the door wide open and were part way into the room before this tableau had frozen them to the spot. It was Alfie who finally found his tongue, initially mouthing silently before anything actually emerged.

"He's supposed to be alive and kicking in Spain. What the fuck is he doing as dead as a doornail in England?"

"He must have come back early!" John dropped into a chair, dizzy with shock. "He is dead, isn't he?"

"If he jumps up and shouts *Boo* we'll know he's not!" Alfie crept into the room as if the noise of footfalls would disturb George, and took a closer look at him. "I think we lucked out. If he hadn't choked on that sandwich he might not have been that pleased to see us." He looked up at John. "Might just have asked us why we didn't ring the front door bell."

John's body temperature had dropped several degrees and the layer of sweat coating him under the plastic was now freezing. He tried to focus on the implication of George's death, but was having a problem. "Sorry Alfie, I feel a bit odd. Give me a second and I'll try and be constructive."

"Take your time. I don't think he's in any rush to go anywhere."

Self preservation came to the fore. "I think we'd better just get out of here."

"Don't be daft." Alfie seemed to be his normal self again. "When you think about it, this is actually good news. There's no record of our being here, and as he's dead he can't try and muddy the waters by saying that the stuff was planted on him." He looked round him, this room like all the others hung like an art gallery. "For all we know half this stuff may be nicked as well. The Vermeer might just be another one."

"Oh come on, we don't need to bother with that now he's dead. I don't need to frame him now."

"Well thank you for including me in your plans, Mr Foxton. Part of the reason we're here is so I can off load the sodding thing. If you want to take it back and hang it over your mantelpiece you're welcome, but I want to get rid of it."

Recovering from the shock, John's brain was beginning to work at last. With George now dead, was there any need for any of this to go ahead? Reggeo and Dragoon would still exist as companies, but as George was very much their alter ego, it was likely that a number of things would fall by the wayside and eventually collapse. But then again, no matter how altruistic the original motive may have been, John's career was still on a knife edge and he still needed the money as much as he ever did, and if George was exposed as a criminal, he might even become the focus of suspicion for the monies going as astray.

"OK, Alfie, let's do it and get out of here." There was an easel in the far corner of the room with what looked like a small Watteau on it, and Alfie made a bee line for it.

"There's no rush. I'm beginning to enjoy myself. We can make a little tableau for when he's found, '*George Stavros the art collecting drugs dealer chokes in his study admiring his latest acquisition.*' I bet there'll be some really good headlines on this one." He took the Watteau from the easel and then carefully removed the cellophane from the Vermeer and put it in its place, standing back to admire the effect. He held out the Watteau to John. "Do you want this as a souvenir? You'll be able to hang it up at home quite openly, he's not going to report it stolen."

Despite himself, John went to the easel and looked at the Vermeer. He was no expert, hardly an art lover at all, but he could see why this simple understated picture was priceless. It showed a Dutch courtyard with a servant girl sweeping it, completely absorbed in her task and her mind elsewhere. There was no drama or passion in the picture, just a quiet depiction of a routine moment in this girl's life, but the very simplicity was where the genius lay. It made him feel inadequate. You could never own a picture like this; you could only ever be a custodian.

Alfie was still holding onto the Watteau. "My misses would love this one, she's keen on sheep." For the first time he noticed the two girls on the TV screen, who, determined to get the attention of the people in the room by some means or other were now doing something with a bowl of custard that was almost certainly not recommended in the instructions on the packet. "I think we could do something to preserve the poor sod's dignity." He picked up the remote and switched the TV to BBC 2. "That's better. You didn't know I had my sensitive side did you."

"Can we go now?"

"Let's just finish the job." Alfie carefully slipped the packet of cocaine into the pocket of George's dressing gown, but then to John's horror took a sandwich from the plate and stuffed it through the letter box in his plastic hood and started to munch on it with apparent enjoyment. "Ham and mustard, John, really yummy. Shall I take a couple for the drive back?"

TWENTY-TWO

HOW WAS HE FEELING? WASN'T sure. Ought to be nervous, but he wasn't really. Numb maybe, sort of brain dead and going through the motions, but otherwise OK. He was even able to feel pleased with his appearance. It was the evening of the party and he was adjusting his black tie in the mirror for the ninth or tenth time, partly a nervous gesture but otherwise as an excuse to admire himself. He lived and died in jeans when not in the office, but with so much depending on it tonight was special and called for a bit of an effort. His dinner jacket looked every penny it had cost him, his shirt was so white it gleamed, and his black shoes were as soft and shiny as sealskin. Even if he was going to his doom, at least he looked his best.

He had tried to eliminate all thoughts of failure from his mind. Everything was in place, and no further preparation could be made. It was now all down to Tracy. She had been briefed a dozen times over as what should be done and she was confident it would go as planned. All that was needed was for her to get an undisturbed half hour on the accounts computer and it should be fine. His job was to make sure that she got it. That at least shouldn't be beyond him.

All the loose ends had been tied up over the last few weeks. Tracy's last day at the office had been a week ago and she had been given a boozy send off at Drums but by mutual agreement he had stayed away. Their clandestine briefing sessions had brought them even closer, and the erotic current there had always between them was now crackling like electricity. A few glasses of wine would be enough to have them stuck together like Velcro, and that had to be avoided at all costs. After tonight, Tracy Spooner would disappear from the face of the earth, very likely with a finger of suspicion pointing after her. Nothing must happen to suggest a link between the two of them.

She was due to fly to Athens tomorrow morning and a first class ticket in the name of Sophia Kostakis had been bought some days ago. She had told the girls in her flat that she was going to see her brother in Australia for an indefinite period so they would not raise the alarm when she went missing. John had felt he must show some additional appreciation and had spent the previous Saturday in Sloane Street and had bought her a set of matching leather bags for the journey which were already packed and piled in a heap on the floor in his living room. He had had a key to his flat cut for her, and the arrangement was that both she and Wendy who would be his guest at the party would come back here after it was over. Wendy would be sleeping with him upstairs, and Tracy would be sleeping in the small bed in his tiny study room. This arrangement made him more nervous than the job itself. Wendy knew that the other person involved in all this was a girl from accounts called Tracy who was going straight off to Greece to get married, but they hadn't ever met, and he had never quite managed to tell Wendy that she and Miss Hot Pants were one and the same. He kept telling himself that Wendy would hardly be justified in making problems about a girl he could honestly say he had never slept with, and who would be gone forever within a matter of hours. Equally, Tracy knew that he was in a relationship with the solicitor for the Saul Liebling School who was the other person involved in the scam. He did not anticipate that Tracy would throw any sort of wobbler over his sleeping with Wendy tonight when the very next morning she was going off to marry another man.

He had not told either of them that George was dead. There was no reason why Tracy ever need know as tomorrow she would travel to another country where it would almost certainly not hit the newspapers. He would tell Wendy tomorrow, but for tonight he wanted her to be as relaxed as possible and able to deal with anything that might occur.

He looked at his watch – six forty on the dot so the taxi should be here in ten minutes. He was due to pick Wendy up at seven, and he was under orders not to be even a second early. There were things a girl had to do on these occasions it was best for a man not to see or know about and she wanted to keep her mystery. Six forty one now and there was nothing else for him to do. He was completely ready having checked his keys and wallet three times over and re-checked in the mirror that he really was as perfectly groomed as he had originally thought. Six forty two. Sod it, he had no choice but to drop into a chair and wait for the door bell which was exactly what he had been avoiding. He had noticed recently that when he let his mind go free, he was tending toward the melancholy. The excitement created by the possibility of his Fantasy Wish List becoming a reality had subsided, and he was now more conscious of what he was shortly going to lose. Ron would be retiring after tonight, so would Bob, and Tracy would be gone forever. Damn it, he would be leaving the firm himself, and possibly giving up the law for good. However it all turned out, his life would never be the same again.

The sudden ringing of the bell made him jump. He checked his appearance one more time and grabbed for his keys and immediately dropped them on the floor. When he bent to pick them up, his wallet fell out spilling all his credit cards. He scooped them up and, hurriedly stuffing his wallet back in his pocket caught one of the buttons of his shirt and pulled it off. Sod it! Not an auspicious start!

* * *

This just wasn't fair; no man alive could deal with this. Certainly he couldn't. He wanted to walk out of her flat and just go on walking till he dropped with exhaustion and madness. Wendy's appearance had the same effect on him as when he looked at the Vermeer, the realisation that he was in the presence of something so inherently superior that although he could admire and appreciate, he could not relate to it as an equal. For a moment he wished that they were strangers so that at the party he could stand to one side and quietly worship but not attempt to engage. She looked so extraordinarily beautiful, so sublimely wonderful she had ceased to be a human being with whom he felt he could have any connection. He knew that women had tended to find him attractive and that tonight he had scrubbed up pretty well, but even dressed up to the nines he was still plain old John Foxton who used to walk to school in an ill fitting blazer that was shiny with wear, not an unapproachable deity. Wendy had somehow taken herself into a different dimension, one that was beyond his reach. Her dress was a long sheath of black silk with a high neck that displayed nothing of her breasts, but the sleeves hung from a precarious thread so her alabaster shoulders were invitingly bare. There was a matching choker round her neck with a pendant diamond and there were diamond earrings dangling from her ears. Whatever she had done to her face managed to be both natural and dramatic all at the same time, and her hair shone like platinum. Until tonight he thought he knew her, but now he felt like a stranger.

He had been looking at her for some minutes before he realised that she was been talking to him, and he came too with a start.

"I said, is there anybody in there?"

"Oh, sorry, I was miles away."

"Well come back will you, we've got a long and important evening together!" She paused and appraised his appearance, a small smile pulling up the corners of her mouth. "I must say, you look dangerously handsome tonight! I can see I'll be fighting them off you."

Nice try Wendy, but it just won't do. "The taxi's downstairs. Shall we go?"

"I thought I looked quite nice too. I suppose I must have been wrong!"

"Oh Wendy, I'm sorry!" He could not risk spoiling her with a kiss, but put his hands out to her shoulders. "You look beautiful. Staggeringly, amazingly, wonderfully, beautiful. You've overwhelmed me. You just make me feel like the organ grinder's monkey that's all. I just can't compete with you."

"Well first of all there isn't a competition, and secondly if I don't get a kiss soon I'll run off with the first man I see at the party. You don't have to do tongues, just a little one to show you're pleased to see me."

He brushed her lips and felt a great surge of affection for her. She was far too good for him, but he would just have to put up with it. "Come on. Let's go and do battle."

* * *

"Champagne, Sir, Madame?"

"God yes!"

They each took a drink from the waitress at the doorway and he downed his in a single swallow, then grabbed a second one to carry round. The party was in the large double boardroom on the second floor, and a temporary raised stage had been set up with a microphone which suggested there would be speeches. It was well attended, most of the senior members of the firm there and a good number of retirees and other special guests, not all of whom he recognised. Sweeping his eyes round the room to see who had already pitched up he instantly noticed Simon, Linda, and Ian who had just been made up as partners, the three of them collectively preening themselves in a self contained group, the expressions on their faces exaggeratedly self depreciating as if they were all about to say in unison how much they didn't deserve it and all the other hypocritical shit that John would also be saying if he were there with them. All going well he would be a millionaire before the night was out, but he was still sick with jealously so he brought down the steel shutters and tried to block it from his mind. On the far side of the room with a couple of the older partners he could see Dan Kleinwort looking tall and rangy if you liked that sort of thing, or awkward and gangly if you did not. John was firmly in the Did Not camp. Dan's dinner jacket was very slim cut and his bow tie was a thin black line across his throat just below his prominent Adam's apple, and as a final sartorial gesture his frilly shirt front was embellished with thin black stripes. Happy to be guilty of stereotyping, John wondered if he might break into a number from Oklahoma before the evening was out. In an anonymous corner and appearing to be loitering without any intent at all was Bob looking uncomfortable in what was clearly a hired dinner jacket, any pretence at sophistication spoiled by his wearing a v-necked pullover underneath it. Hanging on to his arm for dear life was a middle-aged woman, almost certainly his wife, clearly terrified and staring at the people in the room as if they were aliens. Nice to see that there was at least one other person here tonight who was just as wound up as he was. Slightly apart from everyone else were Julia and Chris who everyone knew had something going, the two of them engaged in an intense conversation which could only be about the firm's new and glowing future, and at the centre of an admiring group by the drinks table was Augustus Melville Q.C., so it seemed the firm had managed to snare at least one proper A Lister. If anything Augustus looked even more handsome and distinguished than usual in an impeccable dinner jacket with a large spotted silk hand kerchief casually stuffed up the sleeve thus drawing attention to the two undone cuff buttons and the artistry of his tailor. Had John seen anybody else adopting such an affectation he would have considered it pretentious, but man with such an awesome reputation could make up his own rules. If he had been wearing a lampshade on his head, John would have felt under dressed without one.

Dragging his eyes away from this legal giant he was startled to see another VIP guest, Lord Parker of all people, in conversation with Marcus. Coincidence might have a long arm but this one was reaching out and poking him in the eye. It was the first time John had seen Lord Parker in the flesh, and even from across the room he was unimpressed. He may be wealthy and a public figure but he was singularly unprepossessing with rat like features and small nervous eyes that constantly flickered anxiously round the room trying to see people's reaction to him. Used to assessing witnesses John immediately saw that underneath his carapace of self importance was a fundamentally weak person who needed constant reassurance. On any other occasion this could have been a wonderful opportunity for some mischief making, and it was such a shame he had to be so tightly focussed on what he was here for.

"Thank God for a friendly face." Ron looking flushed and happy clapped him on the back. "They've really gone to town for me haven't they? Must be bloody pleased I'm leaving. What'll they do when I'm pegging out – have a firework display on the Thames?"

"Hate to disillusion you, Ron, but not all of this is for you. Didn't anybody tell you? Three new partners, Desperate Dan taking over the accounts office and poor old Bob destined for the bowls club and day time television."

"Yes, but who give a toss about them, eh?" John with just the one drink inside him could tell that Ron was already well on the way. He was looking well dressed and pleased with himself in a rarely used dinner jacket that had not yet suffered the fate of most of his clothes but his face was flushed and his voice already slurred. "We're forgetting our manners, John." Ron patted the shoulder of the woman with him and introduced her as his wife Clarissa, then looked at Wendy, his face displaying the same mixture of disbelief and awed admiration John had seen on the faces of all the other men in the room when they saw her arrive. "Are you really Wendy, or did John order you from a magazine and blow you up outside?"

"Ron! I rather think that's enough!" Clarissa raised her eyebrows at Wendy and embraced her with a smile. "Sorry about my husband, my dear. He's not used to drinking." Possibly a few years older than Ron, she would once have been very attractive and still had an engaging smile. She had chosen her clothes well and was wearing a loose fitting dress in dark jersey material that subtly disguised a losing battle with avoirdupois. "You must be John. I'm so pleased to meet you at last. Ron always keeps his office friends well away from me in case I spill the beans about him. Do you two need another drink? I certainly do." She took their orders and turned to Ron who was happily staring at Wendy with the glassy smile of a man who had unexpectedly found a girly mag in a heap of House and Gardens. "Could you get us all some drinks, Donkey, there's a darling. We're all still on the champagne."

Donkey! Was that his pet name at home? John would want to know more about this! Clarissa took a good look at Wendy, unselfconsciously assessing her appearance. "You don't mind if I speak out of turn do you, but I've just got to say something." She linked her arm with Wendy's as if they were old friends. "You're with John aren't you? Look, I don't know if you're just his guest or his girlfriend, but can I give you some advice? It's a great mistake to be too beautiful and too well dressed the way you are. Men can't cope with it; it makes them realise how inferior they really are and so they run away to something less challenging. You have to keep it simple for them, all they can understand is mothers and whores." She looked Wendy up and down. "You haven't got a chance like this. If you had cheaper make-up and a short skirt they'd be queuing up for you, it's much less threatening."

"I tell you what I think...." Trying not to laugh too much Wendy whispered an answer that was clearly only for Clarissa's ears just as Tracy appeared right on cue to offer a tray of canapés to the group. Her face was serious but for a second her eyes met John's and they flashed a welcome. She was wearing a form fitting black waitress outfit buttoned down the front, the skirt short and flared, and her legs displayed in sheer dark stockings and high heels. A tiny white pinny in the front completed the French Maid look. Riddled with all sorts of guilty emotions at the sight of her John found himself blushing and he prayed that Wendy was so engrossed with Clarissa that she would not notice.

"A case in point, Wendy!" Clarissa said taking in every detail of Tracy's appearance as she walked away. "That girl's only a waitress, but she'll have every man in the place after her before the evening's out. The only other chance for somebody like you is to aim really high and go for a diplomat or some such."

Wendy was hanging on to John's arm affectionately and smiling at Clarissa's advice, but John felt it was time to intervene. "Well thank you very much, Clarissa. When Wendy has walked out on me following your advice, will you be offering me counselling, or should inferior men like me just go and top ourselves?"

"So sorry, John! I'm sure Ron must have warned you I do tend to be rather free with my opinions. Anyway, now I've stirred things up I'll leave you alone and go and find out what Ron is doing with those drinks."

Pleased to have a second's break John gratefully downed the dregs of his champagne, desperately in need of an alcohol jag. "So what are you going to do, Wendy? Leave me for a diplomat, or start dressing like a tart? Personally I favour the second option."

"I rather thought you would." Wendy was sipping her champagne, looking straight ahead rather than at John. "The sexy little waitress with the pussy pelmet and pinny combo, that's Tracy isn't it."

His throat went dry. "Oh come on! You don't really think she's sexy do you?"

"Clarissa seems to, and she hasn't seen her do her finger sucking routine."

"I promise you, that was ...."

"Your voice has gone thick and you're blushing." She turned to look at him, an inscrutable smile on her face. "Men hate scenes don't they? Now what should I do, slap your face and start ranting, or just pour my drink over your head?"

"Wendy, please...."

"It's all right, I'm teasing. She was before you and I got together but no woman can resist making a man feel uncomfortable." She kissed him briefly. "We mustn't forget what we're here for. Let's just mingle and look natural." Looking round for someone to chat to she immediately focussed her eyes on Dan who had just disengaged from two people John didn't recognise. John couldn't think of anyone he less wanted to speak to but before he could stop her, Wendy had fixed him with a beaming smile. "Hi. We're just doing the rounds. I'm Wendy Vyne. You probably already know John."

"Oh yes, err, yes. I erm, yes...." Dan sputtered on for a moment and then came to a dead halt. John had never seen someone who'd been pole-axed before, didn't actually know what a pole-axe was, but like falling in love, you recognise it when it happens. Dan was done for, rooted to the spot, his eyes staring at Wendy and his mouth opening and closing like a goldfish gasping for air. He may be tall and good looking in a home on the prairie sort of way, but there was no avoiding that he was a complete twat. They didn't have women like Wendy down on the farm, and clearly Harvard and the rest of his career must have been free of them as well. John knew there were times when it was appropriate to pull rank and this was definitely one of them. He kissed

Wendy on the cheek then reaching a hand behind her squeezed her bottom. For a second he considered pissing a protective circle round her but thought that he'd done enough to get the message across loud and clear. "Wendy, this is Dan Kleinwort our new cashier. Dan, my girlfriend, Wendy. How's it all going, Dan? Got to the bottom of the bought ledger yet?"

"That's not exactly… it's Financial Controller, John."

"Oh yes. Sorry. You don't officially start till Monday do you?"

Wendy butted in. "Financial Controller sounds very important. Does that mean you'll be responsible for the firm's financial policy as well as in charge of day to day accounting?"

"That's absolutely right." Dan's face had lit up, his eyes were glued to her and his Adam's apple was going overtime. This was a man in love, and the object of his affections was asking him about his pet subject. No man could ever ask for more. "I'm planning to make major changes in the direction this firm's going, Wendy. The partners are looking to me for leadership and guidance on financial planning, overall strategy, and to create an investment programme as well."

How staggeringly uninteresting! Let's get away from here before I atrophy with boredom. "Look, Dan, we've…"

"What exactly have you got in mind?" Clearly an expert on bringing people out, Wendy looked as if there was nothing in the world that interested her so much.

"Well, my big hope…" He launched into his ideas on embracing what he called the broad community while John looked round the room with glazed eyes, desperate to get the two of them away. They were here to make John into a millionaire but as there was little he could do about that directly, he wanted to at least enjoy himself until the big moment came. Seeing Ron he flashed him a look of desperation then realised it was a mistake. Ron immediately staggered over and started to tug him away as if he needed him urgently which was the last thing he wanted. Wendy was too potent tonight, far too much the object of male attention and he couldn't risk leaving her unsupervised. Wherever he looked he could see men looking at her and he had a problem not pulling his lips back and snarling. Desperate Dan was hardly a rival, but he still wanted to know exactly what they were saying

"What is it, Ron?"

Ron handed him a well needed drink which he downed gratefully. "Is that the woman you asked me about some weeks ago, the one who works for a pound shop?"

"That's her."

"Well, fuck me!"

"Is that all you wanted to say?" A waitress passed by with a tray of drinks and he took another one. There was no way he could get through tonight without help.

"Bit more than that." Ron's voice was slurred, and he fished into his pocket for the remains of a cigarette packet. "I've been doing some more calculations tonight. Having met her I felt obliged, I'm sure you understand." He put on his glasses and attempted to focus on a strange set of scribbled numbers. "It's very complicated. She either comes out at fifteen or sixteen out of ten, or as low as minus three. It's her going out with you that buggers all the figures up; makes me wonder if underneath that glamour she's mentally deficient."

John was barely listening. Alcohol had fired him up but so far had not impaired any of his faculties. In the distance he could see Tracy taking round her tray of goodies, and as Wendy seemed to be engrossed with Dan he risked signalling Tracy with his eye. She flickered an eyelid back and in a few moments drifted over and offered the tray to them.

Ron beamed at her unsteadily. "My favourite girl in the whole wide world. How are you?" He took a canapé and waved it at her. "Not as delicious as you, Tracy, but at least I'm allowed to put this in my mouth."

She ignored him and spoke to John, a not overly convincing smile on her face.

"Are we all set?"

"It's all down to you I'm afraid." He glanced at Ron, but he was muttering quietly to himself and clearly in another world entirely. "When do you think?"

"Not for a bit. There's a lot of pressure on us at the moment and the supervisor will be on to me if I try and slip away. I think about twenty minutes. I'll let you know so you can make sure I'm covered."

He looked at her appreciatively. "You're a gem, Trace. I really mean it."

"You're not bad yourself. By the way, you look really dishy tonight." She was about to go when Ron came back to life.

"Do you realise this might be the last time I ever see you, Tracy."

"How will I ever cope?"

"There's something I've got to tell you, Tracy. Something I've always wanted to tell you...."

Sensing danger she patted him on the arm and hurried away, Ron mouthing soundless words in her wake. He turned to John to tell him what was on his mind, but John was on another case. Looking round for Wendy he saw that Dan was now in conversation with Marcus, and that Wendy was no longer with him. Seeing that John was free, Dan broke off and came over ignoring Ron who stumbled off like a wounded bear.

"That's one hell of a girl you've got there, John. You really are some lucky man."

"Well, thanks, Dan. I won't disagree with you."

"Look John. This is important, and we've got to deal with it tonight. I e-mailed you today about that five million that came in. It's been there for a whole day and you haven't given me any transfer instructions."

John's heart began to beat painfully against his ribs. "Don't worry Dan. I can do that on Monday."

"Its five million John. We can't just sit on that amount."

John patted him on the shoulder, desperately trying to look nonchalant. "Relax, Dan. You're here to enjoy your party. I'll deal with it first thing Monday morning.

Dan's earnest face looked pained. "I'm sorry, I just can't leave it that long, John. I'm not going to start out with a late payment right at the beginning, it'll send out the wrong message. Just give me the instructions and we can go right up to accounts now and send it through."

"Honestly, Dan, it's really not that urgent."

"It'll only take a moment, we can go to your office in less than a minute and get the details. I'm not letting this go"

Desperately playing for time, John tried another tack. "All right! All right! Let me just deal with something else first and I'll let you have all the info in about ten minutes."

Fuck this! He just had to escape. If he could just stay out of Dan's way till it was all over it would be all right. He looked round desperately for Wendy and saw her in earnest conversation with Bob and his wife of all people, the three of them totally absorbed in whatever they were discussing. Bob's wife had lost her haunted look and was looking at Wendy as if she were Mother Teresa. He went across and took Wendy by the arm and she excused herself, turning round to give a last word. "You won't forget what I said, will you?"

"I won't dear. Thank you so much. We've got your card."

With some difficulty John lead her away from them. "What was that all about?"

"She looked so lost I felt I had to go and talk to her, and then I found out about Bob being forced into retirement. I've told them about the Employment Rights Act, and I think he's going to sue for unfair dismissal."

"Jesus Christ!"

"I think they might want me to act for them."

Fascinating as this was he couldn't think about that now. "Never mind that. I think we might have a problem with Dan…"

Before he could finish he felt his arm taken in a powerful grip and found Clarissa on his left side leaning across him to talk to Wendy. "Do you mind if I drag him away for a second, darling. I need to have a word." Overwhelmed, John found himself being lead away. "I think I need a bit of a favour from you, John. Ron's always had a high opinion of you so you might be the only person who can help. I really am very fond of the old sod so you mustn't get any wrong ideas, but just between the two of us, now he's going to be retired, I really can't cope with the idea of having him under my feet day after day." She nodded in the direction of Ron who was in earnest conversation with the water-cooler, waving his hands dismissively as if he disagreed with the answers he was being given. "You can see what I mean, can't you. I've got friends who come for bridge and coffee mornings, that sort of thing, and he'll just be in the way. I know he's keen to carry on doing some work from home, so do you think you could persuade him that if he got himself a flat in town for mid week it would be a lot more practical." She looked at John earnestly. "I know how much he's been looking forward to retiring and putting his feet up at home, but I'm sure if you sold it to him the right way, he would realise it's the best thing. He could meet his chums for lunch and go to the wine bar in the evening if he wanted to. He could even have some of you back in the evenings."

"Well, I don't promise anything, but…"

"Thank you John. I really appreciate it."

Tracy came by again with her tray, her face slightly flushed and her breathing a little staccato. "Would you like one of these, Sir, Madam?" Clarissa took one of the morsels on offer and excused herself leaving them alone. "Look, John, I'm going to try and get up there in about ten minutes. Is that OK?"

"That would be spot on."

"OK. I'll let you know. I'll have to rush now."

He should have told her about Dan, but she had already hurried off. He realised that her calling him "Sir" had left a funny feeling in his stomach but there was no time to think about that now. For God's sake, where was Wendy? Why couldn't she stay in one place for more than a minute? Looking round he could see she had been button-holed by Dan in a far corner, their body language clear even from a distance. Wendy was imprisoned by his earnest conversation and was trying to politely back off. Seeing John beckoning to her she used it as an excuse to escape and started towards him. He moved rapidly to meet her but in a pincer movement from another direction Augustus Melville and Lord Parker suddenly appeared and cut him off. He could hardly say that he was friends with Augustus, but he had done a major case with him a few years before with considerable success and they were on good terms. That Lord Parker had latched on to him was hardly a surprise as he was arguably the only other man in the room of equal status, but seeing the two men together, John could see they were different species. For Augustus, success had simply been the inevitable by-product of his prodigious intellect and energy. He also benefited from enormous personal charisma and positively noble good looks. At forty or so, his head looked as if Michael Angelo had set out to sculpt a Roman Emperor, but was interrupted before he was able to smooth it off. Lord Parker on the other hand had clawed his way to where he was with nothing on his side except his obsession with success. Any normal mortal would look insignificant and parochial next to Augustus, but Lord Parker came off very badly, looking weak and forgettable despite his expensive tailoring. On any other occasion exchanging small talk with these two with the possibility of a little stirring up would be something that John would positively enjoy, but with Tracy planning to do the job in ten minutes he was so keyed up he wasn't sure how he would cope with even being polite.

From their different directions the four of them met up and Wendy kissed John affectionately, linking her arm in his. The other two men's eyes had barely left her from the moment she came into view and he could see how they reacted to this display of affection, his status instantly shooting up several notches.

"John, how very good to see you again!" Augustus put out an affectionate hand and took John by the arm. "Can't wait to do another case with you again. That last one was such fun." He addressed the other two people in the easy patrician voice of someone used to speaking from Olympus and taking the attention of his audience for granted. "John and I did a massive fraud case a while back, didn't we? I don't think I've ever seen so much paper, boxes and boxes of it. John turned over every sheet of it and cross referenced every entry so we could tie the buggers into knots with their own double dealing. I don't think he could have got five minutes sleep in six months with all the preparation work he put in. Brilliant job, and thanks to his efforts we got the bastards."

Oh may this moment never end! One of the great legal giants of all time loudly praising him, not only to the most beautiful girl in the world who was actually sleeping with him, but also to a major public figure, even if something of a tacky one. Why couldn't he have a recording of this to play over and over until he died?

"Sorry....." Augustus sounded unusually diffident for once. "I'm forgetting my manners. Jimmy Parker needs no introduction of course, and Jimmy, this is John Foxton, as you've gathered a quite brilliant solicitor and ...?" He looked at Wendy interrogatively

"Wendy Vyne. Another solicitor. In my case, just an ordinary one."

"I'm sure you're being unnecessarily modest." Augustus' large eyes glowed at Wendy and John was surprised to see her blush. Good to know that she really was mortal. And Lord Parker had been demystified to *Jimmy* Parker had he? Could he risk calling him that? Between the alcohol and the massive confidence boost the last few minutes had injected he felt he could get away with it

"Jimmy, err may I call you that?" John checked Lord Parker's face to see if he resented this familiarity, but it was clearly all right. John was a chum of Augustus Melville and a brilliant solicitor with a girlfriend who even on a bad hair day could launch a thousand ships. His status was suddenly in the stratosphere. It was Lord Parker who had started life eating other boy's brussel sprouts who needed *his* acceptance, not the other way round. This felt good! He could get used to this without even practising. "That painting of yours, the Vermeer. Do the police have any leads? Papers have been quiet for a while now."

"Fat chance, John!" He looked round to see if anyone were listening. "Forget anything I've said on the television, that's just public relations. The police are useless." He took John by the arm and separated them from the other two as if to speak in confidence with a trusted advisor. "What do you think I should do, John? Police won't admit it, but the trail's clearly gone cold. It's not good PR that some tacky criminal has got one over on me. No one's got any ideas. You must have some knowledge of the criminal mind, what would you do?"

Was this for real? John had only asked the question as a wind up, but between Wendy and Augustus he had gained such status that his opinion was being sought by one of the richest men in England. Could he risk what he had in mind? If he pulled it off it would be brilliant.

"This hardly calls for a legal opinion, but I can give you a personal one."

"Please do."

"If the trail is cold and no demands have been made, it's probably been stolen by some art loving nutter who's getting off on it in some secret basement somewhere. If that's the case, you may well never see it again, so you might as well get what political advantage from it you can. You could make a press statement saying that this picture is too important to be lost to the world, and that if it ever turns up you will bequeath it to the Nation. You probably won't get it back, but at least you could get some political clout from making the gesture, you know demonstrating that it's the painting you consider to be important rather than the glory of having it in your own collection."

Lord Parker pondered on this for some moments before answering. "You know, John, I must say…"

He didn't catch the rest of his sentence. He could see Tracy on the other side of the room anxiously trying to get his attention. Shit! It had all seemed so leisurely at first, and now they were running out of time.

"Jimmy, I'm sorry. I've just remembered something very important." He tried to get Wendy's attention but she was deep in conversation with Augustus, so left her to it and hurried across the room. Tracy silently signalled that he should follow her and went out of the room. Immediately outside she slipped into a small room opposite the board room and he followed her and closed the door. She threw herself at him and clutched her arms round his neck. "I'm going up there now."

"Will you be OK?"

"I'm so nervous I could wet my pants but I'm sure I'll be all right." She kissed him hurriedly. "Wish me luck!"

In seconds she was gone, her heels clacking down the corridor and round the corner. He must let Wendy know they were now operational and hurried back into the board room, cannoning into Dan who was just coming out.

"John, here you are!"

For fucks sake! "Hi Dan. I was just having a leak."

"John, those instructions. I was just on my way to the accounts office, but now you're here we can do things properly."

"I'm sorry...?"

"I'd rather do whatever transfer the client has asked you to do, but if you won't tell me what that is, I'll just move the money to a special high interest account."

"Is that really necessary?"

"Listen, John, I'm not going home tonight unless I've done one thing or another with that money."

"OK! OK! Sorry. I got distracted. I'll go and get the instructions right now. I'll see you at the bar in, what, five minutes?"

Dan looked at his watch suspiciously. "Five minutes dead! Any longer and I'll go straight and put it on to high interest, and we can both discuss it with Luke on Monday morning."

"Fine! Fine! See you in a minute." He flew into the boardroom, desperate for Wendy who was enveloped in the joint attentions of Augustus Melville and Lord Parker, their two heads crooked over her like a couple of praying mantis and their eyes glittering like connoisseurs over a new collectable.

"So sorry, I've got to drag Wendy away. Minor emergency...family matter." He grabbed Wendy by the arm and propelled her out of earshot. "Listen, panic stations! You're going to have to be a honey trap. If we don't get Dan away from here this very second he's going straight up to accounts and on to the computer. Tracy's doing her stuff on it as we speak. "

"Honey trap! What do you want me to do, for God's sake?"

"Oh come on Wendy, this is your department! Back him in a corner and stick your tongue in his ear. I don't know, just use every womanly trick in the book to keep him occupied. Once you've got him alone and safe you can plead a headache."

"I might feel like doing it if I have to go that far!"

"For God's sake Wendy!"

"OK. OK. Where is he? I haven't got my glasses on"

"He's over there at the bar."

She composed herself with a deep breath, then head high and taking on the demeanour of a predatory super-model strutted slowly in the direction of her prey as if in time to a heavy blues track. At the bar and all unknowing Dan was drumming his fingers and looking at his watch, his face taking on a look of stunned disbelief when he saw who was coming to talk to him. With half lidded eyes, she took out a cigarette and held it in Dan's direction for a light which could possibly be a mistake with a man far too clean living to approve, but no doubt another five or ten minutes under her influence and he would become a thirty a day man. John couldn't bear to watch the rest of the process and turned away, his nerves like piano wires. How long would Tracy be? Ages yet, probably as she'd only been gone a few moments. A drink! A drink! That's what he needed. One of the waitresses was coming in his direction with a freshly loaded tray and he took one and downed it only to have it explode in the back of his head. Straight champagne had been replaced with champagne cocktail, the addition of brandy and sugar making it way more potent. Pulling his brain back into focus he looked round the room to see that it wasn't just him feeling the effects and that an evening of limitless free alcohol and token food was beginning to take its toll on everyone else as well. There was a hint of abandon in the air and conversation was now free and loud, the polite laughter that had marked the early evening giving way to shrieks and bellows. Surreptitious male hands were checking out the outer boundaries of women who they would normally be too nervous to talk to, and Julia and Chris who everyone knew had a thing going were deeply involved in their first public kiss. From long experience he knew that they would all pay the price on Monday morning but that wasn't his problem. He had his own fish to fry, but what to do while it was happening? He was as tense as a violin string and there was at least another twenty minutes to go. Looking round the room he saw Augustus Melville and Lord Parker in cahoots with Luke who so far he had carefully avoided, but before he could turn away they caught his eye and waved him over.

"John! John!" Lord Parker clapped him on the shoulder like an old friend. "Just telling Luke your brilliant idea. I'll be getting my press secretary on to it tomorrow."

"Glad to be of help, Jimmy." He couldn't resist this bit of showing off in front of Luke who flashed a look of grudging respect in his direction. Shame it was way too late to help his position in the firm, but to his surprise Luke reached out his hand and took his shoulder. "Could I drag John away for a moment, just need to have a brief word? You can have him back in a minute."

What the devil was this? Whatever it was couldn't harm him now. As they moved away he surreptitiously glanced at his watch yet again, hoping that despite an overwhelming urge to poo his pants he could manage to keep up some semblance of normality for at least a bit longer. Looking at Luke however he saw that he too was looking strange and edgy.

. "Look, John," Luke hesitated as if unsure what to say. "I think it's time you and I had a bit of a talk."

Bit of a talk! Didn't Luke know that this very second he was busy ripping off one the firm's clients to the tune of several million? He tried to look interested in whatever Luke might have to say but had a problem simply standing still.

"I've been getting the feeling for some time that you might not be as comfortable with the firm as you could be. Maybe you think it's time you should move on..."

"Luke...?" His concentration was back with a jump.

"I'll just finish. If you were having any doubts about the sort of reference the firm would give you..." He fished into his inside pocket and produced a folded piece of the firm's headed paper which he passed to John who read it in stunned disbelief. The text started "To Whom It May Concern" and went on to describe John's abilities in glowing terms. He may have had a lot to drink but suddenly his brain was in overdrive as he took in what this meant. Diana had actually managed to pull off the impossible, the implications of which shot straight to pole position in his head. Not only was George dead and could no longer cause any trouble, but now he had a reference which meant that he could take his career to where it belonged. The entire scam had been unnecessary but this very second Tracy was upstairs making him both a millionaire and a criminal with every press of the keys.

"Thank you, Luke. Thank you very much indeed." His voice had the artificial sound of a robot whose batteries were running out. "I'll put it in writing on Monday, but please accept my notice with immediate effect."

"I think that's the best decision for all of us. Ahh, here's Ron!" Luke's voice suddenly brightened up. "Now I can make my speech."

He went to across to the temporary stage and tapped the microphone as Ron lumbered across to John and threw an arm round his neck for support, his weight nearly pulling John down with him. Even with what he had put down during the evening, John could tell Ron was in a bad way. His breathing was uneven and he was muttering incoherently. John tried to say something to him, but his eyes were glazed over and it was as if he was unaware of anything going on around him. His brain already overloaded with other matters, John simply did his best to hold him up.

"Ladies and Gentlemen!" Luke's amplified voice boomed across the room, then, looking towards Lord Parker, he added. "I correct myself. Tonight it really is, *Lords*, Ladies and gentlemen! This is both a sad and happy occasion. Sad because we are losing some very dear and wonderful friends who have been pillars of the firm for many years. First and foremost is Ron Makepiece who…"

"Where's Tracy?" Without any help from the microphone Ron's bleary voice cut across the room. Hanging on to John's neck for dear life he craned his head to look round even though it was unlikely that his eyes could see anything. "Where's my lovely Tracy?" He bawled "I WANT TRACY!"

"For God's sake, Ron!" John tried to shush him, but Ron's eyes and ears were closed for business even if his mouth was still all too clearly in good working order. "I'll never see Tracy again!" He yelled, tears now beginning to flow. "I NEVER GOT TO JIGGGLE HER JUGGLIES!"

At the microphone Luke did his best to keep his cool as from all over the room came the unmistakable sound of people trying to suppress laughter, a snort here, a stifled scream there. In the confusion Bob stepped on to the platform next to him, his face still with its standard vacuous expression, but behind the thick lenses of his glasses, his eyes were bright with suppressed excitement. Ron, in his own world, unable to see or hear anything, and his eyes flowing, put his head back and yelled for Tracy with a primeval bellow.

"DONKEY! Will you be QUIET!" From left field Clarissa hove into view and swinging her handbag, caught him heavily across his left ear. It would have felled him had he been sober, but it only had the effect of bringing him back to something like life. Vibrating like a bell he tottered on the spot, looking at her with an expression in his eyes that mixed hurt feelings and confusion with a sort of triumphant surprise that he could still get up to such mischief even at this stage in his life. He balanced there for a second swaying to and fro, desperately trying to say something further but only managing to mouth soundlessly, a thin line of dribble running from the side if his mouth. A couple of trainees seeing the problem stepped forward and took his weight, and then with assistance from Clarissa started to lead him away as he looked behind him in a mute farewell, wondering if this was the last he'd ever see of them all.

"Well perhaps…" Luke seeing him exit regained some of his confidence and tried to make a joke of it. "I think the expression is *'Tired and emotional'*, but we all know he's earned it. I'll come back to the incomparable Ron in a while. Perhaps I should move on. Let's leave the firm's losses for a second and talk about its gains. The firm is in the process of moving forward to a new and exciting future. We have always prided ourselves on our traditional values and always will, but when necessary we are pleased to embrace new concepts, and in particular new technology, and to that end we are particularly pleased to welcome to the firm an expert both in accountancy and in computer technology, Dan Kleinwort our new Financial Controller. Where are you, Dan? Come forward and let me introduce you… "

Heads turned, but the room was a Dan free zone. In a far corner one of the older secretaries made a huge pantomime of looking in her handbag, then yelled, "He's not in here!" Which was followed by a massive peal of laughter. From the back of the room a voice called out, "Perhaps he's with Tracy" followed by another, "I bet he's with Tracy!" and then a third, "Perhaps he's jiggling her jugglies!" An insidious and growing hysteria was beginning to take over the room and as Luke desperately looked round for some non-existent back-up, Bob now exhibiting all the signs of someone who had taken full advantage of the free hospitality took his opportunity to shuffle across and take the microphone. "I think this might be the moment to tell you all," he started, his flat voice amplified round the room, "about the disgusting way this firm has treated me!"

"Here! Here!" His wife called from the front, fired with alcohol and indignation. Before John could see how this was going to develop his phone rang in his pocket and he went outside to answer it, bumping in to Tracy who was just coming down the corridor, her face flushed with excitement.

"I've done it, John! It's all OK!"

"Oh Tracy, you're too sodding wonderful!" He hugged her briefly then pushed her away. "I'll explain later but its complete madness in there. Just get out as quick as you can and I'll see you back at the flat." She kissed him hurriedly, and as she ran off he answered his phone "Yes? Yes? Who is it?"

"It's Wendy!"

"Wendy! Where the hell are you?"

"I'm in the ladies' loo at a restaurant. Dan kept insisting he had to do something in the accounts office so I had to really go over the top to divert him. Once I'd got him on the hook I insisted we went somewhere for dinner first just to play for time."

"You're amazing! I think we might all be going to prison otherwise."

"Look, I don't know how long I'm going to be with this, so don't wait up for me. I'll just go back to my place once I've got rid of him and we can get together tomorrow."

"Come on, it's no fuss…."

"Seriously John, this man's got it bad – it could be four o'clock before I

shake him off. Just get some sleep and I'll see you tomorrow. Must go or he'll get suspicious." She rang off.

He wandered back into the board room in a daze. Could anyone tell he was now a millionaire? Didn't seem so, the whole room was in mayhem and no one took a scrap of notice of his entrance. One of the retirees had taken out his false teeth and was snapping them at the bottom of a screaming secretary, a young trainee had just been sick in the punch, and centre stage Bob was at the microphone giving a spirited rendering of *"I did it My Way"* with most of the room singing along and swaying in unison. Luke and those members of the establishment who were still sober were in urgent conference with panic stricken expressions on their faces, and Julia and Chris who everyone knew had something going had thrown all caution to the wind and were deep tonguing each other in a far corner. As John took it all in, he could see Augustus Melville and Lord Parker pushing their way across the room trying to get to the doorway where John was hovering, the look on Lord Parker's face suggesting that he would never come out into the real world ever again. "Do you want to come with us John? We're going on to the Athenaeum." Regretting that he might never get such an invitation again, John declined using the excuse that it needed someone responsible to stay and put things in order. Looking as if he might want to stay a bit longer, Augustus fixed him with a beaming smile and clapped him on the shoulders. "Wonderful party John! I'm very much in your debt." He indicated the disorder behind him. "Not necessarily what you all had in mind but it could get quite interesting in there!"

Interesting? It was certainly that! He looked at the drunken rabble in front of him, and felt a rush of affection for the place and the people. If it were always like this, he would probably want to stay. Never mind that, it was time to go. He waited a few moments to let Lord Parker and Augustus get clear, then made his way downstairs. He was about to close the front door behind him when he remembered the electricity cupboard behind the reception desk and the big main switch. Well why not? He was a millionaire now, he could do anything he liked. He opened the cupboard door and as he threw the switch, even from two floors above he could hear the yells of shocked surprise as the whole building went black.

That's right, go with a bang. It's the only way!

* * *

"Tracy?" He entered his living room cautiously, not sure if she would already be there, his tie hanging loose and his brain numbed by the events of the last few hours. He felt strangely calm, knowing that he had all the time in the world to ponder on the future. They'd pulled it off, stage one at least, and the rest should be a doddle by comparison. The intervention of the weekend and the confusion that George's death would inevitably create could significantly delay the discovery that the money wasn't where it should be. All going well, it would be a lot longer before there was any hint of where it had gone to, by which time it should have been dispersed without trace.

"Tracy, are you there?"

"Sorry, I was in the loo."

She appeared at the far doorway and hovered there, still wearing her waitress outfit but without the embellishment of the pinny. They were both peculiarly shy, overwhelmed by what they had done.

"You really did it, Trace! That's amazing. Were there any problems?"

"Not really. I've cleared all evidence of it from the office computer, and if I've done what I think I have, at the other end there won't be a hint that the instruction came from us."

"You know you're a hero, don't you."

"Not really, you set it all up. You're putting a ton more money in my direction than I could ever have dreamed of. You're the brilliant one."

It hit him in a big way just how gorgeous she was, so simple and sexy in her little black dress, her face glowing with the quiet triumph of a job well done. If he didn't kiss her he would die.

"Come here, Tracy. I think we must be entitled to a kiss." They met in the middle of the room and kissed at some length, John holding her head firmly in his hands and determined they should not stray elsewhere. Now that the pinny had been removed he could see that the buttons on her dress went from neck to hem and he had to fight a delinquent urge to rip it wide open. Before it could take hold, Tracy pulled away. "Where's Wendy?"

"I'll explain in a minute, but she's not coming back tonight."

Tracy stepped a little way away from him. "I didn't get to speak to her, but she seems really nice. She's very beautiful."

"Yes she is."

"Are you in love with her?"

She was quite entitled to ask, but it was a pity he didn't know the answer. "I'm not sure. I might well be, I don't know."

"What about her?"

"Same answer… you know what I mean."

She looked at him silently for a moment then pointed at the study door. "I get the picture. Look, that's my room for tonight isn't it. In the circumstances you'll understand if I just…"

"Yes of course. I do understand."

He understood all too well. Best to get the elephant out of the room while they had the strength to do so. She left him alone feeling strangely lost, and he slumped back onto his couch. Of course there was tension between them. They were alone in his flat, they fancied each other rotten, but they both had other commitments. He desperately regretted that Wendy wasn't here as her absence had created this dilemma, but he was grateful to Tracy for making the decision she had as he was not sure he would have had the moral fibre to do so himself. Bless the girl! What a little gem she was. Wendy was of course more beautiful, more worldly, more all sorts of things, but there was something about Tracy that pressed some very basic buttons. Fuck it all! He stretched his arms and groaned out loud, wondering how he would survive the night with so much of him on fire at the same time.

"What was that?" She startled him by suddenly re appearing in the room.

"Nothing, sorry. Just stretching."

"Sorry I had to leave you just then. Something I had to do." She just looked at him for some moments then brought out her arm from behind her back, and dangling from her hand was a small pair of white knickers. She gave him a second to focus on what they were then tossed them into his lap. "I thought it best to let you know I wasn't wearing any so we both know where we stood. We misunderstood each other last time and it would be a shame for that to happen again, 'specially with tonight being the last time we're going to see each other." He knew he should say something to stop this, but the power of speech had suddenly left him. He was as much a prisoner as if she had tied and gagged him. All he could do was sit there while she said her piece.

"Wendy's not here and we're alone for the night. You're not actually sure that you love her, and after what we've been through this evening, if she really loved you, nothing would have stopped her coming back to you tonight. I know my future is somewhere else, but Nikos and I might not have one if it wasn't for you, so I don't think that he's in any position to complain if I show my thanks on behalf of both of us. If you think this is wrong, you only have to say so." She took the hem of her dress in her hands and started to undo the bottom button, pulling the two halves of the dress apart as she did so.

"I've hardly started John, so it's not too late to stop me if you really want to. I promise I won't be upset."

But he would be upset, more than upset. In fact he would die if she stopped. He might anyway, his breathing seeming to have given up along with his brain and most of his other functions. Her business with the dress had created a triangle of vision through which he could see the tops of her stockings and a glimpse of her thighs above, and as he was incapable of telling her to stop, she dealt with the next button, enlarging the triangle, and giving centre stage to the central junction of her body. Infidelity had nearly ruined his life which he was at last rebuilding, but maybe he had been pre-programmed to self destruct, because nothing could have stopped him from letting this proceed to its logical conclusion. She undid another button, and now her navel peeped through the apex, its single eye contemplating him silently, and then another, so now there was only one button left. He neither knew nor cared if his eyes or his loins caught fire first, as clearly they must, but if he burned to a fine ash of his own making it would be a fitting way to go. She undid the last button, and with painful slowness she pulled the edges of her dress apart so that bit by bit her entire body became visible, the dress now at the extreme points of her shoulders, loosely held in place by the tips of her fingers.

The silence between them so intense he was being deafened by the sound of his own heart beat, but when she let the dress slither to the floor, he could hear the shimmer of the material against her body through every nerve end. For a moment she did not move, just as much a prisoner of her own performance as he was, then she stepped forward, planting her knees either side of him on the couch and putting her arms round his neck to draw him to her.

"You did once say you'd like to kiss me till I swooned." She kissed him slowly then pulled back to speak. "I hope you're not going to disappoint me."

TWENTY-THREE

HE FELT SICK WITH GUILT and apprehension, hating himself and everything he stood for. What concerned him was not only what he had done, but that when it came to it, he had been powerless to act in any other way. Beyond doubt there were mitigating circumstances, the implication of which he did not want to think about, but nothing could really excuse his act of betrayal. From the moment that Tracy had made her intentions clear, he had abandoned himself to her one hundred per cent, giving nothing else a second's thought until she had finally left at midday Saturday. When at last the guilt came flooding in, it had the additional impact of a coiled spring, hitting his conscience in the face like a baseball bat.

Guilt was not the only thing clogging his emotional arteries. He had so much else to come to terms with. He was a millionaire and he was a criminal, even though it was more or less guaranteed that he would never be found out, and between his legal pedigree and Marcus' reference folded up in his wallet, he almost certainly had the intro to the profession's Golden Circle and all that implied. On top of all that had happened last night, it was too much to digest in one go, and he was trying to put off thinking about any of it until he felt better able to deal with it all.

By six o'clock Saturday evening his body had just about recovered from the previous night. Too much alcohol, too little food and hardly any sleep had between them left him nauseous and headachy, but he had made himself something to eat early afternoon, and afterwards he had managed to sleep for a few hours. He and Tracy had risen late, her flight not till mid afternoon, but there had been little time to linger. They had long agreed that he would not take her to the airport, and he had arranged a chauffeur driven car to collect her at midday. The parting had not been easy, but apart from their both saying some inappropriate things which was understandable with all the strain, it had gone as well as could have been expected. By now she might well have landed, and already started her new life as Sophia Kostakis

After she had gone he had tried to telephone Wendy at all the numbers he had for her, but there had be no answer. They had already agreed have dinner at La Fenice as a celebration and he was to pick her up at eight, but the absence of any contact made him anxious. Later in the day when he picked up his mobile he saw that he had a text message from her that she'd sent mid morning. It simply said she would see him tonight as arranged. Why the devil had she sent him a text message and not called him? The only possible justification he could see was that by doing so she could avoid speaking to him and the thought of that was tearing him apart. Despite his own guilty behaviour he was consumed with the thought that she might have slept with Dan. He could hardly believe that she would have done, but the idea was so abhorrent that even the possibility was enough to make him want to wail and beat his head against the wall. And what could he do if she had? He would have no right to berate her when even after a long bath the smell of Tracy was still lingering on him, in his brain if not on his skin. The one thing he had decided was that when he saw Wendy he would confess to everything that had happened. It was the only way he could live with himself.

* * *

Giovanni showed them to their table, treating them as honoured guests and shaking their hands like old friends. They were pleased to see him and talked to him at length during the pantomime of the evening specials, deliberately prolonging it to put off the moment when they were left to themselves and they had to engage. Wendy had not asked John into her flat when he had picked her up, and they had said little in the taxi. They had both been affectionate, but there was an indefinable distance. At their table they ordered their food, tasted the wine and drank the first glass, looking round them at their fellow diners as if there was little of importance to talk about. It was John who finally broke the spell.

"Wendy, I need to talk to you about last night…"

"I'm assuming it went well. It must have done or you would have said. The money went through?"

"Oh God, yes! I'd be a gibbering wreck if it hadn't. It'll take maybe a few weeks before I can actually start doing anything with it, but you know you'll get back the money you lent me with interest, and the school will get its donation. Don't worry. I promise you'll get back every penny, and everything I said I'd do I will."

She took his hand. "I never doubted that. I trust you completely or I wouldn't have gone along with it."

Why did she have to say that? A knot of lead formed in his stomach and he wondered if he would be able to eat any of his food. "By the way, while we're talking business, there's something you should know." He told her about George's death and what he thought the implications might be including that it might even take suspicion away from Tracy and on to George himself. A combination of the cocaine he'd planted, the Vermeer and the Liechtenstein connection could easily lead the police to think that George had diverted the cash himself for personal reasons.

Wendy took another sip of her wine. "It looks as if Tracy did a good job."

"She did a wonderful job. Look, Wendy, about Tracy…"

"And she's now in Greece on her way to becoming Mrs Papadopoulos or something like that."

"Listen, Wendy, there's something I've got to tell you….."

Wendy silenced him with a hand over his mouth. "Tracy did a brilliant job last night. She got away this morning, and soon she'll be cooking big bowls of moussaka and having lots of olive skinned babies. We both owe her a huge debt of thanks. Nothing else matters, John. Please understand that." She refilled both their glasses and took a deep swallow. "I'm afraid it's me who needs to talk to you, John. Not the other way round."

Had she really said that, the words all men fear and hate? Being sure he knew what was coming did nothing to make it less painful.

"Oh God, you slept with Dan last night, didn't you. I've been waiting to hear you tell me that since I got your text message."

She let out a short laugh. "Slept with Dan? No way!" The relief flooded though him like balm. Maybe, just maybe, the situation could be rescued. "No, John, I'm afraid it's much worse than that."

What was she saying? Simply nothing could be worse than that. "Wendy, for God's sake, I mean…"

"John, I'm deeply, deeply fond of you and I wouldn't have missed these last few weeks with you for anything, but we've never pretended to be properly in love with other. I didn't sleep with Dan last night, but if I had done it would have been one of those drunken one night stands we all have every now and then. I wouldn't have blamed you for being angry with me, but it wouldn't have made any real difference to us. Dan wasn't a problem. He may be very bright in his field, but he's a bit homespun and not my sort at all. I spent a perfectly pleasant few hours with him, but then I just had to let him down gently and get myself home."

He was going mad! "But what…?"

"I had lunch with Augustus today. He asked me last night and it seemed like a good idea. Within ten minutes of talking to him last night something just clicked between us. I don't know, he reminds me of my father, and you know what psychologists say about that." She fixed his eye. "John this is going to hurt. I went to bed with him this afternoon. I'm truly sorry, but there was something inevitable about it. If you really want to know, I think this is something that has a future."

Augustus! The room swam in front of his eyes. Augustus was a good fifteen years older than her, but then, it did make some sort of sense. This was as clear a case of natural selection as anything found in the jungle. They were the same flesh, the same species, two perfect examples of *homo superious*. If David Attenborough put it on television, people would be nodding sagely at the inevitability of it. Whatever he did to his pelt and his plumage, John wasn't the same breed, and a simple sniff of the air was enough to tell that he was an outsider. The irony of it all hit him forcefully. The last time he had had dinner Wendy here he had assumed that her brother was her lover; now it seemed she was in love with a man who reminded her of her father.

Shards of pain stared to cut into his lower abdomen and he put his head in his hands and groaned, trying not to make a spectacle of himself. "Oh Wendy!"

"Listen, John, you must realise…."

"I'll be all right. Just give me a second."

It was just a question of coming to terms with it. Understanding that most basic law of nature that when one door opens, inevitably several more close right in your face. That's how life always works. She was right of course; he wasn't in love with her, not in the true sense of the word. He had to face the truth of what he was feeling, recognise how much was broken heart and how much bruised ego. It still hurt of course, and it was taking a lot of will power not to smash everything off the table and storm out, but he could deal with it. At least, even as he sat here, the dreadful guilt of his own betrayal of her was loosening its strangle hold.

He pulled himself together with an effort. "I hope you'll be very happy, and you know that I really mean that. I suppose I can kiss you?"

She smiled at him. "I insist you kiss me. I do sort of love you, you know. I still want us to stay close."

He kissed her across the table. "And I sort of love you as well. I can tell you that now." She was so beautiful, and it was such a shame, but even trophy girlfriends are human beings and have feelings of their own; just like bims really. That probably meant that Giovanni was a real person too, and so was Luke. Even Marge, and Wendy's impoverished clients. Funny old world!

They held hands and contemplated each other, the silence broken by Wendy. "Now you can tell me about last night with a clear conscience. You probably need to get it of your chest. The two of you shagged each other stupid didn't you?"

He took a deep breath. "How did you know?"

"I knew before you did."

"I'm sorry..?"

"As soon as Augustus asked me to have lunch with him I guessed how things would turn out, and I didn't know how I would be able to deal with it. But alongside that I could see from the way you and Tracy looked at each other what was bubbling beneath the surface, so when you asked me to lure Dan away it gave me an excuse to leave the two of you alone together. It made me feel a little less guilty. You mustn't feel bad about it, John. With all the adrenaline of last night pumping through you, how else could any normal man have reacted being left alone for the night with a sexy young thing like her, especially when it was so obvious that the two of you already had the hots for each other. I'm really sorry she's gone away, but at least last night must have been some compensation."

It certainly had been. He had been feeling too guilty to allow himself to think about it, but he was a free man again and could let his thoughts go where they wanted. Damn it, he was rich and single, he could do and think what he wanted.

"Isn't it time they bought us some food. I'm starving!"

TWENTY-FOUR

OVER THE NEXT FEW MONTHS event followed on event like a computerised jigsaw, all the pieces moving neatly into place with a precision click.

George's body was found on the Monday morning when his housekeeper let herself in. The police had already started to take an interest in George's doings following a weekend tip-off that had produced a stash of cocaine in his Mercedes and further traces in his office. The discovery of even more in his dressing gown only helped build up a pattern. The enquiries that followed from this led to other evidence of drug dealing and money laundering, but it was weeks into the police enquiries before a trainee detective said that one of the paintings in George's house looked familiar and the truth dawned that the picture of a girl sweeping a court yard was Lord Parker's Vermeer. By this time Lord Parker had already made a major appeal on television to whoever was responsible for the theft to give it up, promising that he would donate it to the National Gallery for "The people of this country" if he did. He had been involved in a major public row ever since, as following its discovery he had taken the line that the thief had not given it up, and that therefore it should remain firmly in his ownership. It was one embarrassment too many for his Party who exerted so much pressure that eventually he was forced to donate it to the National Gallery.

It was ten days before anyone realised the money was missing. Clarenden had expected certain action to be taken by Dragoon following their paying over the five million, but initially the lack of action was put down to George's death. Dragoon's accountants and the manager who dealt with the day to day business had no executive powers and in George's absence no one person had sufficient knowledge or authority to do anything. By the time anyone realised that the company was five million short, police enquiries had thrown up the Liechtenstein connection. Tracy had done her job well. There was no evidence that the transfer instructions had been sent from Hart-Russell's computer, and as the bank's computers had been hit by an untraceable virus that had wiped off all relevant data, an over stretched Fraud Squad were all to happy to throw two and two together and assume that George had hived it off for his own reasons.

Clarendon took the view that they had paid over their money and expected the contract to be performed by Dragoon, and as this was clearly not going to happen, they had started court proceedings against them. Within a month Liquidators were called in to administer Dragoon. They initiated a counterclaim against Clarendon on the basis that the money had not ever been paid over, another against George's estate on the grounds that he had hived it off, and finally against Hart-Russell for negligence for not affecting the transfer. Hart-Russell defended the claim on the grounds that they had not been negligent, and also made a cross claim against George's estate on the basis that it was him who had liberated all the money. With all this confusion, there was no question of the proposed development going ahead in the foreseeable future. Martin Fletcher regained his health and was back in control of the council so it was unlikely that it ever would. In the mean time, the Saul Liebling School had received a massive donation from an anonymous source and had identified a new and trouble free site in Belleville for a new local school.

The one square peg trawling for the right sized hole was John. It was his uncertainty about what do with his own future that was the joker in the pack. It had been necessary for him to work out his month's notice as not to have done so would have drawn attention to him at a time when he wanted to be invisible, but it he had only paid lip service to it at best. His heart and mind were occupied with other matters. He found himself working shorter and shorter hours, and during the final week he came in and out as he chose. Nobody expressed any concern. In any event, for three days after the party, barely any work was done by anybody. The place was a hive of gossip about who had done what and with whom, and the partners were occupied with a massive damage limitation exercise. He felt both cut off from all this, and at the same time strangely lonely. Dan could not look him in the eye and only communicated when he had to and Luke avoided him as he had always done. Ron was no longer there, and even Bob's absence left an empty space. Most of all he missed Tracy tripping in and out of his office with her glowing smile and abbreviated hemlines, but the past was a different country and he lived somewhere else now.

At least it was all over and he could start to cautiously test the waters of his new existence as a man with time on his hands and with money at his disposal. He had always had a healthy loathing of shopping so it had never crossed his mind that money would buy happiness, but he did think it might provide a reasonable down payment. He was heavily disappointed. The odd toy apart, he was not particularly concerned with acquiring possessions, but had been looking forward to a lifestyle synonymous with his new affluence, but found it hard to achieve. He was far from ready to start to vegetate in the country, but overnight London started to show characteristics he had not previously noticed. Any form of public transport was of course a torment and nobody who didn't have to would ever choose to use it. Pending the delivery of something more powerful and luxurious he had traded in his no longer young TVR for a nearly new Porsche Boxter, but even in this, crossing London was still unmitigated hell, as no one had yet had the wit to designate certain lanes for the sole use of wealthy bachelors, and it was still impossible to park outside a favourite restaurant or cafe. It was just as bad on foot, the pavements crammed full of people either panicking to get nowhere important, or who suddenly stopped in front of him to conduct a full body search on themselves for something they never seemed to find. Possibly it had always been like that and it was only because he had always been too busy and preoccupied he hadn't noticed. He kept asking himself just how much money one had to have before all these irritations went away, or whether this was just evidence of his being tired of life.

In his personal life, one or two things had slipped into place. He was still living in his Belleville flat, but was in the process of buying a house in Notting Hill. There were a few weeks to go before contracts were due to be exchanged, and he was being kept occupied getting ready for the move. Wendy and Augustus were now living together in Augustus' house in Lowndes Square, and were to be married in the spring. John was high on the guest list. His new friendship with Augustus had given him something that money alone could not have bought him as he now had the intro to virtually every club in London from the Groucho to the Chelsea Arts as Augustus was happy to propose John for any of them that took his fancy. He had also interviewed for five jobs in the Golden Circle, and had been offered two of them, and there were a couple of weeks to go before he had to make a decision. All this had meant he had not been able to even consider a holiday which he felt he needed, if for no other reason than to try and make decisions about the future. Now he could eat every night at China Whites or drink at the Met Bar he was less interested in doing so. Of greater concern was that now he had breached the walls of the Golden Circle, the thought of going back to twelve hour days with his stress metre back on permanent red alert was positively unattractive. His entire adult life had revolved around building up his career to this very point, but now he was here it did not seem to matter anymore, particularly now there was no specific need. Simple mathematics showed that after buying the house and the terrifyingly wonderful car that was on order there would still be enough money left over to produce the sort of income on which he would be quite happy to live. If he chose to, once the move was out of the way he could start in on the peeled grapes and not lift a finger again.

He knew he was in danger of drifting but was not too concerned unless he found himself becoming morose or solitary without a point of focus. To keep himself from becoming reclusive he had re-established contact with friends he had let drift over the previous few months. His libido was at an all time low, but to satisfy himself that all was in working order he paid appropriate attention to a woman called Rosalind he met at a dinner party. She invited him back for coffee then suggested he stay for breakfast, during the course of which he discovered that officially she already had a man in her life so that in his present state of mind, she was everything he needed. She was attractive and interesting and he had now been out with her three or four times, but dining with her tonight at Nobu his heart wasn't in it, so at the conclusion of what objectively should have been an enjoyable evening, he pleaded a headache and got them separate taxis home.

* * *

"Evenings are drawing in."

"Too right!" Unless it specifically involved endorsing the mass killing of homosexuals or blacks, his policy was to agree with just about everything taxi drivers said as this was easier in the long run. Over the years he had applauded the proposals of the extreme left and the extreme right, advocated the cementing over of the entire green belt, and agreed that tattooing the word *Shoplifter* on the forehead of anyone caught at it would certainly cut down the crime figures. This time it was less controversial, the weather being something on which most people agreed. The man was right, the nights were drawing in and autumn was taking hold. His driver was taking the north route, down the Kings Road and across Wandsworth Bridge, and as they went down the Trinity Road through Wandsworth Common, he could see that leaf fall was well advanced and could feel a distinct chill in the air. He hadn't thought to put on the central heating in his flat before he left, so it would be cold and unwelcoming when he got home. Was he getting middle aged? He wouldn't have even given this a thought a few months ago.

"Irish stew tonight."

"What?" The driver's voice had made him jump.

"Irish stew, when I get back. Doing nights I have dinner when most people are asleep or watching breakfast TV. It's not the sleep that's a problem when you change shifts, it's the stomach. Gets itself all set up for Shreddies and suddenly there's a plateful of Chicken Tikka and a pint of Tennants sloshing in. Left here?"

"That's it, and then half way down on the right."

"Behind that Porsche OK?"

"That's fine."

"Yours?"

"Yes."

"Lucky bastard!"

"Some might think so."

He paid the fare with a tip commensurate with being a Porsche owner and let himself in to his flat, and at the top of the stairs opened the upper door with little enthusiasm.

"Don't jump. It's only me."

What the fuck! He was so deep in thought he nearly leapt out of his skin. There were no lights on in the room, but it was illuminated by a fire blazing in the grate, the room glowing in its warmth. Sitting cross legged in front of it wrapped in his dark blue dressing gown was Tracy, her hair wrapped in a big towel and her big brown eyes bright with the glow of the fire.

"What the hell...?" With a million questions to ask he could not articulate a single one of them, and stared at her trying to focus his thoughts.

"Sorry if I frightened you. Are you pleased to see me?" She gave him a vintage Tracy smile, but the question was a serious one, and her voice was uncertain.

"I'm thrilled stiff to see you, honestly. But what on earth....?"

"Really, *really,* pleased to see me?"

He took a pace forward and supported himself on the arm of his couch, needing to ground himself in some way. "You've no idea!"

"Oh yes I have!"

"But what are you doing here? What about Nikos, and the restaurant...? Look...." He took off his jacket and sat on the near corner of his couch.

"Come and sit there, that's right, at the far end where I can't quite reach you. If I even start to give you a hug or anything I might just not stop, so just keep your distance till I know a bit more." She sat down at the far end, a great space between them. They both reached out with their hands along the back their fingers just failing to make contact. "What's with the towel?"

"Oh that. I had a shower and washed my hair. You don't mind do you?"

"Course I don't. You must have kept the key then – I never thought to ask for it back." Watching her recline so close to him he was losing control of his body, but needed to know more. "Don't look at me like that, it makes me go all funny inside. Just tell me what's going on?"

She got up and paced up and down, loosening the towel and rubbing her hair with it. Even in the fire light he could see she had a new glow to her, her skin burnished and darkened by her time in the sun. "I really gave it my best shot, but as soon as Nikos picked me up at the airport I realised I didn't love him anymore. I thought it might be just a mixture of being absent for so long and all the excitement with you before I left, so I really worked at it, but it had all gone. It's funny how clear things can be with hindsight. I wouldn't have been behaving the way I had been with you if I'd properly been in love with him. Anyway, after just a few days I broke it to him as best I could, then went away."

"You took a risk coming here like this. Wendy might have moved in by now."

She looked sheepish. "I knew she hadn't. I've been back a week and I found her phone number and rang her up. We had dinner together a few days ago and she told me everything."

"You what!"

"You know what women are like, John, specially when we've had a drink. She's really fond of you and thought it would be really good if I saw you again. She said you were getting morose"

"Did she suggest…?"

"That I just let myself in like this? No, that was my idea, I thought you would appreciate it." She gave him an old fashioned Tracy look showing she hadn't lost her touch. "If of course you don't actually like finding a freshly showered young girl in front of your fire, I suppose I'll just have to go away and find someone who does."

His body was reacting to her the way it always did, but he needed to make some sense of it all first. "Weren't you afraid that the police would be after you? I know you're officially Sophia Kostakis now, but someone could still have recognised you."

"John, the world's a small place now. I read the English newspapers every day on the internet so I know all about the police blaming it all on George Stavros. You and I didn't even get a mention."

"What about the money?"

"I left half of it with Nikos so he could do his restaurant bit, and took the rest for myself. I felt I had to do that as I had the rest of my life to take care of. I couldn't stay in Zandos as it was so small we would have been tripping over each other all the time which wouldn't have been fair, so I went to Crete and stayed in a taverna for a bit, but I was concerned about just wasting the money, so I tried something completely different. I went across to Sougia and took up with the hippies. That was great. I lived on the beach and barely spent anything for a month. It helped me learn to be more self reliant." She flashed her eyes at him. "I've got an all over tan now, but you wouldn't be interested in that."

He tried to avoid thinking about it. "I don't see you as a hippie."

"I'm not, but it's different there. When it's just sun and sea you can live so simply." She looked at him seriously. "Money's very liberating isn't it. It gives you chance to explore who you are and what you want to do without risking that you might land upon the scrap heap." She stopped towelling her hair and shook it out. "I don't think you realise how grateful I am to you for giving me that chance."

She was different somehow, the same Tracy who had left England three months ago but with a new maturity. In that small interval she had grown up and he realized with a shock that maybe at last he had too. "So what do you want to do?"

"Go back. I told you, I love Greece, particularly the small islands. I want to do what Nikos is doing, buy and run a small taverna. Nothing too touristy, something on one of the islands that only gets a handful of people in the know. I'm good at cooking and organising and I think I could make a go of it." She sat down on the end of the couch keeping the required distance between them, but reached out her hand and took his. "When I left here three months ago you said something. Did you mean it?"

He knew straight away what she was talking about. Had he meant it? Whatever the answer, he had to allow for the circumstances in which it had been said. That day their emotions had been twanging like elastic bands, they had been as thick as thieves for weeks before and he had just spent a wonderful night with her. When they had hugged as she left, he hadn't expected to see her ever again. He had meant it all right, but did that mean it was still the case now? His throat went dry, knowing that painful or not he would have to tell her the truth. "If you're talking about what I think you're talking about, then the answer is Yes."

"You said you loved me." Her voice faltered and she sounded unsure of herself. "So, *do* you love me?"

"'Fraid I do."

"Then *tell* me, for God's sake!"

"I love you, Tracy!" Suddenly it was as if a great weight was being taken off his shoulders and he was floating. "God I love you!"

"And I love you, John. If you haven't been able to work that out then I shall start to wonder just how intelligent you are."

He looked at her across the length of the couch wondering what the implication of all this could be. What would her score be as a comprehensive educated girl from South London with no real qualifications? He didn't give a toss. Tracy was his fate and that was good enough for him.

She looked at him with innocent eyes. "Is it true that men only want what they can't have? A few months ago when you realised I was determined to keep my pants on, you nearly exploded; now I'm here pre-basted and oven ready you don't even give me a kiss." She fiddled with the cord of the dressing gown. "This is a lot easier than a padlock you know. I bet even a thicko who's hopeless with computers could work this out."

He leaned across and kissed her. Two hours later they woke up in front of the dying fire, his dressing gown over them as a cover. She snuggled into him. "I suppose you wouldn't want to come and live in Greece with me, would you. With the money we've got we could do anything we want."

At her words the sun came out in the dark room, and it was full of light. Suddenly he could smell the pine and hear the crickets chirping, and in his mind lemon sizzled on spit roasted lamb. What a wonderful idea! They could have a simple little taverna on the edge of the sea, with chickens and goats in the garden, and a hammock strung between a couple of olive trees. There would be a couple of feral cats and a tumble of multi coloured kittens skittering between their feet as they tried to cook. They could have long siestas together or whatever they called the afternoon sleep in Greece, and get drunk on retsina, and pig themselves on Yoghurt and honey. He could even have a small boat and go fishing for the taverna. And what had he got to lose? A rising crime rate, a transport system that couldn't cope, clogged roads and a rising population in a country already bursting at the seams. Not the most difficult decision he had ever had to make.

"Before you answer, John…"

"Yes?"

"I think that I earned my share of the money, so it's up to me what I do with it. I want to buy the place in my name. I've done this sort of work before, and I know how hard it can be, but I can cook and speak the language and have a reasonable idea of what's involved. What I'm saying is, if we're to make a success of this we've got to take it seriously so I'll have to be in charge, at least to start with. Can you cope with that?"

"What'll you do to me if I make a mess of things?"

She whispered her answer in his ear which set the two of them giggling. He was sure he could cope with it and might even organise the odd deliberate mistake to test it out.

He stared at the ceiling thinking it through. "There's a few practicalities we'll have to deal with. I've got a new car on order, but I suppose I can cancel that, and I can kill off the new house purchase. There's still the Porsche. What'll I do with that?"

"I don't know, give it to Ron. He'll love it."

"You know he told everyone at the party he wanted to jiggle your jugglies."

"He didn't!"

"Very loudly. When you were upstairs in accounts making us both rich."

"The dirty old bugger!"

"But when you think about it, I got to do that and he didn't."

"That's true! I suppose on that basis we should be kind and let him have it."

"Yes, boss!"

Printed in Great Britain
by Amazon

37855033R00138